T0243796

1983

1983

Tom Cox

unbound

First published in 2024

Unbound
c/o TC Group, 6th Floor King's House, 9– 10 Haymarket, London SW1Y 4BP
www.unbound.com

Text design by Jouve (UK), Milton Keynes

A CIP record for this book is available from the British Library

ISBN 978-1-80018-343-8 (hardback)
ISBN 978-1-80018-344-5 (ebook)

Printed in Great Britain by TJ Books, Padstow, Cornwall

1 3 5 7 9 8 6 4 2

For Jean Penchion and all the other inspirational
teachers at Claremont Primary School, Nottingham,
during the early 1980s

'We do not remember childhood – we imagine it. We search for it, in vain, through layers of obscuring dust, and recover some bedraggled shreds of what we think it was.'

Penelope Lively, *Moon Tiger*

1983

Benji

Do I trust my memory? I think I do. With the caveat of the small liberties it takes with chronology, the sellotaping and soldering it does when my back is turned, its occasional habit of mistaking photos for recalled events, I believe implicitly in its truth, maybe even more than I would if it was more meticulous, more of a tedious pedant. So, with that in mind, this is definitely exactly how and where it begins: a road approximately in the centre of England. Not a significant place, unless you happen to be seven years old and live in a house on it. The year is just waking up. Curtains remain closed against an overnight frost just thick and white enough to momentarily taunt any child peeking excitably out from behind them, hoping for snow.

The house is a semi, hard to heat, small but not tiny, built in the 1930s for a miner and his family. I am in the house, in the larger of its two bedrooms, the one where my mum and dad, who are not miners, sleep. I am sitting on the bed, small (but not tiny) for my age, looking at my reflection in the largest of the three mirrors attached to my mum's dressing table, and tears are falling down my face.

Downstairs, there is a knock on the front door. My mum opens it. 'That's strange,' I hear her say to my dad. 'Nobody there. I didn't even see anyone in the road.'

My dad's voice: 'Maybe it was Ethel Troutlock's ghost.'

Outside, on the front drive, the attractive patterns in the ice sealing the five consecutive puddles leading from the pavement to the doorstep remain unbroken.

The dressing table is a Victorian one, walnut, bought second-hand by my mum for a song. My dad's 1940s teddy bear – nameless, like most of my own teddies – sits on it, looking half-alive and asinine with his one hooded eye. Beside him are a selection of my mum's beaded African bangles, which, along with her silk scarves and my dad's big leather jacket, I frequently like to try on. I am wearing a sweatshirt which says SANDYHILL PRIMARY SCHOOL on the front. Or at least that is what I had thought the writing on the sweatshirt said, until a few minutes ago.

The sweatshirt is a present I recently received for Christmas: not one that my mum and dad viewed as being amongst the day's more exciting gifts, but one I have been as pleased with as any of the others, until now.

'Oh dear, what on earth is wrong?' says my mum, arriving at the threshold of the room.

'*Ruined*.' I choke the word out. 'It's ruined. Look!' I say, pointing at the sweatshirt in the mirror, wondering why she can't see what I see.

'It looks lovely to me. Really smart.'

'The words! Look at the words!'

'What is wrong with them?'

'Look! LOO-HCS Y-RA-MIRP LLI-HY-DNAS.'

For a moment, my mum stares at me, bewildered, as if I have begun speaking in tongues.

'Look!' I repeat, pointing at the mirror. 'LOOHCS YRAMIRP LLIHYDNAS! LOOHCS YRAMIRP LLI-HYDNAS! Why? I want it to not say that. Why does it say that? Why doesn't it say what it says?'

Unable to restrain herself, she bursts out laughing, and enfolds me in her arms.

I chuckle in amazement now too, at the recollection, especially with the knowledge that I spent a lot of time reading in the earlier part of my childhood, but I genuinely don't think I'd owned a top with a visible logo on it until then. My parents enjoyed choosing clothes for me, but most of these were bought at the factory shop near my school, knitted by my grandparents or handed down from the slightly older children of my mum and dad's friends. The sweatshirt – part of a one-off batch for kids to wear or not wear voluntarily, printed by the school, which was vehemently anti-uniform – was, if not unique, definitely an anomaly for me in having been purchased new, at full price. Those mirrors on the Victorian dressing table were the only ones in the house beside the bathroom mirror – which was still a little too high for me to see myself in – but it still strikes me as curious that a whole week could have elapsed between me receiving this cheaply made yet hallowed item of clothing and first properly checking myself out in it. I loved my school, which was also where my mum was employed as an English As A Second Language teacher, and I would have felt proud to have worn its name across my chest. This further accounts for the level of distress I felt until, sitting beside me on the bed, she gently explained the rules of mirrors and reverse images. The idea of me wearing a sweatshirt saying LOOHCS YRAMIRP LLIHYDNAS amongst all my friends wearing theirs that said SANDYHILL PRIMARY SCHOOL was deeply upsetting, especially when I was looking forward so impatiently to seeing everyone in Mr Stone's class, and Mr Stone himself, and talking about what we had all got for Christmas, and maybe playing on the new ZX Spectrum computer which Mr Stone might have bought by now with his own money to replace the one that was stolen last half-term when somebody broke into the school.

Was it definitely a knock on the door I'd heard downstairs, not the sound of a doorbell? It was. Several years would pass before we moved to our first doorbelled house. In fact, having gathered little empirical evidence to refute it, at the dawn of 1983 I held the belief that doorbells were something only posh people had on their doors. The door itself, however? That did look quite posh, especially during the warmer months, flanked by the rose and wisteria my mum had planted nearby. Thinking back now, to that house, on that lane, various images quickly arrive, all astoundingly high definition, through the smog of four entire decades: my tyre swing on the apple tree at the top of the back garden, the piss-yellow asbestos garage that my dad told me would kill me if I touched it, the obstinate blocky roofs of the piggery across the road. But what always arrives first is that front door. It had been a naff peeling turquoise when my parents had bought the house, seven years earlier, and the lovely shade of burgundy they chose to replace it seemed like the beginning of a warmth that radiated through the house as soon as you stepped over the threshold. It's a warmth so prominent in my mind, it tends to blot out memories of the actual temperature of the place which, in winter, four years after my parents had central heating put in, remained extremely chilly. It wasn't like the doors of other houses on the road. We weren't like most other people on the road. But at the time, I didn't quite realise that. I just thought we had a nice front door.

The road was called Stringy Lane, which in my head always seemed a good fit. It had a fibrous sort of quality, stretching out like an umbilical cord from the main body of our village,

Tapley Woodhouse, connecting it to a couple of farms, a dozen or so houses, the colliery up the hill, and, finally, Petalford, a neighbouring village which sounded significantly more fragile than it was, being generally perceived as Tapley Woodhouse's roughneck younger brother. Not that Tapley itself was any gentle flower. Pit country. Undeniable. Smellable on the faintest of breezes. Two of them – one still active, the shafts of the other closed fourteen years earlier, but the headstocks still standing – could be found within less than half a mile of the house and several others not far over the brow of every hill the eye could see.

My dad possessed a medium-strong Nottingham accent, often addressed people as 'yoff' – the Nottinghamese for 'youth' – and had grown up in a council house only seven miles south of here, but the Tapley Woodhouse natives soon sniffed him and my mum out for outsiders, what with their Penguin paperbacks, art nouveau posters and cosmic jazz albums.

I remember music being ever-present in my childhood but my only recollections of it playing anything like loud are from occasions when we visited my aunts or uncles or my parents' friends. This apparently was because Barry, the electrician who lived next door, had once heard an Ornette Coleman LP coming through the walls and threatened to kick my dad's teeth in if he ever played it again.

In a decade of living there, I do not remember seeing one non-white face in the village, with the exception of those belonging to my friends Dalton Mellors, Taj Mukherjee, Paul Hashimoto and Errol Watts when they came up from the city to stay for the weekend. These visits marked me out as different amongst the other kids in the village, along with my home-knitted jumpers and the fact that, although I pronounced Tapley as 'Tapleh', I didn't linger quite as long on the 'eh' as they did, with my mouth quite as wide open as theirs. One Monday evening, when I was in the front garden examining some wood-lice under a log, directly after Errol had been staying for the weekend, an older boy called Lee Barrowcliffe from down the road stopped his bike at the end of our drive. 'Been playin' wi' coons again?' he shouted, before riding away, cackling.

School was twelve literal miles, and a few more cultural ones, away, in central Nottingham. My dad drove my mum and me there on his way to other schools where he taught or, if the car broke down, which it often did, my mum and I got the bus: a red double-decker that always smelt overpoweringly of stale cigarette smoke and on whose upper floor I always insisted on sitting, all the way up at the front, so I could pretend I was steering us steadily to our destination from a great and imperious height. I was nearly always pretending I was driving some vehicle or other at this point in my childhood: the muscle cars the male duos in my favourite American TV shows appeared to harmoniously co-own; the Ford Capris and Opel Mantas that broke the speed limit directly outside our living-room window every day; the Morris Marina my dad had bought secondhand to replace the crap half-timbered Morris Traveller he'd bought secondhand before that and the underappreciated Morris Minor he'd bought secondhand before that and the crap Renault 4 he'd bought secondhand before that; and the miniature versions my nan had purchased of them for me from the toy shop in Iron-field, the town a couple of miles to the south where most of our family lived. In my most epic adult fantasy, a recurring dream that I could stop and start at will, I owned a car, which I drove all over the country, purely for the sake of driving it.

Back in the real world, I learned to ride my first bike quickly and impatiently, dispensing with my stabilisers in little more than a weekend, taking grazed shins and knees in my stride and returning instantly to the saddle. My early travels sometimes took me almost a mile from home, which my parents permitted with the proviso that I stayed on the pavement of our lane and entirely away from other arterial roads. Already frustrated by the limitations of even this, I had begun to fold the bike's mudguards against its tyres in order to produce a noise that allowed me to fantasise I was at the helm of a far more powerful machine that could take me to distant places, such as my nan's house in Ironfield, or the farm in Hazzard County where Bo and Luke Duke lived on TV with their cousin Daisy and uncle Jesse.

Christmas had been exciting, especially the day itself and Boxing Day at my aunt and uncle's, when everyone had sprayed their hair with some pink hairspray my cousin Donna had received, then posed together for a family photograph, but to my mind that had been quite a while ago and every one of the seven days since then had been most centrally characterised by the fact that it wasn't Christmas. For me, school could not restart quickly enough. As a rurally situated only child, however, I was adept at amusing myself, especially in the six months since I'd become the proud owner of a bike. Typically, on one of my adventures I would turn left out of the driveaway and head north, past Ethel Troutlock's house, which actually wasn't anyone's house now Ethel had died, then past the Chudleys', then left up the unmetalled pit road. Today, wearing my once-again untainted Sandyhill Primary School sweatshirt and a couple of other layers to protect me from the cold, even though I wasn't nesh like my cousin Donna said I was, I took my usual route, disembarking about halfway between the main road and the colliery at the foot of the gob pile and hiding my bike in the undergrowth. That was what my dad called it, 'the gob pile', but my mum said the proper name for it was a spoil heap. Until she'd told me that, I'd thought it was just a normal hill, but she said it wasn't like real hills because it hadn't been there forever and didn't have nice stuff inside it like soil and worms and seeds but instead contained all the things from the pit that weren't coal and nobody had any use for. Behind the mine, and our house, there was a much larger gob pile. If you used your imagination, this second, more commanding gob pile made it seem in a way like we were living in the Peak District, where my mum and dad often dragged me on walks at weekends, except the gob pile didn't have any ruined barns or rocks or stone crosses on it like the hills in the Peak District. There were trees and bushes on the smaller pile but there wasn't much of anything on the bigger one, especially the back of it, which was a vast and quiet place that I couldn't have reached unless I'd abandoned my bike, climbed a big fence at the back of the colliery, or trespassed across the farm fields behind our house, which contained a scary horse that my dad told me not to mess with.

It was in this quiet spot on the back of the bigger gob pile, I had decided, where the alien spaceship would land.

I was always finding interesting things around the base of the smaller gob pile when I played there: old car seats and bar stools and mattresses and saucepans and once even a car registration plate. I didn't understand why people left them there when there was a tip with lots of room for them only a short distance away in Ironfield, but some of the things came in amazingly useful for the work I was doing in a spinney towards the far side of the gob pile. One night quite a long time ago I'd not been able to sleep and went downstairs for a drink of lemon squash and saw my mum and dad watching a programme on TV about a war that was going to take place quite soon. This war wasn't going to be like the other wars that had happened and wouldn't have soldiers and tanks, but when it was over the only people alive would be the ones who had built shelters for themselves. I didn't see all of the programme because after a few minutes my mum and dad realised I was there in the doorway and told me that it wasn't for children and that I should go to bed, but I saw enough to learn that the best shelters had walls made of old mattresses, ceilings made of doors, bags of sand and lots of tinned food. The war hadn't happened yet, but I was glad to know that when it did I would be protected by my shelter, which had all the things it was supposed to have in it. I might even let my mum and dad stay in it too when the war happened, if they were nice to me, but I hadn't told them, or anyone else, about it because it was a secret. Every time I left the shelter I was careful to cover it up with plenty of leaves and branches so nobody would know it was there. No one ever suspected anything, and I assembled my provisions gradually, so if my mum noticed there was one can of baked beans or rice pudding fewer than she thought she'd bought from the Co-op, it would seem insignificant, and she could blame the mistake on the holes in her busy mind. The Figshaws, who lived across the road, also did not seem to have been missing the bag of sand I had appropriated from their front drive and laboriously dragged up the pit road under the cover of dusk.

After checking on the shelter and seeing that it was just how I'd left it last week, I climbed to the summit of the gob pile and surveyed the landscape. From here, I could see everything I needed to, with the exception of that secret unexplored part of the bigger gob pile where the spaceship was going to dock, or might even have already docked. To the immediate west there were the huge functioning headstocks of the Naghill Colliery, to the south the defunct ones of the old Tapley Woodhouse pit – both of which looked like something from another planet, which I decided would probably make the aliens feel comfortable and even more likely to land their spaceship nearby. Between the headstocks were the farm fields, where I could see the scary horse eating from its trough. Panning around to the north east from there, there was the big pond across the road from our house, the farm where Mandy and Kate Figshaw and their mum and dad lived and its adjoining half-built piggery, and, right at the top of Stringy Lane where it intersected with the road to Ironfield, the bus stop and the Miners' Welfare. Swinging my line of vision back around to Petalford, I could see Lee Barrowcliffe making his way down the pit lane on his bike, so I darted into the trees until he was gone.

I felt pleased with the architectural merits of my shelter and proud that I had done the work all myself, without any help or advice. Last year, for my seventh birthday, my mum and dad had bought me some balsa wood and I'd tried to make a fully functioning two-seater aeroplane for me and my nan to go flying in and that had not been a success, but this was a much better effort. Danny McNulty from school had told me that his mum had said that when the big war came the only survivors would be cockroaches, because of something called radiation, and his mum knew lots about wars because she'd camped at Greenham Common, where they stored what Danny called 'big fuck-off missiles'. But Danny wasn't always as right about things as he thought he was. Last month he'd told me that Santa didn't exist, so on Christmas Eve I'd stayed up almost all night to find out if he was lying and, magically, when I woke up, my stocking had some satsumas, a pair of fingerless gloves, a *Beano* and the latest issue of *Smash Hits* magazine in it. Also, I didn't see how radiation could possibly get into my shelter when I'd built it so well, even adding, with the help of my mum's gardening trowel, a kind of sunken conversation-pit area in the middle to allow me to huddle further still from harm.

When I was sure there was no longer any danger of an encounter with Lee Barrowcliffe, I collected my bike from the bottom of the gob pile and rode back home. Mr and Mrs Chudley were in their front garden, which in a few weeks would be a riot of daffodils. As I cycled past, Mr Chudley asked me if I was practising for the Tour de France. I squeezed the brakes and asked him what the Tour de France was and Mr Chudley said it was a very big and long bike race. Mrs Chudley nodded, to

reassure me this was correct. Both Mr and Mrs Chudley were wearing white boiler suits stained with this winter's soil and last summer's pollen. Sometimes I went into their house for a cup of tea but decided not to today. Their tea was always extremely strong, but not as strong as my nan's, which everyone knew was the strongest tea in Nottinghamshire, and probably the entire country.

I liked the smell of Mr and Mrs Chudley's house, which was a combination of pipe smoke and compost and gas-fire gas, but it was also full of old clocks and paintings and ancient deranged-looking porcelain dogs and it scared me a little bit. Also, the only biscuits they ever had were digestives, which was a crushing disappointment. Unlike my mum and dad, the Chudleys never interrupted each other when they spoke, as if everything they said had already been rehearsed and they always agreed on everything. Once, while Mr Chudley nodded, Mrs Chudley had told me about some boys who were buried in the cemetery up at Petalford: one, my exact age, who had died from swallowing chewing gum (I had been chewing some Wrigley's Juicy Fruit at the time the Chudleys were telling me this), and the others, only a little bit older, who had died in a fire in the Naghill Colliery. I had asked my dad if it was true about the fire and he said it was, but it had happened a hundred years ago, which was a detail that Mrs Chudley had omitted. I wondered if Mrs Chudley and Mr Chudley would be buried in the cemetery soon too, but tried not to think about it because I liked them a lot. Also, even though they were very old, they were not as old as Ethel Troutlock had been when she died. When my dad told me Ethel had died, and I told my dad I was worried about dying too, he had told me that, even though Ethel knew it was about to happen to her, she had laughed about it and told him that when she did die, he could chuck her in the pond across the road and she wouldn't mind. I was fairly sure that my dad hadn't followed Ethel Troutlock's instructions, but every time I rode past the pond, such as right now, I always thought of Ethel Troutlock as being under the water and got the clear image of my dad walking over there with Ethel Troutlock slung over his shoulder, lifeless but with a

contented grin on her papery, bespectacled face.

When I got home, my mum and dad were both painting. My mum was painting the kitchen wall and my dad was upstairs with a much smaller brush, painting some paper. On the table in front of him were two cold almost-full cups of instant coffee and a photo my mum had taken of twenty-seven sheep in the snow in front of a barn in Derbyshire. The coffee in the cups was black because my dad hated milk, ever since he'd had a job delivering it from the back of a scooter.

When they weren't out at work, my mum and dad were often painting. My dad painted walls too, but in a different way to how my mum did. In the flat in Nottingham where they used to live before I was born, he'd painted a nude lady who was totally blue and didn't have a face whose name I thought I'd heard my dad say was Matisse and on my bedroom wall, when I was very little, he'd painted some of the Mr Men, Winnie the Pooh and Rupert the Bear, then, last year, when I'd become too grown-up to have Mr Men, Winnie the Pooh and Rupert the Bear on my wall anymore, he painted the Bash Street Kids and Minnie the Minx from *The Beano* over them. This was his early Christmas present to me but also to himself. I knew my dad got sad sometimes, even though nobody talked to me about it, but painting made him feel better. While he painted, he usually listened to the radio, but not too loud, in case Barry next door came over and hit him in the teeth with his fist. Sometimes the radio played *The Archers*, which made my dad swear sometimes and had a theme tune that made you think lots of fast and exciting things would happen in it even though nothing ever did. Other times it was the news, or the shipping forecast, which I didn't understand but made me think of the sea as a deep and dark and frightening place of complex and nightmareish weather, very different to what I'd seen when I'd crossed the Channel on a ferry with my parents.

I went into the kitchen and made myself a glass of lemon squash. My mum asked me not to put the glass down on a patchwork quilt she'd been making. I worked the arm on the metal coffee grinder while I talked to her, even though there were no coffee beans in it. She had paint in her hair and on her dungarees and there was the smell of crumble, made with the last of autumn's apples, baking in the oven. I asked her if I could enter the Tour de France and she said I'd probably have to wait a couple of years.

School finally began again two days later, and the big news was that over the holiday Taj Mukherjee's mum had bitten her boyfriend's willy and he'd had to go to hospital to get it repaired. Jess Bonner and Paul Hashimoto and I couldn't understand why anyone would bite someone's willy, especially hard enough to injure it, and Taj Mukherjee said he wasn't sure either, but Danny McNulty said he knew about these things and women often bit men's willies when they were especially angry with them. Last year in Miss Buttons' class, Miss Buttons had sat us all down and told us that she wanted all the talk about willies and johnnies to stop, but Mr Stone heard us talking about Taj Mukherjee's mum's boyfriend's willy and didn't tell us off. I told Taj and Danny McNulty and Jess Bonner about part of a magazine which had been ripped and left in the trees on the gob pile which was a photo of a man's willy quite close to a woman's face and said that maybe she was about to bite it, too. Then we played on the new ZX Spectrum Mr Stone had bought for the class with his own money to replace the one that was stolen, which was especially exciting for all of us, since none of our parents could afford to buy us our own ZX Spectrums. We had all enjoyed being in Miss Buttons' class but agreed that Mr Stone's was the best class ever to be in.

I used to view my memory as a sealed metal box of images in my mind. In reality it's a colony of ants, off doing their own thing in a back room while I am busy elsewhere. Also, as everyone knows, sometimes you think an ant is just an ant, but it's actually a flying ant, waiting to sprout wings. Why do I have a recollection of Taj Mukherjee's mum's boyfriend returning from hospital, limping from a car, along a dogshit-flecked pavement, up to the Mukherjees' front door? Perhaps it is because that story Taj told is so fertile, it inevitably tends to breed other images in the mind to back it up. But that particular memory is false: I definitely did not see Taj's mum's boyfriend limping or even walking anywhere after his visit to hospital. I'm not sure I met Taj's mum's boyfriend, even though I certainly met Taj's mum several times, and visited their house: a redbrick Victorian terrace on Priory Drive which was the closest to school of any of my friends' houses.

The street was one I knew well as it was also where my mum and dad's best friends, Deborah and Richard Fennel, lived with their daughter Jane, who – unlike many children a few years my senior – never appeared even for a second to resent being left in my company, and had become a de facto big sister for me, not to mention font of stationery wisdom and music guru, having introduced me – via her bedroom and the shiny, thrilling pages of *Smash Hits* magazine – to the Teardrop Explodes, the Human League, Echo & the Bunnymen, ABC's *Lexicon of Love* album and a variety of excellent pens. I loved going to see Deborah and Richard and Jane, not just because of Jane's coloured fineliners and burgeoning record collection, but because funny things always seemed to happen to them. Once when we went on holiday with them in the Forest of Bowland, they took off for a walk in the snow and returned home twenty minutes later being trailed by a flock of sheep, three of which followed them into the kitchen of the cottage where we were staying. This, I sometimes think, was the same holiday when Richard sat in a chair that was hanging from the ceiling and broke it, but that was in fact a different holiday. Another time, they drove more than 200 miles with a loaf of bread on the roof of their Ford Escort. Deborah read the *Beano* every week, even though she was nearly thirty-six. Like me and my nan and my cousin Donna, she was also a member of the Dennis the Menace fanclub, which meant she possessed a googly-eyed badge in the image of his dog, Gnasher.

The Fennels' house had a smell that I liked, a wholesome one not totally unlike the health store on Mansfield Road where my mum scooped lentils and beans out of big sacks to take home, but also not a foody smell. It is quite hard to pinpoint; I think the closest I can come is to say that it wasn't quite of towels but that I thought of it as being unequivocally under the heading 'Towels'. The smell could also be faintly detected on the hand-me-down jumpers and t-shirts of Jane's that I received. Taj's house smelt not dissimilar. Perhaps it was unique to buildings on Priory Road between 1978 and 1986 because I don't remember smelling it before then and haven't smelt it since

I apologise. Am I going too fast? Are there too many people? Kids tend to know a lot of kids. It happens. They go to school and they inevitably meet them there. But, in case it helps, a brief recap, plus some extra facts:

Lee Barrowcliffe: lived down the road, rode his bike along the pit road a lot, didn't like that I had Black friends, once beheaded my Rupert the Bear teddy.

Dalton Mellors: stayed at my house a bit, once held the coach up with me by getting lost in the woods on a trip to Newstead Abbey, had moved schools by now, briefly had scabies. Lee Barrowcliffe didn't approve of me playing with him because he was Black.

Errol Watts: stayed at my house a lot, pulled loads of excellent faces that made us all laugh, lived in a house where there was a big trunk with lots of shoes in it, had a nice adoptive mum who once woke me up at his house to reassure me that even though I was in a strange place, there was no need to worry and I could soon have some breakfast, co-owned not one but two fully operational space hoppers with his three siblings. Lee Barrowcliffe probably didn't approve of me playing with him because he was Black.

Jess Bonner (he doesn't play a huge part here): wore a lot of stripy tops, always had an asthma inhaler in his hand, didn't understand why a woman would want to bite a man's willy, lived about a mile from school in Mapperley Park.

Paul Hashimoto: didn't understand why a woman would want to bite a man's willy, had a Betamax video player, had really nice hair that I used to like to twiddle in class before I gradually grew out of the habit.

Taj Mukherjee: lived on Priory Drive near school, smelt of something that was a bit like towels but wasn't towels, was taller than he seemed, had a mum who bit her boyfriend's willy, possibly but not definitely because she was angry.

Danny McNulty: knew lots of stuff about life and the galaxy as a whole, had long ginger hair, always brought the thickest brown bread to school, had a mum who had protested the big fuck-off missiles at Greenham Common.

Jane Fennel: transcendental guru of edgy electropop and themed notepads, was already heavily into The Teardrop Explodes before her ninth birthday, all-round lovely person, had an even more reassuring smell than Taj Mukherjee.

My cousin Donna: owned some pink hairspray, used to wrestle me to the floor and pin my legs behind my head when grown-ups weren't around, had all the best bright clothes and toys, sometimes stole Jane Fennel from me and talked about girl stuff I didn't understand, was well known to get irrationally and mysteriously upset when she heard people use the phrase 'in the distance'.

As we speak right now, I am happy because I am looking at a photo taken outside Sandyhill Primary School about eight months before the events I have been describing on these pages: spring 1982, I would guess, although the clothes in it are what many people would probably now think of as more redolent of spring 1979. The photo features a total of twenty-six children – my classmates and me – lined up in three rows in front of a wall covered in legal, encouraged graffiti. I am on the back row in light blue dungarees, being strangled firmly but unperilously by a boy called Aseef who is wearing a tank top boasting a striking geometric pattern reminiscent of the TV Test Card. On my other flank is Errol, who is pulling his customary, painstakingly calibrated googly-eye face, therefore actually does look like he is being strangled by someone, even though the only people touching him – me, and, on the other side of him, a miniature blonde hedonist biker named Barnaby Clough – appear to be doing so quite gently.

On the second row can be found Holly Potter, who by my seventh birthday I had come to think of as very pretty but a little dangerous and would think of in a not dissimilar way eleven years later when I encountered her smoking in the corner of a nightclub down by the Nottingham & Beeston Canal. Taj is two boys to Aseef's right and looks like he has run screaming into the shot from a house on the opposite side of the city where he has briefly abandoned a party that he now wants us all to attend. I don't remember the gawky, tall kid on the far right of the second row with the black flares, polyester shirt and diamond sweater but I very much want to. Danny McNulty is front right, kneeling, grinning, his hair not yet quite grown to the length that made us start calling him 'Neil' after the peace-loving hippie on *The Young Ones*, the most anarchic new TV show of the time. His arm is around Miss Buttons' daughter Emma, who I hung around with a lot directly after school and who, perhaps without properly realising it at the time, I always felt, if push came to shove, and no adults happened to be available, could herself more than adequately take over and steer the class in a direction beneficial to our collective future. If you look carefully, you can see that in her left hand Emma is holding a kaleidoscope.

Not everyone is here. Is that Paul Hashimoto's shiny, beautiful jet-black hair I can see hiding in the second row? Perhaps, but I think not. Where is Jess Bonner and his asthma inhaler? Where is Penelope Myles and the blonde boy whose name currently escapes me who always seemed to trail worriedly in her wake like a lilliputian ecclesiastical husband? I don't know. But nobody here looks unhappy, or shepherded, or reluctant. There's so much energy and colour in evidence. The question is not so much 'Were we wearing school uniforms?' as 'Did we even know what school uniforms were?' The photo is an explosion of colour and life: a small, happy, egalitarian middle-English riot.

That small riot was a result of a moment in history in a particular kind of city, at a particular time in the evolution of pre-teen education, with a particular kind of aroma wafting around that was half post-punk, half post-hippie. But it was also the result of a particular collection of people chosen by another person, and all those people's visions working in harmony under – actually, no, that's not correct: not under, *alongside* – the authority of that person's vision. Not a vision under any official educational banner – and definitely not one of those self-consciously 'alternative' schools – but a vision nonetheless.

Sandyhill's headmistress, Evelyn Wishbone, saw her position less as a job and more as an entire philosophy: the creation of an atmosphere of child-centred learning, encompassing freedom and passion and fun. So, just as kids like me looked forward to going to Sandyhill every day, relished our Towards Mathematics textbooks (I voluntarily finished mine five weeks ahead of schedule, and Maths was one of my least favourite subjects) and impromptu pottery workshops almost as much as we relished the free time we were given to play Dungeons & Dragons or re-enact scenes from popular anarchist sitcoms we were supposedly too young to appreciate, teachers like my mum and Miss Buttons enjoyed the freedom they had to teach what they wanted to teach, and decorate classrooms the way they wanted to decorate classrooms.

While they stayed long after home time wielding their staple guns and putting more love into their jobs, Emma and I amused ourselves in the building's vast echoey corridors and stone stairwells, telling each other ghost stories related to its past as a hospital during the First World War. I wonder: does Emma, like me, now look for elements of that building when she is seeking a house to move to? Does she try to find its high ceilings, its industrial radiators, the covered walkway leading to its nursery, the dented oak herringbone floor of the hall where a screening of *Watership Down* via the school projector terrified the life out of us? Does she too, when back in Nottingham city centre, find herself leaving her family to shop while she nips off to do what she calls 'getting a few things', then set off on a secret pilgrimage of the extensive oeuvre of the building's architect, beginning in the Lace Market and ending at the fitness club that now occupies half of the city's majestic original railway station?

It was about two weeks into January, one of these late afternoons in school, alone with Emma, that I told her my biggest secret.

'I'm from another planet.'

We were in Mrs Callidora's classroom at the time – a youthful-looking teacher, who many children cheekily spoke to using her first name, Georgina – which was on the first floor. The evenings were already perceptibly longer than they had been a few weeks ago, the last of the day's sun was peeking over the red-brick terraces of Priory Drive where Taj Mukherjee's mum and Taj Mukherjee's mum's boyfriend were nursing his penis back to health, and I was sitting warming my bottom on one of the gigantic heating pipes beneath the window ledge. Emma was in Mrs Callidora's chair, which felt somehow entirely normal and correct. I hadn't really been intending to say anything, but I'd not told anyone yet, and Emma seemed trustworthy, and it just sort of hopped out of my mouth. She took the news calmly, chewing it over for a few seconds before she spoke, and examining the kaleidoscope in her hand. She seemed distracted.

'Which one?'

'Which what?'

'Planet.'

'I don't know. I just know it's true.'

'Oh. But I was wondering, because I like Saturn. It's a very interesting planet. It has rings and several dozen moons and you can stuff the Earth into it 760 times.'

'I don't think it's that one, or one of the other ones you would have heard of.'

'Oh, ok. That's a shame.'

'Do you promise you won't tell anyone?'

'Ok, I promise.'

The following Saturday, quite early in the morning, my mum and dad and I travelled into Nottingham city centre in the car. My dad parked in the Victoria Centre's underground car park, right at the far end, directly beneath Safeway supermarket, in a part that he seemed to prefer, which was strikingly dark, with stained walls that looked like they'd been hewn from pure coal. We walked back to the main part of the car park and took the lift, which brought us out in Jessop's department store, which was full of intriguing lights and buttons, including the ones on the lift itself. The most intriguing lights of all were in the café at the top, but we never went in there because my mum and dad said the food was too expensive. On the way to WHSmith I climbed inside the metal grasshopper, which, like the metal snake on the other side, had been in the Victoria Centre for as long as I could remember, and often appeared in my nightmares in a portentous way, but not as portentous as the wooden frog and caterpillar in the Broadmarsh Centre, on the other side of the city, which I genuinely believed would swallow me forever if I climbed into them.

My dad asked my mum if she had the house keys and reminded her not to drop them, because if she did, someone would know they were the keys to our house and burgle it, even though it was eleven and three quarter miles away and the burglar would have to try the keys in thousands of other houses before they reached it. After that my mum and dad said they would split up, which worried me for a moment because their friends Sheila and John had split up then never seen each other again, but then I realised that they only meant for two hours, until they'd finished their shopping. I went to Sainsbury's in the Broadmarsh Centre with my mum and we ate bread while she did the rest of the food shopping, then paid for the empty packet of bread, then she tried on some boots and a skirt in a shop called Chelsea Girl which, like all women's clothes shops, seemed much more interesting than men's clothes shops, but not as interesting as it had been a year or two earlier, when, like everything, it had been darker but more colourful and more mysterious and full of women with fringes. On the way back to the car, my mum and dad went to Habitat, the furniture shop, and talked about some of the things they'd like to buy if they could afford them. In the car, my mum told me that we were going on holiday next month, in a county called Cumberland. 'Technically it's called Cumbria now – they changed it a few years ago,' said my dad. 'Oooh, thank you, sir. Not many of us left!'

'Not many of us left!' was what my dad said when he was driving the car and anyone else driving a car did something kind. When he said it, I always assumed that perhaps he already knew the person driving the other car; maybe they had worked together once, in the fish market or one of the schools where my dad had been a teacher, or last year when he'd become a postman and then driven the milk scooter. I then wondered why there used to be more people like that person and my dad. What had happened, to make them begin to die out? The phrase was – along with my experiences of travelling in my paternal granddad's car – something which formed a picture of an earlier, more self-less age of traffic in my mind, where everyone waved to each other from their cars with gloved hands, stopping from time to time to present their contemporaries with bouquets of flowers or hot drinks from Thermos flasks like the one my dad's mum and dad always took with them on their walks in the Peak District. What was so wrong with the new kind of drivers? What had they done to ruin everything? At the time, my mum was learning to drive. Was she part of the problem, too? I wondered.

We took a long route home, so long that it wasn't a route home at all, past a house in Derbyshire that was for sale, which my dad wanted to look at the outside of, but which he told me wasn't going to be our new house because it was well out of our price range. I was glad it wasn't going to be our new house, because it was even further from school than where we lived now and there was a cemetery behind the garden, and some of the graves were scarily near the back fence. In the car after that I told my mum and dad that the other day my cousin Donna had zipped me into a sleeping bag and briefly shut me in her walk-in cupboard because I'd annoyed her by saying 'in the distance' over and over again and my mum said I'd probably brought my problems on myself.

My mum told my dad she'd forgot to say yesterday that there'd been another knock on the door, while he was out at the pub buying cigars, but there had been nobody there again. My dad said it was probably just kids but my mum said that didn't explain why there'd been no footprints in the ice on the drive. 'Perhaps it was some aliens!' I said. 'Yeah, that was probably it,' said my dad. Later on the journey, we passed a big bull in a field, which made my dad swerve the car while he looked at it, and my mum shout 'Pete!' and reach over to hold the steering wheel. But then we went through a village and passed a house which had been on fire and now only had half a roof and my dad said, 'Do you think that house is semi-dethatched?' and that made my mum laugh a lot.

I would miss my mum and dad a lot when I was gone, I thought.

Just like always, we went to my nan's cottage at least twice a week. The cottage was very small, but bigger than my nan. My mum was always worrying that my nan would be lonely, because she had lived on her own ever since my mum's dad had died, ten years ago, but there were always other people in my nan's cottage, wandering in through the door directly into the living room without knocking: my cousin Donna, my aunt Sue and uncle Jerry, my aunt Sarah and my uncle Tom with my new cousin Andy, and Jerry's mum Pat and Tom's mum Maureen. The cottage had Artex ceilings that reminded me of nougat and a gas fire with pretend plastic coal in it and a kitchen counter with red and white cigarette packets and a googly-eyed Gnasher the Dog badge on it and a bigger telly than ours and backless stairs and a bag of toffee and a glass of water in the bathroom where my nan kept her teeth at night and a mantlepiece with a photo of my granddad, who I'd never met because he was dead, which showed him standing in a river in big wellies holding a fishing rod. Everyone was always competing for my nan's attention, especially me and Donna, and, to prevent us from squabbling, my mum and my aunt Sue had decided that Donna and I would take turns to spend Christmas with her. Now my cousin Andy had been born, though, it would all get more complicated, and I'd only get my nan for Christmas once every three years. The reason my nan had a googly-eyed Gnasher badge was because I had nagged her to join the Dennis the Menace fan club with me, but that was mainly so I could get a reserve googly-eyed Gnasher badge in case mine got lost or damaged. I had thought that maybe the Dennis the Menace fan club might not let my nan in, because she was almost fifty-three, but they were happy to accept her application. Donna could talk to my nan about almost anything, including Dennis the Menace and Gnasher, but she couldn't talk to her about snooker, which was where I had the upper hand. I enjoyed few things more than watching snooker on my nan's telly and even though it was black and white and the balls were all different colours, that didn't matter at all, because we saw them as coloured in our heads while we watched. When summer arrived I also liked watching tennis with my nan, but this month she was sad because one of her favourite players, Björn Borg, had retired, even though he was too young to retire.

My nan never got angry, unless she saw Margaret Thatcher, the Prime Minister, on the TV, and even then didn't swear, although I could tell she wanted to and sometimes was trying so hard not to that tiny bits of spit came out of her mouth. After the first time the aliens had tried to take me back, and I'd been extremely ill in hospital, with tubes in lots of parts of my body, my nan's soft, smiling face had been the first thing I had seen when I woke up, and that's how I'd known that on this occasion the aliens had not succeeded in their mission to abduct me.

The doctors and nurses called what I'd had a 'burst appendix'. They said if my dad had not acted as quickly as he did and driven me to the hospital as fast as he did in our crap Morris Traveller which he'd hastily bought to replace the actually superior Morris Minor, then ran into the hospital with me in his arms, like a quicker version of the way he didn't actually carry the lifeless body of Ethel Troutlock to the pond across the road from our house, I would have been dead because the poison that was seeping into my belly would have become too much for my body to cope with and stopped my heart. I accepted the explanation, and felt lucky to have such a great and quick-thinking dad, but I knew the real reason I'd almost died was because the aliens were trying to get to me through my stomach. After my dad had run into the hospital from the car park with me in his arms, a doctor and two nurses had put me on a table with wheels and taken me to a big white room, then another doctor had injected me with a needle and told me to count to ten, and when I'd counted nearly to seven, and everything was going blurry, I'd seen a man with a scalpel and, behind him, another man who had a normal face at first but whose fake smile and whole face then started to stretch really wide, like it was made of rubber, and I knew that had been one of the aliens. I don't know why his quest to get me had failed and the doctors had won and managed to save me, but ever since then I had been cautious, ready for something like this to happen again, and knew it was purely a matter of time before it did. From my experience in the operating theatre, it was obvious that the aliens were adept at shapeshifting, which meant I had to be extra vigilant.

It had taken many weeks for me to recover from the aliens bursting my appendix to try to capture me and take me back to their own planet. I had been frail for a long time and had to learn to walk again, almost from scratch. That had been almost three years ago and, when I thought about who I was, everything in the time before my appendix burst was a little blurred; the operation was, and would increasingly become, a drystone wall separating one part of my childhood from another. I wasn't yet tall enough to see over the wall, and although there were various gaps, little pockets of air between the stones, it was difficult to find them and you usually had to peer really hard through a kind of thick rain to see what was on the other side. I definitely remembered nursery school, and going to Twycross Zoo with my mum and dad and Donna and Sue and Jerry, and a holiday where all the rooms were in a circle around a big hall, but there was other stuff I was less clear about: a small potato with a face in a fluffy duffle coat standing next to a Morris Minor; a photo of my nan, in tears of laughter, holding a baby in tears of tears. Who was that potato? Who was that baby? Were they both really me? How long had I technically been here?

'Nather,' I said, one night, a couple of weeks before going on holiday with my parents to Cumberland Which Was Actually Now Cumbria. (This was what I sometimes called my nan, as well as 'Nan', 'Muriel' and 'Nantwich'.)

'Hello,' my nan replied. ('Hello' was often her way of saying 'Yes' or 'I'm here' as well as her way of saying 'Hello'.)

'Do you remember me when I was a baby?'

'Of course I do, you silly sausage.'

'What do you remember about me?'

'Oh, you were so sweet. Always so bright-eyed, curious about everything. But you used to cry when you came here at first, so much, and you cried even more if your mum and dad were late picking you up. You'd get on your back and kick at the wall and let rip, wailing your head off, and I'd worry that Mr Jameson next door would think I had been torturing you. The rest of the time, though, butter wouldn't melt. You worried so much when you dropped your panda in the lake at Newstead Abbey – you thought he might have drowned.'

'I don't remember a panda.'

Two cars blasted their horns at each other outside. One of the

27

horns played a tune, the same as Bo and Luke Duke's car *The General Lee* played on TV. I ran across the room and pulled back to the net curtain to see if Bo and Luke were actually there, but it was a man in an Austin Princess and a man in a black-and-white Ford Cortina taxi from Nottingham city centre. They had their windows wound down and were shouting at one another. I thought I recognised the man in the Austin Princess as Lee Barrowcliffe's dad.

'The world's gone mad, son,' said my nan, ushering me away from the window.

While my nan made my bed that night, I studied myself in the teak-framed oval mirror in her living room. Sometimes grown-ups said I was 'sweet' and when the headteacher at one of my dad's schools had seen me she had said 'Oh, who is this handsome man?', but that was not how I viewed my predicament. What I saw staring back at me now was what I always saw in mirrors and photos of myself: a mathematical formulation of a small male human. It wasn't a word that I knew then, but I think the best way I could put it is to say I viewed myself as 'generic'. I saw it at home,

in my head, every day, and I saw it at school, as I looked at those colourful, diverse, interesting-looking children all around me, the ones preserved for posterity in that wonderful class photo, so brimful of life: I was not real. Others, such as my nan, my mum, my dad and my friends, might have been fooled – unless they, too, were in on it, which I had not discounted – but I knew the truth. The evidence was in some innate part of me, and right in front of everyone's face: I looked like an idea of a young boy, one that was a little too neat, which could only have been made by people from another planet trying to make a human. Oh, they'd messed up the nose a bit, made it a bit too squashed and little and weird, but even that, I knew, was deliberate: another clever part of their subterfuge. I might not have any memory of where I was from, and some of the other details were unclear to me, such as when exactly I'd arrived, why I was here, how much my parents knew about it all, and what I'd look like when the aliens came back and got me, but what I did know was that I did not belong here and soon I would return to my home planet.

That night, there was ever such a lot to think about, and I stayed sitting up awake in bed for quite a long time until my nan came in, and told me to 'yhhh mst swwcczzz yyhhr lttt out, zzhn' which I knew, from many other times of translating what she said when her teeth weren't in, meant 'you must switch your light out now, son'. As well as the spaceship and the aliens, there was the shelter, and the danger of me leaving it unattended for a week while we were in Cumberland Which Was Actually Now Cumbria. Also, what if the new war started before the aliens arrived? What if it came, and nobody else survived apart from me and cockroaches, and I was lonely, just sitting there in my shelter with nobody to talk to, and no way of getting back to my original planet? Additionally, there was the even more pressing question of which friend I was going to take with me on holiday to Cumberland Which Was Actually Now Cumbria.

I was leaning towards Danny McNulty or Taj Mukherjee, but, on the downside, neither of them had nice hair that they would let me twiddle, like Paul Hashimoto. It was all going to take a lot of careful consideration and planning.

The next morning, my nan and I walked over to my aunt Sue and uncle Jerry and cousin Donna's house on the other side of Ironfield and met my mum and dad, who had stayed there and drunk lots of wine after going walking. I asked if we could all spray our hair pink again but Donna said all her hairspray was gone and Sue said that was just a special thing, for Boxing Day, and it was a new year now, and people couldn't just go around with pink hair all the time, especially when most of them had jobs to go to. Afterwards Donna told me to come upstairs and showed me some pens she'd got, which were good but not as good as Jane Fennel's, then she played me some good songs I'd also heard at the Fennels' house and pinned my legs behind my head and tickled me. When we went downstairs, I asked my mum if I could bring Taj Mukherjee on holiday with us but she said there probably wouldn't be room, because Deborah and Richard Fennel would be coming, as well as my mum and dad's other friends Steve and Penny, and that also meant Jane would be coming, which made me happy and compensated for the bad news about Taj Mukherjee.

My uncle Jerry had a new car, which he told my dad went really fast, and a new record player, which was shiny and silvery and wasn't made partly out of wood like his last one. He played some records on the record player, which my dad said he liked, but later, when we were home, my dad told my mum he didn't think a couple of the records were all that good. Jerry and Sue's house was always really nice, with stripy cushions and bedsheets and a sofa from Habitat that was twice as big as ours, and a garden the same length as ours but much wider, without an asbestos garage. We walked to the top of the garden and through the back gate and over a stile and into the cow field. First my mum and Sue put their coats on and laughed when they realised their coats were the exact same kind. This was something that happened to them and my mum's other sister Sarah a lot with clothing, even though they never planned to buy the same things as each other. In some ways, it was as if all three of them were all the same person, although, unlike me, they didn't look like they'd been created to look a certain way by aliens. When we reached the top of the hill I said I was cold and everyone told me not to be so nesh. Far beyond us we could see the big dark wall of hills where the Peak District started.

'Look!' said my mum. 'I'd never noticed that before. You can see Crich Stand, all that way away, in the distance.'

'La-la-la-la-la!' said Donna, stuffing her fingers in her ears. 'Don't say that!'

'Sorry,' said my mum. 'I forgot.'

Parents

'Fucking hell, I was a right miserable bastard back then. Look at me in this photo here. What a young git. I never should have had that bloody moustache.'

'I think you look nice.'

'You must be mad. That's why you're still with me. Anyway, yeah, that holiday in Cumbria. It was a weird house with all rooms around this big hall and then this cockpit at the top and there was us and Deborah and Richard and Sue and Jerry and Steve and Penny and all the kids and Steve made a soup with a chicken carcass and there was the woodsmoke and the combination of both made the whole place smell brilliant and we listened to that Dick Gaughan LP and it was just the perfect ambience. But it was bloody freezing and the owner in the house next door kept the heating controls locked and wouldn't turn it on properly, so Jerry got his toolbox out and sorted it. Richard and Deborah went out for a walk in a blizzard then came back about twenty minutes later, being followed by a load of Herdwick Sheep, which scared Deborah out of her wits. Four of the sheep wandered all the way into the kitchen, by which point Deborah was upstairs hiding behind a copy of the *Beano*.'

'No, you're thinking of a different holiday in the north west. You're talking about the Forest of Bowland. That was the one with the sheep, and the big hall, and when Benji played a trick on you and locked you out in the snow. That was a few years earlier. This was Dentdale. The one with the big white cottage and the icicles and Mother Shipton.'

'Ah, right, yeah, Dentdale. With the viaducts and the mills. We got there, it was the middle of nowhere on his massive bastard hill in the snow, and I got really ill straight away. Breakfast TV had just started and Jeremy Paxman was on it but everyone said he was too posh so he wasn't on it for long and Richard kept making me these hot whisky and lemon and honey drinks to make me better. Every time we got the fire going, the room would fill with smoke, so we had to open all the windows and the Cumbrian wind blew in and it just got even colder.'

'I remember you were sweating a lot and I could see your sweat freezing on the bed sheets. There were these big cold York flagstones on the floor. It was just like being outside. I don't know how we'd stand that kind of cold now, we're such wimps. I also remember bringing some hazel catkins in and seeing that there's a female flower that's next to the catkin that's absolutely microscopic and pink. That's the main thing I remember about that holiday. What about this picture, of the road? I don't remember where that was taken.'

'You would have taken it from the passenger seat because you hadn't passed your test yet. We were in all that snow, on this treacherous lane way above everything that Steve took us on because he liked frightening everyone. That's his car in front. We were on the way from Dentdale to Mother Shipton's Cave, over near Knaresborough. I told Benji about her, that she was a witch and she'd predicted the Great Fire of London and the end

of the world, and he wanted to know if the End of the World would be because of the radiation and how she had known about radiation in the 1500s. Apparently she said the End of the World would happen in 1991, and Benji said that would be fine anyway because he wouldn't be here by then. He was always saying stuff like that. He had some strange certainties about his mortality for a seven-year-old. Anyway, Mother Shipton was wrong about the world ending in 1991. Or she wasn't. It depends who you ask.'

'A lot of those stories about Mother Shipton's prophecies were made up by some bloke in the 1800s. Yet another case of men being the ones who rewrite history. Benji got quite obsessed with Mother Shipton after the holiday. He borrowed a book about her from the library and started drawing pictures of her when we got home, a little comic strip. I just remembered something else, which was really strange, and I haven't thought about it in yonks. Mother Shipton had a moth named after her, and when we told Benji he thought we meant just one moth, not a species of moth. So then he drew Mother Shipton with her moth. Then when we got back from the holiday in Dentdale,

the first thing I saw when I opened the door was a moth flying around the porch, even though it was February. But I don't think it was a Mother Shipton moth.'

'That's right. That was it. And Benji rode off on his bike to his den on the gob pile but it had been wrecked by that rough lad down the road. The Barrowcliffes' kid. What was his name?'

'Lee. Benji didn't think we knew about the den. I was always finding tins of spaghetti hoops and rice pudding that had gone missing, and I saw a couple sticking out of his rucksack, but I never mentioned it. I thought it was resourceful of him.'

'It's good for a young lad to have a den. I had loads when I was that age. I'd sit in them with my Davy Crockett rifle, waiting for Red Indians, as we called them then. Then developers built the high-rise flats over them. The dens, not the Red Indians. Anyway, not long after we got back from that holiday we saw Colin moving his stuff into Ethel Troutlock's place.'

'Was it really then that Colin moved in? I thought Ethel was still alive at that point. But I don't remember all that much about her, really.'

'No, she died in late autumn. I remember because there was mist over the pond across the road that morning and Benji was playing conkers. I'd found him using kebab skewers to make the holes and I told him he was going to stab himself and grabbed them off him and did it for him instead. Ethel had been a bus conductress when she was young on some of the first buses in Nottinghamshire. She had her own weird names for vegetables, some old family thing. She called courgettes 'courgyjets' and carrots 'orange noses'. I remember one time she heard a Black family had moved to Ironfield and she moved all the valuable stuff in her front room so you couldn't see it from the window. It turned out that the Black family was Marvin Morris, who I used to teach, and his mum and dad and sister. His mum was a nurse. His dad had been the manager at the hardware shop in Sneinton. I used to give him lifts to school sometimes.'

'You're making up stories. I don't remember that. How do you remember this stuff?'

'Honest truth. It all happened. He was a brilliant boxer, won tournaments, but one of the most peaceful kids you could ever meet. He would have never started a fight at school. He was a bloody good lad, Marvin. Anyway, that was a lot earlier. Colin moved in, and suddenly we weren't the weird ones on the street anymore. All his instruments and hats and paintings and aeroplane parts and those robots he had. Cars slowing down on the street, watching it all happen. I remember people in the village thought we were from another planet because we had a herb garden, so fuck knows what they thought of him. I can't imagine he ever went to the pub. I used to go in there to buy cigars. It would all get dead quiet when I opened the door, and then someone would say "How's your *herbs*?" and everyone would piss themselves laughing. It was like walking into a cave full of early, part-developed human life. You expected to see pictures of woolly mammoths scratched into the walls. Colin wouldn't have lasted three minutes in there. I think he'd had quite an interesting life in the sixties, been in a band, I can't remember their name now, and directed a little film and all sorts, but then he'd fallen a bit on hard times, which probably is why he'd ended up next door to us. He wasn't part of the hippie generation, though. He was much older than us. He would probably have been sixty by then.'

'No, not that old. Forty-something? Fifties at most. Fifty looked different back in the early eighties to how it does now. He had one of those faces, like a wise old woodpecker. It did seem strange that he ended up there. I think it might have been something to do with a woman. That's ringing a bell, but maybe I'm wrong. I asked him if he might like to bring one of his robots into school to show the kids and he gave me a long explanation about why he wouldn't be able to, how difficult it was to move them, which led to a very long lecture about exactly how he'd made all three of them, put all the wires and metal together, which I didn't understand at all. It would have been great, though, and nobody would have had a problem with it. It was that kind of school. Someone would have seen a frog at the weekend and then you'd spontaneously have a whole day of learning about frogs because you could. Such imaginative kids. Miss Buttons would push all the chairs together around a table with a huge sheet of paper and everyone would add their own drawing to it until it became an epic story. Benji's contribution would usually have an alien or some kind of strange creature from the woods he'd made up – probably something he'd dreamt up on of our walks in Derbyshire. He'd be drawing on this big piece of paper with a felt-tip in one hand and with the other he'd be twiddling Paul Hashimoto's hair, which was this incredibly shiny jet-black hair, and Paul would be sitting there, entirely placid, like it was the most normal thing in the world.'

'Ah, look at this. That fucking asbestos garage. Benji and his friend Errol next to it.'

'Errol! I remember his house. He was very boisterous, a lovely kid. Imaginative, like Benji. Lots of brothers and sisters. In his house there was this huge trunk of shoes, usually from different pairs, like you were supposed to grab any shoes you could find, as long as you had a left and a right, then get on with your day. You can see that they're lost in their own universe here.'

'They're a bit bloody close to the garage. I told them about that. Awful fucking thing, it was. We sanded it and painted it before we knew just how dangerous it was. I'm surprised we've lasted this long. And the lorries thundering past all day long, making the windows shake. They were all cracked at the corners. And then the subsidence. Benji's snooker balls always falling to one side of the little table he played it on. And how cold that living room was because of the void under it. But in a way I don't think we were actually there in our heads. We were imagining we were in some kind of French farmhouse, which was a bit of a stretch. I was miserable for a lot of the time. I didn't want to be there. Your rhubarb would have been coming through then. It's just out of shot.'

'I don't know, we did our best. I thought it was quite fancy when we got there. It had a phone, and I thought that was really posh, and a garden. We'd never had either of those before. We would have had a washing machine too, but the hire-purchase man at the Co-op wouldn't let me get one because you weren't there, and they wouldn't let a woman buy one if her husband wasn't there to give official permission.'

'The phone was a party line at first. You'd pick it up and there'd be some strangers on it, having a chat. We didn't know who the strangers were until this woman walked up the hill when you were on the phone to Sue, knocked on the door and asked if I knew how long you would be because her husband had just had a hernia from lifting some tyres down at the garage and she needed to call the doctor. It also made things difficult when I wanted to call Richard Fennel and see if he had any weed.'

'I think I do remember some of that. But that was only for a while. We had our own line by the time this photo was taken.

Do you remember that time when I picked the phone up and there was just this voice on it that sounded like me? Actually, I was convinced it was me. "Who is this?" I kept asking and it just said "Who is this?" Everything it said, it just repeated it, but I also knew that I was speaking to someone, and that it wasn't just a technical fault, and then right at the end, when I got frustrated and gave up, just as I was putting the phone down, I heard it say, "Don't worry – everything will be all right." And that was said in my voice too but very softly. That was what I heard me say to me.'

'Ooh, look at this pic: Mr Staythorpe and his cow, Daisy. He used to walk her through the village on a rope. Grazing the long acre, they call it. And here's Mr Chudley with his daffodils, looking proud. I took that picture with the camera we got from Leicester. Best camera we ever had, still is to this day. He had emphysema from the mines. Hated Thatcher even more than your mum did. Later, when the strike was on, he'd walk up the road and take flasks of tea up to the miners on the picket line, down under the gob pile. His onions used to win awards.'

Benji

Because it made sense, in travel and babysitting terms, I had started my school life a little earlier than the other kids. Seeing all these older children, these strangers, acting like my mum was theirs and then my mum being totally unfazed by it threw me off balance at first, but it was not long before I came to accept it and ceased to interpose my tiny body between them and her as a protective shield or to shout 'Leave my mum alone and go and find your own one!' in their faces. I don't remember seeing much of her at all by the time I graduated from the nursery to the main building, probably because she was always busy, firing up the kiln to make some pottery, applying hot dripping wax letters to a cloth or staple-gunning the photos from the school's Diwali or Eid Festival to the board in the foyer. Upon being released from the back seat of the Marina, I'd belt through the arched Victorian front door ahead of her, keen to start my lessons.

I don't remember ever willingly taking a day off, apart from on the afternoon the BBC's *Play School* programme came to film our Harvest Festival: a sudden 'stomach ache' (Errol, who'd been my partner in rehearsing the Harvest Festival song, was not happy) which I still regret, and marks the beginning of a shyness around TV cameras that remains to this day. I had learned a bit about adult illnesses by this point: the main ones were flu and hangover, both of which were like having a cold but worse. On the rare occasions my mum took a day off due to illness, I always still attended, being dropped off by my dad, then heading directly for the office of the school secretary, Theresa, to report on the exact nature of my mum's suffering. 'My mum told me to tell you she isn't here today because she has a hangover!' I announced to a packed staffroom one morning in spring, before eagerly bouncing up the back stairway to Mr Stone's classroom. *Was that right?* I wondered to myself. *Or did my mum say flu?* I decided it didn't matter, as I knew they were pretty much the same, in that they made you ache a lot and have to stay in bed, the only difference being that you recovered more quickly from hangover. *Who had my mum caught hangover from*, I wondered. I decided it was probably the Fennels, whose house she and my dad had gone to over the weekend.

Even though the decade was already three years old, the main light that eventually illuminated it – what everyone I knew called 'the big light', the one hanging from the ceiling – was just properly coming on, when before it had only been the twenty-watt lamps beneath it. I could see it in the newly permed hair of my mum and Deborah Fennel and Miss Buttons and my aunt Sue and my aunt Sarah and my cousin Donna. I could see it in some of the new cars on the road, who had different faces from their predecessors, more suave and determined to reach their destination. I could hear it in the music I taped off the Top 40 every Sunday, which was more hedonistic and apolitical than it had been a year or two before. On *Top of the Pops*, I saw George

Michael from the band Wham! and thought he looked like someone I might like to be friends with one day, but who would probably be far too busy talking to pretty girls to have time to talk to me. Like George's, my hair began to rise and take a more vertical shape, as if drawn inexorably towards that new big light that was making everything more vivid and compelling. In the school's performance of *Bugsy Malone*, in which I had a minor role as a barman, I gelled it for the first time. I found the crunchy feel of it later, as it dried, extremely satisfying, and, in the Fennels' bathroom, stared for a long time at the way it defined my parting, reinventing myself in my mind as one of the pop stars on Jane Fennel's wall, many of whom were now wearing shinier clothes than they had done before.

A couple of new computers arrived at school, with big noisy keyboards. In the city, the finishing touches were being made to a multi-storey car park that reminded me of the Death Star from *Star Wars*. Someone from outer space, I thought, would be happier to land in Nottinghamshire now than they might have been a short time ago.

I could even see the effects of that newly turned-on big light in some of the more recent friends I had made: kids who hadn't been around last year in Miss Buttons' class. Kids such as Jess Bonner and Matthew Woolcroft, who lived in bigger houses than my other friends, over in Mapperley Park – a fairly grand, largely Victorian settlement just under a mile from school – and had shorter hair and clothes that, under the glare of the light, you could tell were new and had not been handed down from an older sibling or family friend. Sidetracked by Matthew Woolcroft's BMX – the first I had ever laid eyes on – I forgot about my invitation to Errol's birthday party, and we were never quite as close ever again. Newly fascinated with my own hair, my interest in running Paul Hashimoto's through my fingers began to ebb. I remained as close with Danny McNulty and Emma

Buttons as ever, and with Taj Mukherjee, further united by our discovery of the word 'typical', which we found could be used to summarise a vast range of predicaments in life and used with alacrity as our joint catchphrase. I felt strongly that it would be either Matthew or Danny who was most likely to be the next friend to join me on a family holiday. Matthew had the BMX and was good at running but I was leaning more towards Danny, on the whole. He had a brother, Ian, who could fit three snooker balls into his mouth and was already a proper actor who'd been on TV, even though he was only twelve and three quarters. He also knew loads of great stories, such as one about a boy he used to know who got his goolies kicked up into his stomach in a fight and had to go to hospital to get them sucked back down into their sac, then learned karate and absolutely battered the kid who did it ('Typical!' said Taj Mukherjee), and another who had got his arm sawn off by a gang when he was walking through the notoriously dangerous Hyson Green district. I memorised these stories and, outside of school, they, and the unknown friends of Ian who starred in them, became mine.

'Did the doctors really suck his goolies back down out of his stomach?' asked Jane Fennel. 'I didn't know they could do that.'

'I swear,' I said. 'No lie. They did it with a special machine. Ian told me, and his friend was the one it happened to, so he should know.'

At breaktime, football, which was yet to evolve into a game of tactics, was sometimes played. Forty children chased a ball as fast as they could towards the wall on one side of the playground then chased it back towards the wall on the opposite side. Tired of that, and the limited scope it offered for artfully curled free kicks, I stood off to one side with Taj, Matthew and Danny, absorbing the knowledge about the ever-expanding outside world that Danny was kind enough to pass on.

'Do you know what a hard-on is?' he asked us.

We shook our heads.

'Well, do you know what being on bonk is?' he asked.

We nodded, not totally confidently.

'Ok well it's just like that.'

To our left at that moment, you would have found Emma Buttons, Ishrat Darpan and Holly Potter playing on the slightly faded hopscotch court, colourfully painted by the children who'd left for Big School the summer before. To their left: the bike sheds. Behind the bike sheds: nothing (a fact that confused me whenever I heard the phrase 'behind the bike sheds' since when I did I only imagined a wall). To the left of the bike sheds: the steps that would lead us back to class, never a thing to be dreaded, no better or worse than playtime. On either side of these steps: iron railings. Many were the times that we had looked at the gaps between these railings, which were roughly head-sized, and almost succumbed to curiosity, but managed to resist. However, a boy called Waheed in the year below us, who had once made the mistake of calling Miss Buttons 'mum' within earshot of her entire class, had let temptation get the better of him. The margarine that Mr Stone had located in the staffroom hadn't worked and the fire brigade had taken almost an hour to arrive. In the interim, a lot of staring and pointing occurred and I made a note to avoid a similar situation. The one consolation for Waheed was that thereafter he was no longer primarily known as the boy who'd called Miss Buttons 'mum' by mistake.

These were what I understood as the main rules of getting by at school: you didn't wee or poo yourself, you didn't call a teacher 'mum' or 'dad' (even when a teacher did happen to be your mum or dad), and you didn't get stuck in part of the school's architecture or furniture. Up to now I had been doing well on all three fronts, but that spring I let my guard down.

There were two types of seats in Sandyhill's classrooms at that time: the soft, square brown pleather pouffes that were scattered on the floor in the reading corner, and the metal-framed, opened-backed chairs with the plastic bar across the top that we sat on when we were doing work at a table. Plenty of warnings were issued about just how dangerous the pouffes could be but, despite our penchant for using them to build pouffe walls to hurl ourselves through when the teachers weren't looking, I never saw anyone get injured by one. The metal chairs, meanwhile, were generally portrayed as unthreatening, which perhaps accounts for my complacency when, one fidgety afternoon in Mr Stone's class, I allowed my legs to slip further and further through the hole in the back of the one I'd been kneeling on, until finally I became one with it.

Ishrat Darpan was the first to raise the alarm. 'Look, Benji Moss is stuck in a chair!'

'He's wearing his chair like it's some shorts!' said Jess Bonner.

'Typical,' said Taj Mukherjee.

'Now calm down, everyone,' said Mr Stone. 'I'm sure Benji can get out of his chair easily enough. Benji, can you twist a little bit, then step out of the chair?'

By now the entire class had encircled me, laughing and pointing. I writhed and twisted and shuffled, and even hopped a little, but the chair was stuck fast, so in the end I merely stood before my friends, like some case study in boy-furniture hybrids. Miniature scientists without lab coats, they prodded and analysed me. Meanwhile, Mr Stone, who had failed in his gentle attempts to disentangle me from the chair, sent Holly Potter to fetch Stanislaw, the stand-in school caretaker, and his toolkit. He took around twenty minutes to arrive, which is a long time when you are not quite eight, and while we waited, a new normality began to set in. Danny McNulty and Taj Mukherjee started a game of Connect 4, sitting on the pouffes, and I watched uncomfortably from above, my new extra torso digging into my hips. I wondered if this was it: would I now be part of a chair forever? How would it limit me in everyday life? Would the aliens still want to take me back to their home planet, now I was part metal?

'Did you cry?' Emma Buttons, who had been off sick on the day of the chair incident, asked me that weekend.

'No,' I lied.

We were on the back seat of my mum and dad's car, on the way from Emma's house to mine. Through the window, the Nottingham suburbs began to fade away in a series of scattered outposts of pebbledash terraces, the landscape changing, its innards rising to the surface. We passed a pub my dad always said we couldn't go to because the garden was full of dog crap. High above us, over the hill which hid the village, headstocks turned against a nothing sky. Behind it: the north of England, looking like one big dishcloth that had all the colour wrung out of it.

'Danny McNulty said that while you were stuck in the chair you did a big fart,' said Emma.

'Well, he lies about everything. He said Father Christmas is make-believe.'

'It's perfectly natural. My mum says everyone does it and it's nothing to be ashamed of.'

'Mum,' I said to my mum, who was in the seat directly in front of Emma. 'Why does Danny McNulty's mum go on holiday camping on her own, away from him and his dad, to a common with missiles, instead of to Cumberland or Norfolk, like us?'

'Cumbria. It's because she's a feminist.'

'What does that mean?'

'It means she wants equality,' said Emma.

'What's equality?' I said.

47

'It means that men and women should be able to do all the same things and have access to all the same things,' said my mum.

'You mean access to things like missiles?'

'No, Danny's mum is protesting the missiles. That is part of being a feminist too. But it's complicated and long to explain.'

My dad had pulled the car into the drive now. Our new neighbour, Colin, was in Ethel Troutwick's old front garden and waved to us from behind a rusty horse trough that he was filling with compost.

'So being one is good?' I said, getting out of the car.

'Definitely,' said my mum. 'I'm a feminist too, and so is Emma's mum.'

'So why don't you both go camping at Greenham Common too?' I said.

My mum reached down to pick up the crisp packets and drink cartons that Emma and I had left behind us on the back seat. 'It's because we don't have the time because we have such messy children.'

I liked it when Emma stayed over and she was probably the girl I most enjoyed being friends with, apart from Jane Fennel, but, when Emma came to my house it always felt like there was a bit less to do than when my male friends came to stay. I wanted to ride my bike up the road but Emma didn't have a bike of her own, so that wouldn't have been fair and would have demonstrated a lack of equality. So the two of us got some good felt-tips that the Fennels had bought me for Christmas that were just like Jane's, and drew some of the dinosaurs in a book my dad had borrowed from Nottingham library called *The Big Book of Dinosaurs*. I drew a Tyrannosaurus Rex and Emma drew a Stegosaurus and a Triceratops because she was much quicker than me and said she preferred herbivores. 'Did you know that much less than half of the dinosaurs actually ate other dinosaurs?' she said. 'Most of them just ate plants, like Danny McNulty's mum does.'

I talked to Emma about the big lake in Scotland where some people had seen a dinosaur, most probably a Diplodocus, living right now, even though dinosaurs had died out hundreds of years ago. I told her about the pond across the road where my dad hadn't thrown Ethel Troutlock when she died and said maybe a Diplodocus lived in there, too, but nobody had ever seen it because it was smaller and better at hiding. Sometimes I imagined that the Diplodocus lived in the pond with a shark who was trying to get it, but the Diplodocus always outsmarted it. When the shark was trying to get the Diplodocus, it always played the same tune as the shark in *Jaws* did when it was about to eat someone, even though I now knew that it wasn't Jaws itself who played the tune, because Danny McNulty had told me it was played by some musicians who helped make the film.

'Who do you think would win in a fight between Jaws and a Diplodocus?' I asked Emma.

'I think you've created a false opposition,' said Emma. 'Great White sharks didn't live at the time of the dinosaurs. Megalodons were the old kind of shark, but they were much bigger and first lived on Earth twenty million years ago. The dinosaurs had been extinct for over forty million years by then.'

'I don't believe you,' I said. 'DAAAAAADDD!'

My dad appeared at the doorway, smoking a small cigar. 'You called, sir,' he said.

'How many years ago did the dinosaurs die?'

'Ooh, a long time ago. More than sixty million. Humans are just a tiny little footnote at the end of that. There have been so many time periods since then. The Paleocene, the Miocene, the Pleistocene.'

'Pleistocene? What was that?'

'Oh, that was a really special era. It was the time when tiny humans made out of modelling clay roamed the Earth.'

That night my dad cooked what he always cooked when he cooked for me: fish fingers, peas and chips. His chips, which he cooked in the deep fat fryer, were always darker than anyone else's chips and were my second favourite food, after radishes. My dad shouted to my mum, who was in the bath, to check that she hadn't drowned in the water, even though that would have been quite difficult to do, because the bath was quite small. Emma and I left clean plates. Emma, who was always very polite, tried to wash the pots but it was too difficult, because she could only just reach the sink, and also my dad told her to be careful because there were knives in there and he was tired from work and didn't want to have to drive anyone to hospital. I continued to leaf through the dinosaur book. At the front, I noticed a library card with dates stamped on it in red letters. '7 September 1978' was the most recent. 1978 seemed ever such a long time ago, but when I thought about how long sixty million years ago was it made my head hurt in the same way it did when I was trying to imagine what it might be like to not exist anymore or go up into the stars and try to find the place where outer space ended.

To everyone's surprise, a shaft of evening sun broke through the sky, which was still made of nothing, and my mum, who was now out of the bath and restoring an old chair she'd found at the tip, poured some lemon squash into two thick tankards and suggested that Emma and I go outside and enjoy the last of the daylight. We walked up to the top of the garden, to the tyre swing, and while I swung on it I tried to decide whether or not to tell Emma the secret I had discovered about next door a few weeks ago. It was quite an amazing secret, somehow not surprising at all and eminently surprising at the same time. I hadn't told anyone at all about it but since I had told Emma my really big secret, the biggest one of all, she hadn't told anyone, so I concluded I could tell her this one too.

'I have something to show you but you can't tell anyone about it,' I said.

The hedge that separated our garden from Ethel Troutlock's house where Colin now lived was turning green, thickening up. As we followed it down along the boundary from the compost heap, occasionally we saw what looked like tiny globules of saliva stuck to the leaves.

'My cousin Donna says that's called cuckoo spit but it doesn't actually come from cuckoos,' I said.

'Why can't I tell anyone about that?' asked Emma. 'I already knew.'

'No, not that,' I said. We had now reached a small gap in the hedge, down near the back of the asbestos garage. 'Look.'

Emma joined me, crouching in the gap, careful not to touch the garage, and peered through the hole.

'Can you see them?' I asked her. 'It's the aliens. They've come to take me away.'

Headteacher

I have to confess I have no recollection of Benji Moss getting trapped inside the chair. I actually thought it was Taj Mukherjee who that had happened to. But it definitely wasn't unusual for one of the school caretakers to be called in to use his tools to remove some pupil or other from part of the building. Those railings near the playground were lethal. Then there was the time that Ishrat Darpan got stuck upside down with her leg behind one of the big industrial pipes in Mr Stone's classroom, on the top floor. I have no idea how she got into such a position in the first place.

Everything was on a grand scale in that building, not least the pipes. It was a big echoing place full of nineteenth-century iron. You opened the windows using these big winding handles. Not everyone was strong enough to do it. Mrs Moss and Miss Buttons would throw lengths of fishing line over the big metal beams near the ceiling then peg the children's paintings onto it. Everything was nicely decorated, anything but minimalist, and a lot of that was down to the teachers themselves and their passions. They brought in the babies of the spider plants and cacti they'd grown at home. Drapes were pinned to the wall, trailing onto tables, where they were weighted down by various displays: pop-up models children had made out of cardboard, fossils, battleships and planes and old food tins brought in from the educational resource centre. We got some of the stuff from the shop in Lincolnshire that Thatcher's family used to own. There was talk amongst some of the more politically inclined children about burning it. There was a lot of nice fabric around, Heal's and Laura Ashley; what would these days probably be quite expensive and considered 'vintage'. We all dressed stylishly. All the female staff had lovely hair, at least until perms began to come in. Looking back, I realise I had some very attractive staff, although of course that wasn't why I picked them. I did choose them with great discernment though. I was very sure about what I wanted the school to be.

The building had been built as a school, then during the First World War it became a hospital, then a school again, a boys' comprehensive this time. In what must have been 1975 or 1976 there was a fire. I don't remember the cause, only that it happened on a weekend and nobody was hurt. It provided the catalyst for the comprehensive being moved to a bigger building on the other side of the city, which is something that had already been talked about anyway. That was when I was brought in. Before we reopened I had dozens of hours get to know the place, to think about what I really wanted it to be. I spent a lot of time listening to people. I held meetings with parents of potential pupils, asked them what they wanted, what they thought was lacking in other schools. I was amazed at how many people turned up; that big parqueted hall, full of bellbottoms and saris and ponchos and turbans. Central Nottingham in the mid-seventies meant an extremely diverse catchment area. I found secondhand chairs and tables in salvage yards, painted walls, even helped knock one down to make the staffroom lighter and airier. I'd been teaching for almost a decade by then and, as I assembled the workforce, I made sure I had lots of conversations with people I'd got to know and trust. Who was inspiring? Who was passionate? Who believed in what they did?

It was eight lovely years, in the end. Of course I see that as the Golden Age: it was the only one that happened there that I had firsthand experience of. I am not the person to ask, but I heard that everything became much more rigid and conventional afterwards. Several of the staff I'd brought in moved on not long after me. It was only three years after that when the National Curriculum came in and that changed everything forever. The last thing we had ever viewed children as was statistics. No child was ever put down at Sandyhill. We wanted every single one of them to feel like they could be anything they wanted to be. We nurtured them and we nurtured our staff, gave them space for ideas. If they wanted to show children how to churn butter, they were wholly encouraged to do that. If someone wanted to use a spout to pour hot wax onto batik, wonderful. I was living with an artist, Malcolm, back then. He painted a gargantuan mural of the building on the wall in the main hall, very meticulous and psychedelic. In each window in the mural you could see children busy with something or other. He said that, as he painted it, he reimagined the building as a woman: a giant Earth goddess, feeding the minds of everyone who encountered her. I confess that I was flattered by that. We both saw ourselves as creators, making things exist that hadn't quite existed in the same way before. We were equals. But when he decided he wanted to move to Cornwall, I followed. About a year later, he left me for a fashion student, the daughter of an oyster farmer whose boat he'd been asked to paint.

I'm still down here, in spite of some opinionated parts of myself, after almost four decades. At times I can scarcely believe it. It has always felt to some extent like a betrayal. You won't find many less ethnically diverse parts of the UK. Not much I see in my immediate vicinity is any barometer of something the average British resident might describe as reality. My head is in the sand in a way it never was in my youth, sometimes quite literally. Malcolm came down here for the light but the water was the big draw  for me. Not a lot of people know it, but I won medals as a swimmer in my teens. I might even have tried out for the Olympics if I hadn't gone to teacher training college. Next year will be the big eight-oh, and I'm still at it, pretty much every day from late February to early November. Wetsuit? You must be kidding. What do you think I am? Some big southern jessie? That said, I do sometimes allow myself a woolly hat, if the sea is extra nippy.

My bungalow is the last in a row of terraces in a clever sort of zigzag design that makes you forget they're not detached. 'Built in the 1960s and would benefit from a schedule of renovation,' the ad said when I bought the place, six years ago. 'Sounds familiar,' I thought. 'I'll take it!' Next door is the village primary school: C of E, entirely white. I hear a lot of happy sounds coming from its playground. At the moment there's one kid who can be heard above all the others at breaktime who clearly believes he is a terrifying monster. He seems extraordinarily committed to the character, and the lack of visual accompaniment somehow makes it more vivid. The headmaster looks about sixteen to me. I'm not convinced that he even shaves yet. When I've chatted to him in the lane, he's made gentle inroads, tried to convert me to Jesus, but it hasn't happened yet. A courier delivered a package for him here once by mistake, and I redelivered it, standing in an unnervingly bare-walled foyer and lingering while he opened it. It was quite big and I was intrigued at what sort of educational device or prop it might be. It turned out to be some kind of gaming device – an Xbox, I think they call them, don't they. 'Brilliant!' he said. 'That's my evening sorted.'

The drive to the coast takes no more than a quarter of an hour. The general rule is: the harder to get to the cove happens to be, the better it is. June is what it's all about, when you live in this place. The month you try to hold in focus during the harder ones. The time you keep your hands clean and dry for because you don't want any of it to slip from your grasp. That peculiar melancholy mid-Cornwall carries in winter and early spring obliterated in one big screenwipe of rampant wildflower, lamb and blackbird. Blue skies and weekdays not yet stolen by tourists: precious, transient gold dust.

I go to bed but, with the windows open, feel like I've still not left the garden. Night isn't so much night as a brief deepening of the lovely days. A surround-sound animal serenade pulls me out of a soft sleep. Thrush, wren, robin, sheep, hedge-munching cow, neighbour's parrot, despotic cat. I drive the lanes that twist their way from here to the beach, beeping before the triple-sharp bends, reversing down a farm track to make way for the occasional courier or BT Openreach van. I walk to my favourite spot from the car. Sea thrift and chamomile above the rocks. The water is green and it reminds me of one of Miss Buttons' old projects with her class because it looks like someone has lightly glued it and is shaking glitter on it from a jar. Floating inside it, I am green too. I let the waves pick me up over their heads and dash me to the ground like wrestlers. They come at me again and again, eternally winning. But I don't lose. There are no losers in this game. A bit like Sandyhill, really.

I remember a June day much like this that seems like last year but is in fact probably a little over a decade ago, when I noticed a young man on the other side of the beach. I say 'young'; he was probably in his mid- or even late thirties. Young to me. Tall. Nice broad, sharp shoulders. I confess I might have looked at him a little longer than was polite or subtle. After his swim, he rooted around the far side of the cove, picking up objects, placing some in a plastic bag and discarding others. I dozed off, I'm not sure how long for, and when I opened my eyes was surprised to see him standing over me.

'Miss Wishbone?' he said.

'Erm, yes,' I said.

'Errol Watts. You were the headmistress at my school. The best time of my life. I am not kidding. Hand on my heart, it genuinely was.'

Once, quite late in my career, I had two colleagues in adjoining classrooms who were surreptitiously at war with one another. The reasons why – mostly a difference in philosophy, leading to an escalation of misunderstandings, at a very different school from Sandyhill – aren't important enough to detail here. Let it suffice to say that by the time term ended, the milder of the two colleagues was at the end of her tether. Her summer holiday could not come quickly enough. She chose a Greek island, one of the less famous ones, Lipsi. On her first night there, as she sat down with her husband for a meal at the restaurant near their hotel, she felt a tap on her shoulder. You've guessed: it was her nemesis from work, who was staying less than a mile away. Coincidences happen. But still, who would have thought it: one of my favourite ex-pupils from the depths of inland Britain, here, in my most secret of secret places, on the edge of everything? Errol talked about the Harvest Festival that the BBC came in to film and the brief breakdancing craze of 1984 – which I have to admit I had forgotten – when the hall was full of children spinning on their knees. He remembered Holly Potter and Taj Mukherjee and Mr Stone and Miss Buttons and Mr Dodds and Mrs Callidora and Mrs Moss and her son Benji, who he said he was still a little miffed with for forgetting to come to his eighth birthday party.

Beach glass. That's what he said he was looking for. He collected it from all over the UK's coast, and plenty of places from abroad too, and turned it into jewellery. And not just beach glass; other objects he found on the beach. He'd made a necklace from three Paraguayan Guarani coins and a pentagram from driftwood. It was not a highly remunerative trade, he said, but he was starting to get by, and happier than he had been for years. He remembered an assembly taken by Mrs Moss when she'd brought in lots of things she'd found on the beach in Suffolk. 'It all goes back to that, really,' he said. I could not stop smiling. I felt in talking to him that I'd briefly got lost in one of my own dreams: a surreal episode that was deeply interesting to me but would later bore a close acquaintance in recounting over breakfast.

Errol did not look like someone who made his living in the craft industry. He looked like exactly the person I'd imagined he would, back in his childhood: a diver or an explorer or the kind of heroic fireman a local newspaper would write gushing articles about. His face had more hair and a few extra angles, but it was still obstinately his eight-year-old face.

'I doubt I'd be doing what I'm doing now, if not for Sandy-hill,' he said. 'I mean that. It was a whole way of life. You don't forget it.'

Do I sound like I'm flattering myself? Flattering *us*? Probably. I am aware that not every child who attended Sandyhill in the late seventies and early eighties went on to do exactly the exciting or creative job they wanted to. The world doesn't contain all the compartments which would allow that, even though there was a point in history when some of us ardently hoped that it one day would. That said, it's astounding how often I hear the same story: the terrible let-down of secondary education, the stumbling around in the confusion of early adulthood, the throwing off of the shackles of something and the realisation of a dream, the invocation of an early attitude, something instilled at a mouldable time and never lost. I go back to Nottingham every year and meet up with the old staff, the ones of us who are still here, and we exchange our news heard via the parents we remain in touch with. The didgeridoo player, the actor, the truant-turned-diplomat. No, do not let us be smug, but can we be permitted to revel a little, to let our hearts fill up with this wild and reassuring life-size montage of the tiny people we once taught? Malcolm can travel the country and see his own paintings, knowing most of them will outlive him. What we leave behind is less tangible, but I like to think it is no less real. The changes we made are more fragmentary than our original vision of them, but many of those fragments float forward, undying, into the future.

When I emerged from the restaurant after our last annual meal together, I realised I had a spare half an hour, so I took a detour past the school on my way back to the car. From the street it didn't look a lot different, save for a few more parking restrictions and a lot less dog shit. Same red brick, same belltower, same enormous arched door, same 'BUILT 1884' engraving above it. I decided not to go inside, although I'm sure I could have swung a little tour for myself. 'Kerrie-Anne, there's a crazy old woman here in reception! Can you come out and see to her? Reckons she used be the Queen of the School or somefin'.' I'm not one for that whole L. P. Hartley the-past-is-a-different-country stuff and, besides, nothing physical would make me remember every centimetre of that building better than I already do. I swear that there's a whole wing tacked onto the structure of my mind which is a precise scale replica of it. I spent so much time in it, when it was empty and when it was full, so much time listening to all its sounds in both states, hearing it fill up with life and laughter and tears, then deflate so all you could hear was the echo of its old creaking bones, coming at you from every side.

Now, in the frail depths of the night, when the structure of everything is tissue-paper thin and I feel in many ways closer to my previous life than my present one, it's those big empty rooms that I find myself in, more often than any swimming pool, any office, any ocean. I'm dressed in a pencil skirt and heels, a big floppy hat I bought from Birdcage or Chelsea Girl. I check to see if an old kiln is still functional, then try the stiff door of a Victorian cupboard, one I'd never noticed before, which turns out to be full of cricket balls and wooden clipboards. I imagine the tidal river of children that will flow into the empty spaces. My footsteps echo for miles. They speak to the building and the building speaks back. Then, much later, I'm in my office, making a plan for tomorrow's assembly, one of only six people remaining before one of the caretakers locks up for the night. I can hear his brush, sweeping the internal courtyard between the entrance hall and the nursery. From the playground, I can hear the chatter of Benji Moss and Emma Buttons. Upstairs, the rapid fire of the staple guns wielded by their mums, my two most painstaking and committed outlaws.

Even then, especially in the emptier times, when there was no smell of boiled carrots — 'good for the eyes' we always said in those days — or incense or teacher perfume or child swarm to obscure it, you could still smell remnants of the fire that had put an end to the school's previous phase. It was always strongest in the paper storeroom, where it was said the fire had started, and heavy rain would somehow tease it out of the building's guts, into the open. I remember one especially atmospheric evening, at the end of an eerily still early summer's day, when there was a violent thunderstorm. As the rain pounded on the Perspex roof at the back of the nursery, we few idealistic stragglers left in the building felt like the whole edifice was under attack. Afterwards, everything was bathed in cobalt light for a brief spell, almost as if a giant metallic lid was gradually being closed on us and everything we did. It was truly unusual and fleetingly overwhelming. Crows huddled on every window ledge: lines of them. We all noticed and made our remarks but, being people who passionately believed that we worked in a place where anything could happen, swiftly put it behind us and continued with our lives.

Colin

I ended up there because I'd been wanting to go to a place nobody expected me to go, not even me. The Back of Beyond? No, that wasn't the idea at all. That was a place that held zero appeal for me. You take a trip from a place that's noticeably Somewhere to the Back of Beyond and you soon realise that lots of other people escaping from Somewhere have exactly the same idea. Before long, it's 'Ooh, how funny seeing you here, darling.' You're running into the exact people you wanted to get away from, or at least other versions of them. I didn't want that. I did not purchase a convertible with a zippy engine. I did not don a pair of tight stonewash jeans. I did not cultivate my first beer gut and ponytail. I had no wish to buy into the conventional idea of what an artist or filmmaker or musician would do on the back of a 1980s midlife crisis, had no yearning for the familiar recuperation hotspots. So I chose to escape to one of the places people escape from. 'He's gone way up north,' I knew they'd be saying, incorrectly. 'Yorkshire, I think. Somewhere like that.' I enjoyed the idea of their incomprehension.

I'm stubborn like that. My name isn't even really Colin. Not that it matters. By that point in my life I'd already been called more names than I could remember. The Mad Professor, Crowley, Warlock, Einstein, Mr Roboto, Wizard, Moon Man, Gastronaut, Woodpecker, Spaceman, Scarecrow, Robot Fucker – yes, even that.

I had started out in adulthood as an electrical mechanic, working on planes, just after the war. That's where I fell in love with the logistics of flight. I reckon if I had continued on that path, and it had been Britain, not America, who'd carried off the moon landings, I'd have been one of the astronauts. Instead I was hospitalised with TB. After recovering, I went to art college, joined a band. But my mechanical knowledge came in useful in 1965. There was a big poetry event in London at the Albert Hall and I had an argument with the organisers: they said I couldn't take a model of the *Venus de Milo* on stage and destroy it because poetry isn't visual. So, using aeroplane parts, I built a robot called John Silent who went on stage and made farting and belching noises. Soon after that he went through gender modification and became Rosa Bosom. Her name is an acronym. It stands for Radio Operated Simulated Actress, Battery Or Standby Operating Mains. A couple of years later she served as best man at my second wedding. I had initially asked a close human friend to be best man, but Rosa had become such a part of the family already and I was sad at the thought of her being left at home and not taking part. She played the bridal waltz, kissed me with her big red lips and blew confetti over us from the top of her head. She's still here, although now she has more friends to keep her company. There's Clockface, who I made from an old grandfather clock and a Victorian vacuum cleaner, and Electric Man Mk II, a hermaphrodite robot I once threw knives at during my cabaret show.

I don't see myself as an inventor, just as I don't see myself as a musician, or a druid, or a satirist, or an actor, or an artist, or an aviator, although it could be argued that I have been all of them. I'm really a mucker-about, more than anything so specific. I like to go in and mess things up. A lot of people have a childhood, then they have adulthood with all its responsibilities, then sometimes have a second childhood. My goal was for my first childhood to never stop. I believe the child in us is who we really are. I wanted to follow my instincts, follow all my little fantasies. I didn't want to become fossilised, like most adults. So I tended to be restless, never in any one artistic milieu for too long. I appeared on screen fleetingly as the gardener of a famous musician in a well-known film. I made props for TV. An influential folk-rock band wrote a song about me. I was the first to do a lot of things. The Sex Pistols, desecrating the Union Jack for a record cover in 1977? Old hat, my love. My band did that in 1962. 'The ultimate toilet paper,' we wrote on it.

The cogs of the fame machine worked so differently in the early 1980s. People couldn't look you up like they can now. Where would they have done it? A microfiche in the local library? If you'd loitered on the edge of lots of things, even lots of culturally significant things over a long period of time, you could easily slip through the cracks. I knew nobody in the village would know who I was when I arrived. Using a fake name had nothing to do with that. Calling myself something different for a while was mostly a gesture I made to myself to signify a fresh start, a springboard for whatever piece of work would come next. But anonymity? That doesn't come easy when you look like I do and wear what I do and carry what I do from house to house. In a small mining village in the East Midlands you're always going to struggle to go incognito when you have a section of the fuselage of a Second World War bomber in your front garden.

Unsurprisingly, there were the comments from the lads

outside the pub and the chip shop – 'poofter', 'woofter' (I never quite understood the difference between the two), 'bumboy' and the like, or sometimes just 'HAIR' – but at the beginning I got on with most of the neighbours. There was a big bloke next-door-but-one, Barry, who worked for the East Midlands Electricity Board, who I could tell right from the off didn't take to me – maybe he was envious of how big my circuit boards were – but there was also Cath and Pete Moss next door, and nice Mr and Mrs Chudley on the other side, with their jungle of daffodils, which were just in their last throes of glory when I moved in. Cath and Pete had a little lad, Benji. Sweet kid. Sort of boisterous, but strangely girlish, too. Endlessly curious, especially about anything related to space travel. I caught him in my garden one day. He'd come through the hole in the hedge, close to the bench where Rosa Bosom and Clockface often liked to sun themselves, and was staring at them in such fascination and wonder that he didn't initially notice me. When he did, he asked if they were aliens. I told him they were just robots and gave him a demonstration of some of Rosa's skills, using my remote-control handset to make her blow confetti all over him from the hole in her head. After that, I couldn't keep him away. Sometimes he came over with his little friends at weekends: a sinuous-looking boy of Asian descent with a runny nose who kept saying 'typical' in response to everything, and a girl who seemed to know far too many big words for her age, asked lots of questions, carried a little red kaleidoscope around with her and had the kind of haircut you might see on the mayor of a small town. Both were polite and they all always remembered to wipe their feet before they entered, which struck me as amusing, considering the state of my floors. Everything was different back then, in terms of children and how far from home they were allowed to stray, but I made sure Pete and Cath knew about Benji's visits and that they were ok with it.

'Just so long as he's not bothering you,' Cath said. 'Send him straight back if he is.' She gave me some radishes she'd grown from seed. I noticed she was extraordinarily creative, building raised decks and gradually reshaping their garden into a series of intriguing rooms without walls or ceilings. She reminded me a little of my ex-wife: always busy, always softly teeming with ideas. I hadn't come to the village, Tapley Woodhouse, to be living alongside artistic people. I thought it would be more of a tepid 'England for the English' kind of crowd. Jingoistic flags and soggy chips. And I would soon find that was very much present too. But definitely not next door. Sometimes Cath's younger sisters would arrive, and their mum, and you'd see the four of these small busy women all lined up in the gardens with their easels, or making mosaics out of old pots. Often at least a couple of them would be wearing the same dress or anorak.

Pete was more withdrawn, more frequently indoors. On many weekends when I was in the garden I could see him in the upstairs window, working on his own paintings. He addressed me as 'duck' or 'yoff' or 'dad', was inordinately fond of word-play and curiously fearful of milk. When he saw me with the garden shears or wire cutters, he always told me to make sure I didn't hurt myself. He was either one hundred per cent up for a chat or one hundred per cent not. No middle ground for him. When the warmer nights began and guests were over there for drinks in the garden, his voice was always the most enthusiastic, the final one I heard laughing as I drifted into the realm of sleep.

My house was the mirror image of theirs, and the six others on the row: same shitty deathtrap asbestos garage, same serving hatch in the kitchen wall, same single-glazed corner-cracked windows that rattled every time a truck went along the road. On the whole, they still made houses intended for poor people pretty solidly in the 1930s. If only that was still the case now!

Even though I had the slight sense I could push it over, I never felt like the place was going to fall down from natural causes. But then, that summer, all of us found out that the buildings had subsidence, which made me realise that on those nights I poured myself some wine and thought it looked a little lopsided in the glass it hadn't just been my mind playing tricks on me. It was hardly a surprising revelation, when you considered what was beneath us. Miles and miles of seams and shafts. Less than four months after I'd moved in, the Coal Board was offering to buy the building off me. But I was in no rush. Thanks in part to them, I had other notions, new fertile creative avenues to explore before I decided whether to accept their offer.

I never have to dig too deep to get my ideas. I usually just give the jar a little shake, do something that's the opposite of what people expect me to, and the ideas swiftly suggest themselves. Soon after I'd moved, I began to think more and more about the planet directly below me. I realised that in terms of my working life, it was a natural progression. For years an obsession with the sky and everything beyond it was my theme. In 1971, I made the film *British Landing on the Moon*, in which my wife and I dressed as astronauts and played football, drank tea, picked flowers and collected rock samples in Union Jack bags. A few years later there was *Stella Superstar and Her Amazing Intergalactic Adventures*, a multimedia performance piece where she dressed up in a space suit, a little like Jane Fonda in *Barbarella*, and I played a black hole who was chasing her around the galaxy. Then at the Ariel Fair, at Herringfleet in Suffolk, she dressed up in the suit again and we held a flying competition off the top of a hill – something not easy to find around there – and people dressed in capes and tried to fly, landing in hay beneath a ramp we'd set up. I think many of them believed they would genuinely soar off, up over Great Yarmouth Pleasure Beach and into the heavens. We went to most of the old hippie fayres in Suffolk and Norfolk; they were great opportunities for creative minds to get together and experiment.

In 1982, my wife left me for another man. For twenty years, she had been my goddess, so at the Rougham Fair that year I drew a seventy-foot woman on the ground with a vagina made from branches and stripped naked and began to woo this gargantuan deity, caressing the ground with a brush, whispering words in her ear, then coming up between her legs. I climbed through the vagina, and as I did it I scraped my dick and balls on the branches and hurt them a bit, but I didn't mind. It was all therapy for me. I fertilised the legs. I became a baby in the womb of the giant woman, then danced like a baby learning to walk. My wife was there watching, with her new lover, who drummed for me. The drumming got louder and loose dogs were wandering about and people were chanting and the chanting rose and then more and more people were dancing with me. It was my greatest earth ritual, the ultimate. And where was there to go after that, except further down into the earth?

Getting rid of the car before I moved was probably a mistake. The Co-op was a forty-five minute walk, and not a mung bean in evidence. 'PAKIS OUT' scrawled on the side wall of the newsagents. Pine-scented air fresheners dangling from car dashboards. Bellicose conversations on doorsteps. White dog shit on the pavement. Surprisingly good library. Confoundingly high number of electric substations per yard. I usually came back the long way, hooking back through the colliery and the woods behind the reservoir, skirting the edge of the big estate with the manor house paid for by coal and dark claustrophobic death, unsettled by a bitter taste that was always on the breeze but pressing on dauntlessly with my rucksack full of pasta and lentils and Twixes and local history. Pete said there was a 'rum lad' who walked some of the same footpaths, dressed in the authentic Edwardian teaching costume of D. H. Lawrence. A poet or two, also. I never saw them but it was good to know I was not the area's only wandering eccentric.

In the forest above a ruined abbey I often found the shredded pages of pornographic magazines. Why were they there? Who were all these people, wanking off in woodland where I rarely saw another human? I collected some of the torn pages and, back home, made a collage from them, juxtaposing them with old photos I'd found of the local mines: those that had closed and those, judging by the way the Coal Board seemed to be heading under the Conservative government, that seemed soon likely to follow them. It was hot, that summer. Muggy grey hot. When the rain finally came, the soggy pages I did not collect would sink further and further into the ground, just like everything. I imagined them seeping through the earth, onto the heads of ghostly miners and then onto the heads of the ancient spirits below them, who were not shocked by tits and arse and cock and fanny, but were thoroughly bemused by the exploitation of the earth's natural resources. The ground, in my mind, became nothing but a thin crust I walked on above a complex maze that held the keys to all history. In a field, a mile from home, I put my head flat to the dry cracked earth and listened. And then I proceeded over the brow of the hill and saw in the valley below me the house I was suddenly responsible for, in this greatly foreign place in the centre of England, and, above it, the big metal wheels that continued to own the horizon, upon which I sometimes would imagine the devil sitting, sharpening his fingernails.

Benji

The way my parents tell it, I was a latecomer to reading but, when it finally clicked, there was no stopping me. Not a single one of the kindly yet ever so slightly sinister vehicles-with-faces in my foxed copy of *Tootles the Taxi*, formerly Donna's, had an engine to rival my own. Books, previously the domain of tired adults who at bedtime could never quite cater to my boundless enthusiasm to be lavished with stories, became all mine to escape into, to vanish with. They were kingdoms I inhabited fully, incautiously gave every fragment of myself to. After I'd finished *Little Red Riding Hood*, an army of wolves in spectacles – or 'wolvers' as I had originally called them – marched on me from the bottom of my bed, never quite reaching my face to bite it off and achieve their ultimate goal of stealing my pyjamas.

My feelings regarding *The Gingerbread Boy* were greatly ambivalent. On one hand, I too would have liked to travel across a river on the nose of a psychedelic fox. On the other, the Gingerbread Boy came across as a little thug with a touch of the Lee Barrowcliffes about him, and if those buttons on his chest weren't made of raisins or currants, which they didn't seem to be, then what exactly *were* they made of? *The eyes of his victims?*

In *The Big Pancake*, the central food 'character' was more abstract: fundamentally just a faceless alien blob with uncanny powers of rolling, belying its non-aerodynamic shape. As, too quickly for my own good, I ate the pancakes made by my mum on Shrove Tuesday, the animals from the book stood around me in a circle: a sad pig who'd believed the pancakes would be his to gobble up, a disapproving hen, goose and cat, and a cow who seemed to be mentally elsewhere.

My original anti-wolf stance shifted upon reading *The Wolf and the Seven Little Kids* and seeing a wolf, far less slick or together than the one in *Little Red Riding Hood*, get stones sewn into his stomach by a vengeful mummy goat then, due to the weight of them, fall into a well and drown.

From the get-go, I was ardently on Team Fox and deeply troubled when, in *The Sly Fox and the Little Red Hen*, a vixen and her cub were graphically scalded to death with boiling water from a cooking pot. My allegiance grew upon reading *Fantastic Mr Fox* by Roald Dahl, then reading it again, and again, and again. When, at around the same time, my mum pointed out a fox skulking across a field behind the pond across the road which didn't contain Ethel Troutlock's corpse, my imagination went into overdrive, remembering the network of tunnels the foxes negotiate beneath the farms in the book. This Nottinghamshire Colliery Country fox now ducked down a hole and scurried into a fascinating tree-root and mine-shaft labyrinth between our house and Colin's and the Chudleys'. He opened his special trap door into the mine shaft, stole a salty chicken sandwich and a Jacob's Club bar from a pit worker's lunchbox and took them back to four hungry cubs and a thankful, fluttery-eyelashed fox wife.

For my parents, books were a great way to get rid of me for a while and buy themselves a chunk of time. Hand me one, or a copy of the *Beano*, and I could be relied on to be elsewhere in a parallel dimension until every page was fully digested. It was one of many ways that I was in fact The Kidded, while going around  believing I was The Kidder. I fell asleep on long car journeys and, even though I woke up when we pulled into our drive, pretended to still be asleep, as I knew it would get me a lift into the house, slung over my dad's shoulder, but I was fooling nobody. On a holiday in Norfolk, Jane Fennel, Donna, Taj Mukherjee and I – not much liking the look of that night's kebabs, laid out ready for the barbecue – snuck off to the campsite chip van with our pocket money. We believed the adults were none the wiser. Much later, we found out they'd known exactly what we were up to. Of course they had.

I was a basic 1980s preteen chip fiend and fishfinger hound, a culinary explorer of no place exotic, but, if I was nonplussed or unenthusiastic about a foreign-looking meal, for a long period my mum and dad only had to answer 'wildebeest' when I asked what it was and I would zealously gobble it down. I find my philosophy here hard to explain. I certainly did not wish wildebeest to be harmed. In truth, I did not know the reality of what they were. I saw them as semi-mythical creatures, not unlike dinosaurs: beasts from a fantasy realm that I might somehow get closer to merely by the process of consuming them. My relationship with wild boar during summer camping holidays near the home of our Italian relatives was not dissimilar. Still to process the fact that their journey to my plate had involved events no less dark than those befalling the foxes in *The Sly Fox and the Little Red Hen*, I saw eating them as a way to get closer to them, or at least to their habitat: the intriguing woodland high above the dusty terraces of our Italian campsite, where we also heard wild dogs howl through the night.

If you are an adult, inventing your own language can be a useful tactic in calming the enthusiasms of a small boisterous child prone to run full pelt into any new passion or hobby. 'Nadging' was another word whose meaning I hadn't yet gleaned, which my mum and dad used a lot. 'Shall we go nadging this evening?' one of them would ask. 'I don't know,' the other would reply. 'It could be busy, and Jerry might be coming over with those paving slabs.' They knew that if they used the common word for what they were talking about, 'swimming', instead of the one they had invented to replace it, they would never hear the end of it from me. Give me the slightest sniff of chlorine, the distant lap of wave or current, and I would become the most insatiable pain in the arse.

So much about water, and the culture of moving through it, fascinated me. I heard some adults who were good at swimming talk about a 200-metre butterfly. I had seen some big butterflies at a butterfly sanctuary we had visited but none anywhere near that big. Perhaps I would see one, if I started to truly excel at swimming? In my impatience to leap into the pool at the local leisure centre, while waiting for my mum and dad to get into their swimming costumes, I could often be found splashing around in the footbath at the threshold of the changing rooms, despite repeated warnings that doing so was squalid and inadvisable on various health grounds. One day a large man from the local tip, covered from head to toe in dirt, arrived at the pool, causing a mass evacuation of every other human there when he entered the water. I was the last of his fellow swimmers to get out – reluctantly, even then. One of my strongest memories was being guided into the same pool for the first time by my mum when I was barely a toddler, the simultaneous feeling of safety and freedom as I bobbed about. But was it a real memory? Or something that had been planted cleverly inside me by the aliens who dropped me in this place?

My mum didn't always join my dad and me in the pool. Instead she sometimes went into a tiny room nearby and, for reasons that remained largely opaque to me, shut herself into a strange futuristic coffin, emerging half an hour later as a slightly different woman: more orange and somehow, alongside it, less trustworthy. Outside the door was a robot, which I guessed to be about thirteen, due to it being shorter than my dad and taller than me. It was worse than Colin from next door's robots, because it didn't walk or have a face, but better than them because if you put money inside it gave you a can of 7-Up or a packet of Skips. On the sloping ramped corridors, milling around, could be found men with neat moustaches and hair that looked it was a flyscreen for a secret door in the back of their head. Dressed in tracksuit tops and trousers cut expressly to show off the bright whiteness of their socks, they bounced balls on squash rackets and winked at me and at ladies heading to the badminton courts, or scrubbed bubblegum and dog-poo stains out of the worn blue carpets. In a short time, much to the consternation of my aunt Sue, Donna and her friends would one day come here purely to try to attract the attention of these men's similarly attired successors, sometimes receiving lifts home with them in their low-slung cars.

Directly next door was the comprehensive where Donna was already becoming one of the more popular pupils amongst her peers, far more popular than I would ever be in my time there. Upstairs, directly above the crisp-giving robot, a room full of immovable plastic seats and lockers serving part time as a youth club awaited that summer's school discos. These would be fuelled by Carlsberg Special Brew and its nine per cent alcohol content, which so many fourteen-year-olds of the area – including, one day, me – would, having little experience of the universe outside north west Nottinghamshire, grow up believing was an entirely normal beverage to ease a person into their drinking life. What a simultaneous assembly line and scrapyard for dreams this building would become. A table tennis career stalled. A black thatch of early pubic hair noticed and puzzled over. A jumble-sale t-shirt ridiculed. A geography classmate kissed. A promise made. A heart broken, taped back together then taunted. A metal locker headbutted (that Special Brew again). A sixth former mooned over. A football elegantly backheeled. A dickhead decked. But for now, for me, it was all about the breaststroke, and by that I don't mean the kind that, with Special Brew in the veins and 'Pump Up the Jam' by Technotronic on the turntable, would one day in this very building become not a totally far-fetched idea of an outcome for an evening in late spring.

The pool at that leisure centre in Ironfield – the nearest to home – wasn't the best, but it certainly wasn't the worst. The latter accolade went to the one about a mile from Sandyhill where we were sent for lessons with a menacing half-squashed goblin called Mr Grubb, who barked at us in a way no teacher at the school ever did and had been reliably witnessed on numerous occasions – though not by me – to flick his own bogeys into the deep end. Unrenovated since around 1903 and prone to wobbly tiles and cockroach infestations, it was a hugely uninviting environment to get wet in, characterised by a suspiciously furry-looking diving area so dark and mysterious in its deepest depths that rumours circulated that the remains of Victorian sailors and their ghost boats could be found there, provided you could hold your breath for long enough. I never built up the courage to try. Instead

I dreamed of the light, clean pool on the other side of the city with the freshly installed flume which, after lots of swerving of the issue, and diversionary conversation on the theme of nadging, my parents finally took me to, on what the pool's owners called 'Family Night'. It cost fifty pence for the four of us: me, my mum, my dad and my temporary brother, Danny McNulty. That got us three joyous, eclectic hours of badminton, squash, table tennis, five-a-side football and the highest quality nadging available in the whole of the Greater Nottingham region. The one catch was that everyone had to be related. This led, in subsequent months, to me gaining a number of new siblings of dramatically varying different sizes, shapes and colours; a pattern that was never questioned by staff, who probably pictured a culturally rich but cramped home life in a one-bed terrace nearby. On the weeks where Danny McNulty was with me, I am sure nobody would have concluded that I was the elder of the two brothers. He was a good year or two ahead of me in physique and at least seven ahead in ideology.

'My mum says Thatcher and God are the modern world's two greatest evils, and I think she's right,' he told me during a pause in a table-tennis match.

'But aren't there lots of different gods?' I asked. 'They can't all be evil.'

'Yep. Every one. My mum says so. They're responsible for virtually all the suffering in the world. And they somehow manage to do that without existing. Emma Buttons says you're an alien from Saturn.'

'I can't believe she told you that. I made her promise not to tell anyone. And it's not Saturn. I don't know what the planet is. The aliens sucked that memory out of my mind, I think.'

'We were at her house when she told me. She's got a video player now. We watched *The Empire Strikes Back* then we watched *The Empire Strikes Back* again then we watched *Panorama*. Her mum videos it. Emma and me and her mum were talking about the ice planet Hoth and what it would be like to live there and about the future of British Rail. Her mum and the people on *Panorama* said it's hugely uncertain. Don't worry. Emma trusts me. I won't tell anyone else. Oh and her mum knows too. But she won't tell anyone either.'

I smashed a serve past him and proceeded to win by 21 points to 6, but that week the Tory Party manifesto had been published, with worrying plans to abolish the GLC and six metropolitan counties, and there was a rumour Michael Foot was poised to resign as Labour Party leader, so I suspect he wasn't giving the game his full concentration.

At school, Danny had lately introduced some of his classmates, including me, to a game called Dungeons & Dragons, which was harder and different to other games we played, such as Connect 4 and Downfall, and, unlike them, carried on in your brain hours, and sometimes even days, after you'd stopped playing it. Nowhere more than here did we get a measure of just how far ahead of us he was, in so many ways. As he led us through swamps and forests, where we fought hellhounds and mind-flayers and received glowing amulets from helpful elves, I jiggled around excitably in my chair, careful not to slip back through the hole in the back of it. Under Danny's guardianship, the games would stray into even more exotic areas than those recommended by its designers, containing a different kind of mystery and peril.

'Ok, Son of She of the Gnashing Teeth,' said Danny to Taj Mukherjee. 'You're now finally in the Swamp of Zugod. You see a night hag, who has just returned from an underground passageway where she fought off over a hundred gelatinous cubes, using all her cunning. She has her jugs out and has sex energy from her battles. She says she can take you to the Mountain of the Leaf Men, but she has long nails like knives and you are not sure if you can trust her. What do you do?'

'Can I go back to the Labyrinth of Retallick?' asked Taj. 'And do I have to be called that?'

'No. And yes. You are fully on bonk now and she is touching your leg with her knife nails. You can see her jugs are really big and long. What do you do?'

'But where am I at the same time?' I interjected.

'You are thousands of miles away, living as a moss-covered stone, in the Woodland of Moles. You have to wait until a female rust monster sits on you, because only the touch of her brilliant fat bum will reawaken you and return you to your true form.'

'So I just have to sit here? That's not fair. I rolled a twelve. You said that was enough for me to bribe the Ghost Ferryman and get across to the good side of the Million-Year River.'

'SILENCE. Do not question what the Dungeon Master decrees. Now a great rain made of sweat has fallen on the Swamp of Zugod and an army of girl elves has arrived to assist the night hag in her campaign, and Son of She of the Gnashing Teeth is tangled amongst the elves, covered in sweat and even more on bonk than he was before. What does he do?'

Although many parts of the games – not least the carnal ones often introduced by our Dungeon Master – made no sense to me, I fell increasingly under the spell of the epic folkloric universe that Danny transported us to. Back home, it pushed me a little further from home on my bike rides, in the direction of the woods near the reservoir. Here I had sword fights with orcs, yugoloths and frost men. I was less interested in my den on the gob pile now, especially since it had been found and mostly annihilated by Lee Barrowcliffe. My attentions turned instead to the more arboreally rich landscape in the opposite direction. In my bag I took with me *The Forest of Doom*, a new book which was better than all other books because I could actually be in the book and choose what I did. I imagined Tapley Woodhouse as Stonebridge from the book and the gob pile as the hill where the evil hill trolls lived, coming down periodically to attack the local dwarves.

One day, as I twirled through the trees, twigsword in hand, I was shocked to see a dead elf on the ground in the distance but, to my relief, realised it was just Colin. He didn't notice me and something about the intensity of his concentration told me he shouldn't be disturbed.

'Mum,' I said to my mum that evening. 'Why does Colin listen to the soil?'

'It's because he's a Pagan.'

'Can I do it too, if I become a Pagan?'

'No, you'll get your trousers dirty.'

'What's a Pagan?'

'It's when you believe that the real God is in flowers and bees and rivers and that when we die we all come back as an animal or part of nature. Maybe a nice flower.'

'But Danny McNulty's mum says all gods are evil.'

'Not this one. This one doesn't want anyone to have any wars. It just wants everyone to get on.'

'I don't want to come back as a flower because flowers die really quickly.'

'Well, yes, they do, but it's ok, because after that you'd come back as another flower. Maybe an even nicer one.'

Sometimes I went over to Colin's house and he let me play with some of his old aeroplanes. He said one was from so long ago it had existed before my nan was even born, which made my head hurt to think about, although not as much as when I was thinking about how long ago dinosaurs existed. He was always busy, reading or writing or taking telephones and clocks apart. I wasn't allowed to go in one room of his house because he said there was an important project he was working on, which wasn't for children. Every room had books in, but unlike in my mum and dad's house, a lot of them weren't on shelves; they were just piled up on the floor, between all the other things Colin owned, such as old helmets and records, and small chubby guitars and big capes and hats, which he let me try on. On one wall there was a big drawing of the human body, a bit like ones I'd seen at school, but with tiny astronauts floating all over it, examining the various organs and parts. I asked him what it was and he said it was a diagram for an orchestra he'd invented that played all the sounds of our internal systems. 'You mean like burping and farting?' I asked. 'Oh, definitely,' he said. He told me that really he was just playing silly buggers, which confused me, as that was something my nan had told me not to do.

He said his house was sinking into the earth, like my mum and dad's, and I wondered if that was because all the things he owned were too heavy. He didn't have any animals that were alive but he did have some dead ones, including a fox and some birds. I asked him why he had them and he said it was to remind him of man's cruelty. 'Because men are crueller than women?' I said. 'Well, I mean "men" as in "all humans" but . . . yes, I mean that too,' he said. I asked him if he had a wife and he said not anymore, and that he used to actually have two, but not at the same time. I asked him if that was because he didn't like the wives anymore and he said that, no, he still liked them a lot. I asked him why both of them didn't still live with him now, then, and he said it was complicated and that also sometimes it was nice to live alone and that you couldn't live with everyone you liked because that would be impossible. I decided he was right after I thought about my nan and my cousin Donna and my aunts and uncles and Jane Fennel and Taj Mukherjee and Danny McNulty and Emma Buttons and Mandy and Kate Fig-shaw from over the road and my other friends from school all living inside my mum and dad's house with us. I reasoned that it would probably give me no time to read *The Forest of Doom* or the *Beano* or *The Warlock of Firetop Mountain* and also that the house would become far too heavy from all the people in it and sink even further into the ground.

As I talked to Colin, he kept taking wires and bits of metal out of an old radio, then putting other wires in it, but talking to me didn't seem to make him any less good at it. He always looked like he was concentrating, even when he was just having a cup of tea or stroking the head of his dead fox, but he never got frustrated or angry. One time when I was riding my bike along the pavement then up to our front door I saw him standing on his doorstep, listening to Lee Barrowcliffe's dad shout really loud at him. I couldn't properly hear what Lee Barrowcliffe's dad was shouting about, because all the words seemed to get eaten by each other, although some of them were definitely something about flowers. Colin seemed really calm the whole time, even though Mr Barrowcliffe's spit kept landing on his face. He just kept saying stuff like, 'Keep going, my friend, let out your rage. I'll just stand here until you're tired.' I couldn't understand it, because if I'd had robots, like Colin did, I would have set the robots on Lee Barrowcliffe's dad and got them to karate chop him with their metal arms. Then he would cry, and be sorry, and he'd also make Lee rebuild my den on the gob pile.

I believed Colin when he told me that the robots weren't aliens, but that didn't make me any less vigilant. I knew, especially from my experience in the hospital of nearly dying, that they were unusually clever and liable to take many forms. They'd probably know I was onto them by now and be devising a new disguise. One afternoon when I was up in the woods, fighting some elves, I walked a little further than usual and came to a field at the back of the woods where there were some goats and some sheep but then behind them were some other animals, much taller, with strange faces and big teeth, which I decided must be animals from another planet, maybe even aliens, because the only animals I'd seen that looked anything like them were the tauntauns on the ice planet Hoth in *The Empire Strikes Back*. But then a few days later, when Donna and Sue were over here, my mum got some chopped apples out the freezer from last year, which she didn't want to use for a crumble or pie, and let them defrost, then we all went up to feed the apples to the animals the aliens were disguised as, which my mum said were called alpacas and came from far away, although not a whole other planet, just South America. I remained suspicious, though, and resolved not to let my guard down.

Another photo I like, probably taken within a week or two of that day when we fed the alpacas: seven children in my mum and dad's garden, including me, playing at the far end, closest to the gob pile, on the climbing frame my mum and dad built together for me, close to the stable where the scary horse lived. The day of my eighth birthday, probably around 11.30 a.m. The first arrivals. There's Mandy and Kate Figshaw from the farm across the road and Brett and Philip from the house two doors up from them, who I have started playing with more lately. Donna can be seen in the photo too, holding a tray of cheese and pickled onions on sticks which she has helped my mum to prepare. Kate is hanging off the climbing frame, wearing a jumper with a sheep's face on it. I'm wearing a yellow t-shirt with a red smiling sun on it that says NUCLEAR POWER? NO THANKS. I have not got scared about it when I have seen it in the mirror and it says something else because I know what mirrors do to writing now. I almost certainly got the t-shirt at the CND fair beside the River Trent earlier that month, which comprehensively blew the minds of me, several of my schoolfriends and dozens of the other offspring of Left Wing Nottinghamshire parents by virtue of featuring a giant inflatable that you could not only bounce on but *actually get inside and walk around in*. I have decided that the day inside the inflatable was the best day ever, but today has not finished yet. Colin has not yet come over with several of his hats and cloaks and flying helmets, acccompanied, to my surprise, by Danny McNulty's mum, and my mum has not yet given me my birthday present of a cape she had made with a 'B' for Benji sewn into it, like the 'S' on Superman's cape. Colin has not yet set up a platform at the summit of the garden, the hay bales and an old bean bag have not yet been placed beneath it, and the first of us has not yet soared off the platform, in the genuine belief that he or she can keep on going into the pure blue directly above us.

Is it any wonder I still love June so much and surely will forever more? The world is a table set just for you when you are an eight-year-old with plenty of friends and a safe, loving family, and, in summer, the spread on that table is more lavish still. As you get older, those days, which did not exactly seem short on expansiveness at the time, will only expand further until they go marauding over the cooler, greyer days that flank them. Summer is childhood memory's greatest ally, its accomplice in the battle against all the tedious reality checks of winter. So, keeping this in mind while I look at this photo and a few others from the same day, I now turn back and try to imagine an alternative view, from behind the scenes.

I go, as my adult self, down the crazy-paving path past the asbestos garage, through the back door, past the supermarket-brand lemonade and unprepared jelly and powdered mousse on the kitchen counter, over the sausage-dog-shaped draught excluder and into the front room, where I find my dad, staring off into space, his chin resting on his left hand. His glasses – his only pair – are held together with sellotape. In front of him on the coffee table is a bank statement which he has recently placed there, hoping – having ruled out other solutions – that it might magically disintegrate. He hears a knock on the door and answers it. The drive is empty, as is the road directly in front of the house. He goes upstairs, takes two paracetamol for his headache, then, by my mum's request, unfolds the stepladder to get to the loft and locate Donna's old paddling pool, which my mum thinks might have a puncture in it but also might not. He flicks the bolt of the loft hatch and, just as the hatch swings down and hits him on the head, there is another knock on the front door. 'Pete, can you get that?' says my mum. 'I have no hands.'

It's Jess Bonner's dad at the door, with Taj Mukherjee, Holly Potter, Emma Buttons and Paul Hashimoto. Jess Bonner's dad says hello and makes a mean joke about the rust spreading up the side of our Morris Marina. As he does, the phone rings. It's my aunt Sarah, who is bringing my nan and my baby cousin Andy to our house, but who is calling to say their Volkswagen Beetle has broken down near the plant-hire firm, just down the hill from the Chinese takeaway, and now they're standing on the grass verge and don't know what to do, and also my nan is having

one of her dizzy spells. 'Hold on, I'll come and pick you up,' my dad says, but then remembers that the clutch is just about gone on the Marina and he and my mum are waiting until pay day before booking it in to be fixed and also neither of the left indicators are working, so it's technically illegal to drive, but he thinks sod it and grabs the keys anyway.

On the way from the porch to the driveaway, he notices that the Barrowcliffes' German shepherd, which the Barrowcliffes choose to exercise simply by unchaining it once a day and letting it out to roam anywhere it wants to, has come up the drive and crapped exuberantly on the lawn. He knows it is almost certainly the German shepherd because of the size of the shit and the fact that no other dogs anywhere near that big live in our part of the village. As he's looking at the shit and thinking he should clear it up, so no children tread in it, he steps in the other part of it that he hadn't spotted.

It's now five hours later. Nearly all the party guests have left. Barry next door has been over to complain about the noise the children have been making in the garden but hasn't punched anyone's teeth out. I'm still outside, with Taj, whose mum works long hours at the hospital and can't get here to pick him up until this evening. My dad is feeling grumpy because my uncle Jerry took the piss out of his cardigan and moustache. He's not cleaned up the stain where Jess Bonner dropped ice cream on the sofa. My mum is in the kitchen with Donna, washing up, but is itching to get back to the antique chair she found at the tip last week and is halfway through sanding down. She's thinking about something my nan said about something the doctor said yesterday about her heart, and about that bank statement, and worrying that Errol Watts might have accidentally touched the asbestos garage. Hearing a piercing scream, she and Donna run into the garden, overtaken by my dad, who is a faster runner than them. I'm on the ground, clutching my arm, near the back wall of the garage. Taj is standing over me, shrugging and showing his teeth in a concerned way. Blood is gushing out of the underside of my arm. 'What happened?' my mum and Donna keep asking. But I don't seem to want to tell anyone. All I keep saying is, 'I'm not going back there. They'll get me.' My mum is asking who 'they' are and Donna has gone to find a bandage and Taj is opening his mouth to speak. But by now my dad has the keys: the ones to the car that will probably work, just like it did earlier. The blood keeps coming, which is a concern, but he is sure that everything is ok and that, as he keeps telling us, it's just a matter of everyone staying calm. He's done this journey with me before. He knows the rules now: it seems frightening at the time and you have to go very fast and look out for the police along the way, but everything works out in the end.

Authors

After he'd dropped from the sky and been through customs, he took the road past the power station: the one where parts of a TV show with spaceships had once been filmed. It wasn't the most direct route, but he was ahead of schedule and wanted to look at his old haunts, swim for a while in what they triggered. The edges of the city were a different shape, different even from the shape they'd been last time, which had only been eleven years ago. The painting he held of the city in his head now depicted a different place, not prettier, just different and painted with a finer brush. Everything he saw looked so big and uniform, it made it hard to slip beneath the heavy corporate top layer of the palimpsest and into the past. A beautiful summer day, though. High-definition scenes. The Beechdale Retail Park branches of Pepe's Pizza and The Tanning Shop had surely never looked better.

He wound down the windows and let in the smell of the afternoon: hot tyres and ketchup. All the missing jigsaw pieces of the suburbs had now been found. No gaps remaining to show the messy green carpet underneath. When the car finally exited the jigsaw, brick changed to stone and the walls of the land went up on either side of him. He breathed, remembering they did have some countryside halfway up the length of England. He noticed that the breath had a flutter to it, as if it possessed brittle, defective wings. Nerves. Absurd. He'd once told her he'd like to marry her. They had been eight years old at the time.

He parked where he could, walked up a rocky path. There was a brief anomalous breeze, like a hand giving the world a little shake to wake it from a nightmare. It stripped the petals off the foxgloves at the bottom so they swayed in the wind like tall, blushing men.

She had prepared black-olive focaccia with a little rosemary from the garden, and iced coffee. After a thorough clean, the house, though naturally dark, appeared to be full of reputable summer air. It resembled the place she wanted to live in but, due to the realities of time and work and fatigue, usually only did in the company of visitors. At more or less the exact second he was due to arrive, she noticed the dog had puked on the sofa and rushed to the kitchen for a cloth, then caught herself, slowed her walk to something almost comically calm and mellow. There was nobody to impress here. She was the one who'd won the award, the one with the film option, the one the book clubs talked about. The day was not intended to be the beginning of anything. You chatted about some stuff that happened forty years ago, then you promised to keep in touch but didn't. Certain lessons learned about reconnecting on the internet, though, informed her anticipation of the day: a regrettable meeting with an old boyfriend from the distant past at a vulnerable time. The shrivelled sad state of the bloke. Anecdotes like slow leaking burps that kept squeaking on out into the air long after you thought they'd finished. Clogged ears and opinions like an old dustman's brush. Her polite forbearance. His apparent belief that he had been part of a totally different evening to her and his absurd expectations for its conclusion. Not at all relevant to today's encounter. But still.

She had in fact been the one to establish contact and set the chain of correspondence in motion that had led to today's meeting. They'd been connected online for a while, just by chance, she can't remember how, and she'd barely noticed him, had no suspicion of anything that linked them outside of the digital slop bucket too many people mistook for reality. But then she'd seen him talking about the book he was writing: a memoir about a childhood in a place that sounded familiar. The more she heard about it, the more she wondered. 'I might be wrong and being a total weirdo here, but I think you used to live across the road from me,' she wrote. 'I think you were the Dungeons & Dragons kid? You used to talk about it all the time. I remember thinking it seemed such an interesting world.' He responded as if a little bruised by the pigeonholing – 'I only really played it for a few months' – but something pleased him about it, too. He had known she was a writer, a historian, but a little more investigation revealed a short-story collection. A new surname. Not a lukewarm review in sight.

As you read these stories of East Midlands toil and struggle, an eeriness grows. Part of it comes from their desolate rural-industrial setting but the other comes from the sense that Nottinghamshire-born writer Amanda Clark is somehow listening in on us all, in our most private and fraught moments.

Reading the sparse, at times furious prose of Colliery Girls, *there are numerous sounds that can be heard constantly, stridently in the background – the turn of headstocks, the chug of tractor engines, the scrape of metal against metal as fire grates are cleared – and one more, more subtle, always going on just beneath them: that of D. H. Lawrence shivering in his grave.*

She said they'd got it wrong: she'd actually been born over the border, in one of the wards in the Royal Derby, but, yes, it hadn't been a bad thing to wake up to. She said she had some photos he might like to see, letters, a couple of other things he might find interesting. They danced around the idea of meeting for a while, making sure nobody would be stepping on anyone's toes, creatively speaking. He said he was overdue a trip to the UK to see his parents. He could pop by, then carry on, an hour or so east.

Her tiny garden backed up to the limestone cliff at the edge of the village. Sitting in it at this time of year, with its rampant wisteria and honeysuckle and clematis, reminded him of the comfort of fabric-dominated rooms from his past. As a child, he'd liked to hide behind blankets pinned to walls, enjoyed being taken to carpet showrooms. Today he wore an Indian block-print shirt, which she noticed was buttoned incorrectly, so one side of it hung down too low. It was part of a series of realisations that gradually remade him as the boy she'd once known. At first, his hair, greyer than in the photos she'd seen, had come as a shock, but that was mostly because of the part of her that believed that every adult from her past she ever would be rekindled with would be twenty-five, which extended directly from the other part of her that was herself forever twenty-five, a twenty-five that believed in twenty-five as a sort of plateau where everything stayed the same forever. She glanced at the apple tree which hung over into her yard from next door. In only three months, the fruit on it would fall.

'It's an old miner's house,' she said. 'Hard to believe, but it used to be even smaller before the couple who sold it to me knocked it through.'

'Perfect for you, then,' he said. 'With your interests. My

parents always wanted to get a house over this way when I was a kid but they couldn't afford it.'

'Mine too. I feel guilty sometimes. Not that I'm living like Queen Isabella of Castile or anything.'

'You seem to be doing ok for yourself. I watched a clip of you getting the award.'

'Oh God, why did you watch that? I have to admit it came along at a useful time, but it didn't change my life. And you? I mean . . . Italy! Wow.'

'It's good, though not as perfect as some people probably think. Nowhere is. It was hard at first, especially before I learned the language. We missed friends and family. Still do. There are all these houses with swimming pools but winter is cold, just like here, sometimes colder. My place was cheap, though. It was a way to take the pressure off work-wise, not push so much, at a time when I felt a bit ruined by it all. I write a book, a few people buy it, then I write another book and the same few people buy that too. Meanwhile we pay the mortgage and don't have to beat ourselves up if we buy a bottle of our favourite wine instead of the other wine that's cheaper that we don't like as much. And there's the sea, which is only ten minutes' drive. That was the other big draw.'

'You said you're married now?'

'Yes. Coming up on six years now. Allesandra owns a bakery down in the village near where we live, which is also where she's from. I met her in Long Eaton. She used to work at the big Tesco there. You?'

'Was. Mechanic. Full of piss and vinegar. Less vinegar and more piss, these days. Our daughter is at his place this weekend. I'm stuck with his surname now. It's on the books, so no point changing it. But, yeah, going back to the sea thing. It doesn't surprise me at all that you've ended up near it, to be honest. I remember that day we went with your headmistress – what was she called? – on the trip to Lincolnshire, and you and her were the only ones brave enough to get in. I don't know why I was there, or why I wasn't at my own school. I guess you all just let me come along.'

An old dog, with eyes somewhere inside its fur, emerged from the upstairs floor of the house and stretch-slumped on the hot paving slabs near her feet. 'This is Praisegod Fairbones,' she said. 'The name comes from a lay preacher in the seventeenth century called Praise-God Barebone. I misheard it as a child. I prefer Praisegod Fairbones anyway, even if he didn't exist, because he didn't suck up to Cromwell or oppose freeborn rights. I always knew that one day, if I ever had a dog of my own, I would call him that. Even if he was a her, which, as it turns out, Praisegod Fairbones isn't, unless I've been chronically unobservant for many years.'

'Bloody hell, I'd forgotten about that,' he said, giving the animal's head a rub, tentative in case something fell off it. 'I don't think it was a proper school trip. Just a few of us at the weekend. Miss Wishbone. My mum worked with her. That would probably have been Saltfleet, near where you can see the seals have babies on the beach every November. She was like one herself. No, not the right shape. More like a tall otter, really. It must have been fucking freezing. Not precisely the Adriatic. I don't know if I'd do it now. Too spoilt by my environment. It can still be frightening, though, over there. I have this way of blocking out what might be in the water with me. I actually got stung quite badly a few years ago. Thought I was paralysed at first. Portuguese man o' war jellyfish. It swam all the way around the bottom of Spain, just to have a go at me.' Was he talking too much? He decided he probably was. 'How is your sister?'

'She's well. I honestly think she's the happiest person I know. Still the brightest light in a room, still likes sheep. I wondered if you knew that she still has a quilt that your mum made her.

Every panel has a different breed on it. The Zwartbles are her favourite.'

'I had no idea.'

'I remember she was always busy with some project or other, your mum. I sort of had it in my head that she had built your entire house with her bare hands. She seemed a bit miraculous to me.'

'Do you still pay her to let you squeeze her spots?'

'Your mum? No, I haven't seen her in absolutely ages and she hates it when I sabotage her face. I'm kidding. You mean Kate. No. I'm into her for two grand already for the repairs after the shower leaked and the living-room ceiling fell in. She's a head-mistress herself now. More of a managerial role, as has become the way. Responsible for five different schools.'

He showed her the photos of her and Kate that he had brought with him: one from his eighth birthday party; another from the time his parents took everyone to a butterfly sanctu-ary; one of her, him and Kate and the two little Christian boys from up the road having a picnic in the wildflower field on the other side of the reservoir, him doing his googly-eyed face, pat-ented by his friend Errol. Another, peopleless, taken from the top of the valley, looking down across the farm where his dad once worked for a summer, showing both of their houses, and the gob piles in the background.

She showed him a copy of an old magazine the four of them had made that she'd kept. 'STRINGY LANE CLUB BUGLE' written across the top of the front page in red felt-tip, the letter-ing uneven, hanging down too far on the right, just like his shirt. Some drawings of a caveman named Alf. A list of favourite songs. Reports on her and Kate's adventures. After a few pages the handwriting changed, became neater and more technologic-al: '4.35pm: fed pigs. Checked around the back of the barn for marshans with Benji. There wasn't none.' She told him that was her bit. 'My prose has come on a bit since then but there's still a long way to go.'

She opened a chest of thin wooden drawers and pulled out some clippings she'd saved, from a project she'd worked on a few years ago: historical info about the collieries, local-newspaper reports about the strikes in '84 and '85. An older picture of Thatcher in a hard hat, down in the shaft, looking quasi-interested. 'Planning her apocalypse. Devastating. I won't linger on this as it will just make me angry,' she said. 'Please feel free to borrow anything you need.'

She brewed some tea, stronger than he liked it, and they returned to the garden. The sun felt like a big bright pause button in the sky. 'Oh, and I don't know if it will be interesting to you, but there's this as well,' she said, lifting a curtain of wisteria to reveal a large rock resting on the wall, with an emerald tinge to it and a hole in the centre. The hole formed an almost perfect circle. She told him to pick it up. When he did, the wholly unanticipated lack of weight to it made him stumble backwards. 'Isn't that totally bizarre?' she said. 'Even my nan could still pick it up, not long before she died. And she was only four foot eleven and had pretty much the same diet as a sparrow. Do you think it's green? I do. But some people look at it and say it's blue. I know a lot of geologists, because of work, but I've shown it to all of them and they seem flummoxed. One of them said it looked like some kind of intergalactic hagstone. He's in a stoner rock band and decided *Intergalactic Hagstone* would be a really good title for their album. I think he's actually going to record it. Anyway, I am pretty sure it's something to do with the mine, but I'm not sure what. I found it just off the pit road in the undergrowth one day when I was walking with Kate. Near your den that that horrid boy set fire to. Wasn't his dad a member of the Nazi Party or something? I think you might have left by the time we found it. I'm not sure. It's been with me ever since. I call it my lucky charm.'

She asked him how he was fixed for time, and after doing some spontaneous maths they decided to drive the ten miles south east to Tapley Woodhouse: two writers on their way back to the place that had formed them, the place where nobody ever thought anyone could be a writer, despite significant historical evidence to the contrary. They were different people of different genders who lived in different countries and wrote different books, but if you'd met them, you would have got the same feeling of encountering something approachable but containing a little ash at its centre, hot to the touch. On the short journey, he was aware of something wasted between them in the years since they'd last seen each other, although whatever it was wasn't quite tangible enough to lament. They passed the chip shop and the black gateway which used to have the orange NCB sign next to it. He said he used to conflate it with the NCP signs of a similar shade that you saw at the front of car parks. 'Fucking hell, me too!' she said.

The old asbestos garage was gone but the house didn't look all that different if you ignored the rubble and upturned early-2000s computer in the front garden. They climbed the gob pile, which now carefully hid its dark past and reinvented itself in front of newcomers as just a hill. No baggage. No hang-ups. The sort of easygoing mound you might want to get to know and spend your life with. Opposite them was the barn whose hay they had fallen deep into together while Kate watched, her sandalled feet dangling from the ledge above them. There was a sign with some public information about the welfare of bees. At the bottom of the incline, an abandoned quad bike was buried snout-deep in the earth. 'Rewilding,' she said. 'Of a sort.' All around the earth seemed to be wearing a new heavy coat, inappropriate for the season. He decided not to correct her about the ruined den, inform her that there had been no fire. Or had there? They looked across at the headstocks to the south – the one set in the immediate area that had been retained, though solely for historical purposes – and floated on the thin surface of the longest silence of the afternoon.

'The land grows weary of its inhabitants,' she finally said to someone. He thought it was perhaps a quote, but it might not have been. She said a lot of good things.

Daffodils

'We remember t'party, don't we. We were out in t'garden at t'time. Yer'd look over t'right, two hedges away, and every minute or three yerd see a young lad or lass in the sky. This being back in t'other time, when we were tall enough to look over t'hedge. It were right lovely to see and to listen to. Course, we didn't get an invite. But we wouldn't 'ave expected to, being owd folks. There were a bloke living next door on his own at the time. Some kind of scientist or summat. I think it were his idea.'

'I went round his house once, to tek him some potatoes. Yer told me too. It was cos you said you thought he looked right skinny.'

'Ger out. Yer didn't tell me.'

'I did. You've forgot! Yer always forgetting stuff. I remember when I went over there he had this thing on the wall, one of them collage thingies. It had a picture from the papers, of *her*, of Thatcher, down Maunsley Pit, in her hard hat. Then above it there was this letterin' from summat else. It said . . . ah, I'm embarrassed to tell yer.'

'Yer embarrassed to tell me? Yerv known me 103 and a half years. And take a look down below. In case you hadn't noticed, we're nekkid. There are no secrets here, me duck. Dunt be so bloody soft.'

'All right then. Don't say I didn't warn yer. It said "BORED HOUSEWIFE SLAGS WANT IT HARD IN THE BACK DOOR".'

Parents

'The foxgloves came and went so quickly that summer. By the time of Benji's birthday they were pretty much gone. Just a few hanging on, almost stripped to the bone.'

'I thought you said you found it hard to remember when things happened. But you remember *that*?'

'I always remember plants and flowers. It's just the way my mind works. It's like that streptocarpus over there on the window ledge. Remembering what's it called is easy: I just think 'dinosaur with a bad throat'. I can still see that garden, like it's a map in my mind. Near the top there's the compost heap, then the raspberries and gooseberries. Then the leeks and courgettes and onions and radishes in the beds halfway up. Then the rhubarb, down near the house. I was trying to get fleabane to self-seed into the little wall below that, above the patio, but it never wanted to.'

'You could say it was the fleabane of your existence.'

'It's amazing you didn't try to become a stand-up comedian. I've never understood why that was. Do you remember the wildflower verge, on the other side of the road? As soon as he moved in, Colin went straight over there and threw down a load of native wildflower seeds. Poppy and purple loosestrife and corncockle and ragged robin and loads more. It was just starting to come up really beautifully – it had been quite a drab and industrial view, before that – and attracting all these bees and butterflies and then Dave Barrowcliffe went over and sprayed pesticide all over it. What an absolute bastard.'

'He did. And then you must remember what happened after that? Colin went over to his garden while he was out and stole all the rest of his pesticide out his shed and got rid of it, emptied three or four bags of sugar into the tank of Dave's lawnmower while he was at it. And then there was that awful break-in at his house. We were abroad at the time. So we couldn't help. He had no proof but it wasn't hard to guess who'd done it. Do you remember the time when Barrowcliffe was out on the pavement walking his dog and I caught Benji looking at him through the tines of one of our dining forks?'

'I don't think I remember that at all, no, but I feel like I should.'

'I asked Benji what he was doing and he said he was pretending that Dave Barrowcliffe was in prison.'

'I liked Colin. I often wonder what happened to him. Do you remember he came with us to vote? We all knew it was a lost cause. There was such a sinking feeling around that point. It was in the gap between the Falklands and the start of the strikes, all the tar barrels burning up on the pit road. What a fiasco that was, the Falklands. Then all those Union Jacks everywhere. Thatcher's voice coming out of every radio and every TV. You couldn't get away from it. When the invasion started most of that lot in Number 10 didn't even know where it was, did they. Had to get the atlas out. I remember being surprised, even with the way he was and the way he dressed and the books he read,

that Colin didn't vote Tory, which is a measure of my naiveté at the time, my preconceptions about southerners. I hadn't met all that many. He turned up at the polling station with Elaine McNulty. I think they were having a thing for a while. She knew his ex-wife from Greenham Common. She walked there all the way from Scotland. His ex, that is. Not Elaine. Julie Christie came to her house once.'

'He was good to us, Colin was. I feel a bit bad about it now, because maybe I wasn't as grateful as I should have been at the time. How generous he was with Benji and everything. He did actually have kids of his own, but we never saw them. He was there and gone in a flash, really, it felt like. He mended the car for us a couple of times. It wasn't just a matter of lending me some jump cables. He seemed to be able to just magic parts for it out of thin air. But he didn't have a car of his own. Or maybe he did, later. I know he walked everywhere. Probably twenty miles a day sometimes. I once saw him wandering up the hard shoulder of the M1. It was only when I had gone past that I realised it was him and of course I couldn't reverse because it was the motorway. He looked like a baffled wizard. Do you remember that collage he had inside his house, all those pictures from the mines, and then that stuff from the porn mags? He said it was an art piece he was working on, about the purchase of people's bodies.'

'Nope, sorry. Don't remember that at all. I can't believe that car got us all the way to Italy, and not just once, either! It couldn't get us to bloomin' Canning Circus roundabout most of the time. You were really worried about it that summer. Especially with money being so tight. We all were all looking forward to going so much, especially Benji, and we thought we probably wouldn't be able to. And then Benji slipped when he was playing with his friend and put his arm through the garage window. I felt terrible. The thing was in an awful state and we should have taken the glass out of it long before that. But it could have been worse. The reason he cut his arm open was because he was shielding his face. Imagine if he hadn't done that.'

'Yep, and then, just as it was all healing up, and we arrived in Italy, on our first trip to the beach a wasp came and stung him inside the wound. A Tuscan bloke ran over and sucked the sting out. That seems quite weird, now I think back on it, but I'm sure his motives were innocent. But, yeah, I suppose the point is, looking back, it was all a struggle, but we still managed to do some nice things. We probably have forgotten exactly how much of a struggle it was.'

'I haven't. I remember that as clearly as the fleabane of my existence.'

'You were the one with the staying power. I wasn't. I was pissed off that by that point I hadn't already become a stand-up comedian or a subversive cult alto saxophonist.'

'You couldn't even play the alto saxophone.'

'That's what would have made it subversive.'

'I didn't want to be an alto saxophonist. I just wanted to not

be worrying about finding a way to pay the mortgage every month.'

'Teachers' pay was so shit back then. This was before the strikes, when everything got a tiny bit better. A tiny bit. We definitely went into it because we wanted to make the world a better place. I don't know if we even thought about the pay. We probably just assumed society would value it more highly as a job. I managed six years teaching in Radford, but that was all I could take. One of the kids in the class next to mine was killed in a knife fight. My wallet got stolen twice. Once by a fellow teacher. My Vietnam, that place was. And every time the month ended we'd gone overdrawn. It felt for a long time that we couldn't make it work, no matter what we tried. We didn't go to the pub or eat out. Lots of home-brew. I did a milk round, then while I was doing it I came off my bike and hurt my leg. Do you remember when I stacked hay bales as well? Or when I worked on the fish market? That lasted all of a fortnight. Then I got some work supply teaching. Which paid a bit better. But doing that you had to make yourself seem a bit intimidating as soon as you walked in or the kids would eat you for breakfast. I knew a bloke who walked into a class and as soon as he did, his false teeth came out his mouth. There was no coming back from that for him. That was how we made it to Italy that summer, that extra bit from supply teaching. Not that going there was expensive, like it is now. Cheap petrol, cheap camping, cheap cheese and cold meat and fruit. And the occasional bit of wild boar. We listened to *Remain in Light* by Talking Heads over and over again until the cassette broke. Before we set off I bought a big stack of old *Beano*s from a junk shop for two quid. Gave them to Benji and we didn't hear a peep out of him until we saw the first Alp on the horizon. The ants were massive and strong with these fat black arses. They could carry a whole baguette over their heads. And there was the biggest toad I'd ever seen living under a grate near the tent. Then all the lizards running about by the swimming pool. And then when we got back to our garden on Stringy Lane all that was there was these two big fuck-off crows up a tree trying to kill a squirrel. And I thought, "Eyup, we're home, then."'

'Hold on. You're going too fast.'

'. . . And do you remember your uncle Giuseppe with his giant cucumber? And the little car with no proper doors that went on the beach. And Nonno standing in the middle of the traffic and making it stop. And the peaches by the roadside. I can't help it. I was born this way. It's all right. I'll be quiet soon. I'm coming back as a brick in my next life.'

Cousin

My granddad died when I was four. There are a couple of photos of him holding me, plus a few others; one of us, probably taken by my mum, sitting together on a wall near the sea at Skegness with my nan and my aunt Sarah and my aunt Cath. But I think my memories of those times are memories of the photos rather than real memories. My mum would have been only just out of her teens when he died, my aunt Cath twenty-three, and my aunt Sarah only eighteen. With time I'm struck more and more by the raw fact of their youth. I suspect the family pulled even closer after it happened. I could not say for certain. We were all just close and that's the only way I'd ever known it to be. In a lot of ways it was like my mum and her sisters were a single entity. They'd often end up wearing the same perfume without planning it, buying the same cushion covers or shoes. My aunt Sarah would come around and see a plant pot my mum had bought at a garage sale down the road. 'Oh,' she'd say. 'I spotted that at the garden centre, then I came back to buy it, and it had gone. I might have known it was you who bought it.' Everyone was constantly over at each other's houses and going camping together. My nan couldn't often join us on the holidays, because of her health, but she was always at the centre of everything. Us kids wrangled for custody of her. Sometimes it got ugly, especially as there became more of us.

At first, though, it was just me and my cousin Benji. He was always outside, one of those kids you meet who are permanently tumbling about the place with bloody knees. He'd have barely recovered from a wasp stinging him inside a wound on his arm and he'd be falling headfirst from a climbing frame. There was a rumour children had died on the roundabout on the park up the road from his house. I don't know if that was true, but I know that when it broke it just got abandoned, hanging half off its base, looking like a stolen car that had been driven into a ditch. In my head it was that way because of Benji. He was boisterous, hard to keep track of. Not that I am exactly one to talk: I arguably wasn't the best influence. My dad would walk along a narrow windfallen log balanced precariously across a river and I would follow, with Ben never far behind. Then it was up to my mum and her sisters to fish us out of the water.

My dad was the daredevil of the grown-ups, but my uncles were all 1980s men's men too, each in their own way. There was always a lot of talk of cars and gadgets, a fair bit of physical sparring. Who could chop the most wood. Who was best at table tennis. That sort of thing. My uncle Pete was the least sporty of the lot, beardier, constantly worried about people hurting themselves, the one you'd most often find with a book in his hand, but he wasn't above all the showing off. He once told me and Ben that 'Danger' was his middle name.

Even when he was as young as four or five, Benji was always looking for something new to explore, especially if it involved outer space. In autumn everyone always went to Goose Fair, down Notts. One year – it was the same year a girl got killed

after falling off a ride, I think – Benji managed to slip everyone's grasp and get lost, having been distracted by a ride that looked like a flying saucer. Eventually a kindly lady in her sixties got him back to us, with the help of the Tannoy system. When she'd found him sitting on the grass behind the helter skelter, crying, she'd asked him what his dad's name was. He'd told her it was Pete. 'But what's his full name?' she'd then asked. 'It's Pete Danger Moss,' Benji replied.

My dad and my uncles all had strong accents appropriate to the region. Ours are there too but it's like somebody put them under the water butt in the garden for a while. No shampoo or conditioner, just last night's rainwater. If it had been solely up to our dads, you'd probably hear that bit more coal and injustice in our words. My mum and her sisters, proper northerners who'd grown up in Liverpool, poorer than any of their spouses, in a big house with their own cousins and aunts and uncles, were the ones who encouraged us to speak marginally less like we'd just emerged from a hole in the ground. It wasn't snobbery or social climbing; it came out of their natural yearning to learn and expand their horizons, and their hope that we would be able to get on quietly in the world, with as little as possible standing in our way. That 'quiet' part was something of a religion for them; not that they'd have ever told you that in any sermonising way, because they were too busy being self-effacing and discreet. But when you were brought up by them, you knew the importance of it, innately, and eventually it couldn't help but become your religion too. Gardening. Ceramics. Carpentry. DIY. Oil painting. Embroidery. Do it, master it, move on. No bigheads allowed through the door because they wouldn't fit.

Looking back at my life at that point in the eighties from now – a time when the shouters and the braggers are in the driving seat, when the praises of self-love are sung through the microphone of every other mobile phone – it's this that seems possibly the most quaint and vintage thing of all: the philosophy of going away on your own and doing something well and not telling anybody about it. Some people called it The Me Decade, which is something someone calls every decade at some point. But for us it was more like The Don't Mind Me Decade.

I suppose a bystander might have claimed that as a family we were in the process of graduating to the middle class, but if we were, it was in a natural and organic way, with no real aspiration behind it, or at least not the kind concerned with labels or status. The shift in that direction was a natural byproduct of easier foreign travel, wider varieties of food appearing on the supermarket shelves, job opportunities that took our parents out of the sphere of drudgery that their families had been trapped in for decades. We called our dinner 'tea'. We accused each other of being nesh if we complained about the cold too readily. We called the big light 'the big light' (because that's what it fucking is). We ate the bread while we were pushing our trolley around the supermarket then paid for the packet. But we went to Italy and learned what polenta was. We made pakoras. We looked at our wallpapered

1970s rooms full of fag smoke, stripped them down and aired them out, stencilled their edges. We overcorrected our hairstyles and quite a few other items on and around us.

The country that my mum and each of my aunts came from was called the UK, but they also came from another one, much more than they came from that one, and it was called the 1960s. That meant Women's Lib. That meant – albeit somewhere far from here – civil rights. That meant more opportunities for young working-class people than at any point in living memory. That meant your mum, in the car, making it move, on an actual road, not just waiting for your dad to give her a lift somewhere. It meant her at home, mending a fuse or putting a broken sideboard back together, while your dad watched, looking admiring and useless. But it's not quite that simple. You don't all just start again and fumigate the air of the cultural past in one easy go. There'll always be some lag and drag, a miasma here and there. Especially if you lived where we did. It was a cloudy place. 'Glass of wine? Put it down an' 'ay a proper drink, you big poof.' 'Got a problem wi' me, or summat about me? Ger outside now and let's see which cunt decks which other cunt and thar'll be the end orrit.' 'Shall us go down t'chippy tonight, or t'chinky?' 'Are you sure you want to wear those, love? They don't make you look very ladylike.' Lamping someone outside your local branch of Woolworths was still viewed as a very normal way to settle ideological differences. A small male you knew quite well, let's say a cousin, who wore nice shoes that could, by certain sectors of his peer group, be perceived as girls' shoes, and who expressed a minor enthusiasm for botany, could expect to quickly become an ostracised small male human with blood seeping from his nose. Certain household duties were still not generally expected of men. A wife, even a wife with many many progressive ideas of her own and a mostly considerate husband in the top three per cent of husbands in the region, could still be widely perceived as an annexe of that husband. Behind the scenes, genuine female superheroes could frequently go uncredited, especially if they happened to be particularly self-effacing female superheroes, schooled from birth in the art of not being a bighead.

If I did not know what genuine superwomen my mum and her sisters were back then – and I think some part of me, under all the other mostly obnoxious thirteen-year-old parts, always did know it – I certainly do now. It can be quite intimidating, if I am totally honest. You'll be in one of their houses and you'll see a sculpture or painting you haven't seen before. 'Where did this come from?' you'll ask. 'Oh, that's just something I did on Tuesday,' they'll say. 'I'm not happy with it at all.' The menfolk will be there, with this look about them that says, 'Yeah, I sometimes misbehave, but I know which side my bread is buttered.' You sit down for a Sunday lunch, and look at the size and range of what they put in front of you, and you wonder when the other three hundred guests are arriving. You go out into the garden and realise how little distance a lot of it had to travel to your plate. You

see the colours and smell the smells and everything beyond the boundary with the house next door melts away.

In my most frequent recurring dream, my mum and her sisters are all living as a family of octopuses. My aunt Cath opens the door to their lair, dressed in paint-stained eight-legged dungarees. It's a lovely deep-red door, the one to their old house on Stringy Lane. My mum and my aunt Sarah are inside the lair, which is also an attractively landscaped garden, and they're sitting on some rocks, and it turns out they're all in a band, and they're making this big orchestral sound, which they are capable of making because, being octopuses, they can all play several instruments at the same time. Benji and my nan are there too. Both of them are wearing silver spacesuits. 'Can you see the fish dancing, in the distance?' my nan asks me. 'Don't SAY that!' I reply, wincing. But suddenly everything makes sense, all that self-effacing creativity over all those years, maintained in conjunction with the weathering of life's tragedies, sticking out full-time jobs, child-rearing, man-soothing. It was always because of the extra limbs.

I don't know where that whole 'in the distance' thing started. I do remember that it went right through me like a rusty nail when anyone said it. It was one of those weird inexplicable childhood phobias or obsessions, like Benji hating miniature dining forks or going around for a while telling people he was from outer space. But on second thoughts, perhaps there was a little more to it than that. Where we lived was unextraordinary, the most middle of places, but there was also this darkness to the rim of everything while you were there. We'd be playing in our gardens and you'd look over towards the spoil heaps at the far point of your eyeline and wonder what was beyond them and you couldn't help being a bit afraid. I'm sure what I knew about my other granddad, my dad's dad, and his brother, must have contributed. Both of them died in a tunnel fire in one of the mines, before I was born. I heard some ponies died in the same fire. I always avoided the pit road when I was out on my bike or my rollerskates. I'd been there once and it resembled the end of world. Actually, no, more like the end of another world: what everything looked like when the evil lord in one of those fantasy games that Ben played back then had vanquished all the forces of good. Of course, in reality, it, along with the other mines nearby, was the lifeblood of the region, and many would say that the truly scary time came directly after it got closed by the government.

How do you accurately shade complex events half a lifetime in the past when you're running out of ink? What I could do with right now is one of those fancy pens our friend Jane Fennel used to have, where you clicked a button on the side and it changed to a different colour. It was the darkest of times, it was the lightest of times. We all dressed in brighter clothes that year. I got my first deely boppers and fluorescent legwarmers. My dad drove us all the way to Italy in his new bright red car, with my aunt and uncle and my cousin behind us in their older much less bright one, which somehow didn't fall to pieces. In the gelaterias, we chose from a rainbow of ice-cream flavours, our brains almost exploding at the realisation that we could even have *several of them in the same cone at the same time.* In our bright-striped swimming costumes and clean white t-shirts we went to the beach with our multicoloured boules and our bright orange tennis balls and, as we played with them, tried to avoid the piles of litter that people had flippantly left in the places where they'd been sitting, which seemed shocking and awful to us, although not shocking and awful in the same way it seems now that we know what we know, now that we live an era of ecological enlightenment, an era when we don't any longer believe in the magical curative powers of the pedal bin, an era that is the lightest and the darkest in totally different ways.

Even our birthday presents seemed to give off more light that year. It didn't matter if you didn't come from a well-off materialistic family; you became aware of the availability of a growing number of objects that might temporarily enhance your life. The greater number of these objects meant a greater  number of older objects could be found on kerbs, in gardens, in woodland. A widespread faith in the new had emerged, seemingly overnight. Even the most thrifty of us were converted. Antique shops sat on dark streets with downturned mouths, bemused by the plastic promise in the air, biding their time until their day came again.

But the casting-off of the old objects that the new objects replaced made the world darker on its margins. Far more arcane pieces of machinery could be found on the average street than today. Far more chairs. Far more car parts. Automobiles passed into the official ranks of the elderly as quickly as dogs. In their death they piled up, as common as hills. My mum and her sisters went to the tip and, with their creative eye, took away old chairs and hot-water bottles and hairdryers and cupboards; selected them in the way that they might have been selected by knowledgeable magpies from the future who'd passed through a curtain in time. A large hairy man, covered in apparent soil, jumped from skip to skip, sorting a river of rubbish that was constantly in spate. You sometimes saw him at the swimming pool, too, and everyone would get out when he got in. 'Is that a real gorilla?' I asked my mum, the first time I saw him. But no actual gorilla could ever have been as busy as him. The old

toasters and fireplaces and Sindy dolls and sofas and plastic dinosaurs and Action Men and asbestos dressing tables and Bakelite
hairdryers and rusty scissors and bags of shitcaked cat litter and
fridges and newspapers and rusty scissors and shredded wall-
paper kept arriving.

The tip smelt bad, but not vastly worse than most areas directly beyond the tip. The new brightness we had embraced was
not generally reflected in the air we breathed. Cars belched past
us and left us temporarily invisible to our companions. We were
good at holding our breath while under water because we'd had
plenty of practice in public toilets. The odour of pet food made
no attempt to disguise the unfortunate journey that had led it to
our dog's or cat's dish. The fart of the boy who sat next to you
in Maths could put you into a brief coma. Silent had never been
more violent. The aggregate smell of the places where we played
and walked was a threat and an enigma, always with us.

Machines looked at you with happier, more open faces than
before, but what lurked behind them in their wires remained a
dark mystery: a jet-black tunnel, inaccessible, full of fuck knows
what. One day, my mum picked the phone up to hear my aunt
Catherine's voice, telling her, 'Everything is going to be ok.' As
she listened, she watched Catherine through the window in the
garden, talking to my nan about the most effective way to
tie tomato plants. She puzzled over the incident, especially
when she discovered that my aunt Sarah had received an oddly
similar phone call on the same day. But, being pragmatic women,
they found some way to rationalise it. It sort of made sense to
everyone, since they were more or less psychically connected
anyway and the language they spoke was nearly always one of
soft reassurance. Also, maybe it was easier to accept the inexplicable, in the era we lived in. As far as technology, and its
concomitant flood of information, was concerned, we were the
savages, muddling through the Before Time, telling ourselves

stories in the dark. We flicked off the TV at night and a white dot sucked all the glamorous people on it back down into the tunnel behind the wires. We switched on the Top 40 with our finger hovering over the record button to capture a song and make it ours. We pleaded with our mums not to use the vacuum so the song was captured without interference. But then, when we had captured the song, what could we do with it, apart from listen to it again and again until it was burned into our brain? The personalities behind the songs often remained impenetrable. It was all in that black tunnel in the wires. I pictured the voices who sang to me from that tunnel, trying to imagine their lives. Many of them, particularly the men, sang like they were being lightly strangled. That made sense to me because I imagined the tunnel as a scary place where robbers and muggers might lurk on every bend.

You might be forgiven for imagining that, as far as information was concerned, school was a little less opaque. I don't remember that being the case. I brazened it out, fell in with the popular crowd, found that a bit too exhausting, slept through the remaining years in the company of nerds. School gave me no sense of how many people and places there were in the world. If I had any sense of that, it came from my family, from TV, from what little I managed to find out via magazines and record sleeves about those people who sang my favourite songs. I remember a general outlook, coming from the teaching staff, of 'Ok, if you're lucky, and you work hard, you might one day get to work part time in the post office.' Maybe a full-time job as a plumber or an electrician, where the boys were concerned. Not that there's anything wrong with being a plumber or electrician. It pays bloody well. Better than any job I've ever done. I remember there was one kid in my class, extremely gifted and ahead of us all, who wanted to be a diplomat. The careers advisor told him to join the army.

Those kids who went to Benji and Cath's primary school, though: you got the feeling that all of them were going to follow their own weird little path, and nothing was going to get in their way, even if secondary education was going to do its best to shake the inviduality out of them. I hope my kids feel the same. I think they do. It's so different now. No barrier between them and the true size of the world, the true extent of the opportunities it could still contain, despite the people in power's attempts to make them ever more inaccessible to those without inherited wealth. They only have to look down at the device in their hand to realise the state of play. Which is a good and bad thing. Dark and light, once again.

You can't grow up around the women I grew up around and not have the creative bug. I print, I paint, I make. I forage in the same meadow my mum and her sisters took me to forage in as a kid. I write, too, although that's just for my eyes at the moment. 'You should try to get this published,' a couple of friends have told me. Are they just being kind, saying the stuff friends are supposed to say? It's hard to tell. Whatever the case, that level of potential public scrutiny is not for me, much as I admire those brave enough to put themselves through it. I'd rather just go quietly about my business for now. I surprise myself with how eerie some of the stuff I come up with is. It gives me a chill. I make myself a bit nesh, just from typing words. I wrote one story about a man who dies then realises he's not actually dead but locked in a giant container full of everything he's ever put in a bin. It's all there, like a rancid archive of his life as a consumer: ring-pull Pepsi cans he drank out of while he was on holiday as a kid, half a plate of mackerel from the hot summer of 1989, sellotape ripped off forgotten birthday presents from long-dead relatives, a computer keyboard with a faulty space bar stuck to a Findus crispy pancake that didn't quite taste right, and a mouse that his sister's cat half-ate in 1997, every crisp packet, every old perforated sock and teabag. I would not say that I wrote it so much as it wrote me. The process was more a matter of exorcism than anything, since it was inspired by a real nightmare that I kept having, for many years, and I decided that if I wrote it down maybe I could make it stop.

I didn't succeed, but I do only have the nightmare occasionally now. I'll be in there, in that container, crawling slowly over the mounds of rubbish, confronting hard the facts of a reality beneath everything, the underside of some of my happiest memories, but then, just sometimes, a door will open at the back of the container. A lovely deep red in colour. I'll sigh with relief, because I'll know that, behind it, I'll find three octopuses, ready to welcome me into their lair.

Benji

We arrived in Italy only three days after school finished for the summer, which was earlier than we'd said we'd arrive to my aunts and uncles and cousins who lived over there, who weren't my aunts and uncles and cousins in the same way as my Nottinghamshire aunts and uncles and cousins were. We would have arrived even earlier if it had been up to my dad, but Donna and my aunt Sue and my uncle Jerry and Donna's new boyfriend Kev wanted to stop at a campsite in France on the way. The first one we found had really smelly toilets and a building on it that looked like the science block at Donna's school, so my dad drove off to another one he'd seen a sign for nearby, to see if it was better. 'It's like blummin' paradise!' he told us when he got back. 'You could eat your dinner off the side of the swimming pool.' I immediately fixated on the image, which I found appealing, and was disappointed that, when we got there, we didn't in fact eat our dinner off the side of the swimming pool. But there was a fast river beside the campsite where Donna and Kev and I took turns to go down the rapids in a rubber dinghy

Jerry bought Donna from the hypermarché, and a man you could watch making pizza outside, then putting it in an oven that cooked it even faster than I'd once seen Taj Mukherjee's mum cook some chips in a cardboard box in a special oven she had that Taj Mukherjee said operated on nuclear waves like the ones they were going to use in the war that I'd built my shelter on the gob pile to hide from. I would have liked to stay longer, even though I was desperate to get to Italy and liked it better than France, but my dad said it was important that we got to Italy as quickly as possible. I didn't understand why it was important, because we had three whole weeks to do anything we pleased once we got there, but I understood that driving was important to my dad, as was the planning of the most efficient routes for that driving. It was a way in which he could look after us and keep us safe, amidst the more numerous ways which my mum looked after us and kept us safe.

The first thing we did when we arrived at the town where our Italian relatives lived was to fill up with four star at the garage they owned. Being early, we thought we'd surprise them, pretending we were just normal tourists in our car, on the way down to Rome. The surprise worked, because my cousin Frank, whose job it was to pour petrol for customers, saw Donna walk across the forecourt towards him and poured petrol down his own leg. The Italian air smelt thick and oily, like you could fill a baguette with it and eat it, and I ogled the cars on the forecourt and tried to decide which one I'd most like to drive. After we'd helped Frank clean his trousers and said hello to everyone else, we went straight to the campsite, where, before our mums and dads had even put the tents up, Donna and I ran straight over to the swimming pool and dived in, with Kev hanging back, hesitant. Donna told me Kev wasn't her boyfriend, but I didn't believe her, because if she'd decided she just wanted to bring a friend with her on holiday, not a boyfriend, she would obviously have brought a girl with her instead.

Up some steps above the swimming pool there was a restaurant where we could smell pizza baking and Donna and I asked if we could have some, but my mum and my aunt Sue said it was too expensive, and that we had perfectly nice food back at the tents from the shop in the village at the bottom of the hill. Donna nagged my aunt Sue some more and she said that if we were well-behaved maybe we could go and have pizza once, in a few weeks, as a treat, just before we went home, which was to me the same as if she had been saying that if were well-behaved and polite we could maybe have pizza sometime after the turn of the century.

People drove differently in Italy to the way they drove back at home; it reminded me of a cartoon TV series I watched called *Wacky Races*, which was full of vehicles of all shapes and sizes being driven creatively by a variety of exciting humans and human-adjacent creatures. As soon as we'd crossed the border from Switzerland, we'd seen a stream of cars reversing at top speed down the hard shoulder to escape a traffic jam, which was like being shown a sign that said, 'Hello, you are in Italy now!' It seemed to me that Italian people drove the way my friends and I probably would, if we could drive, which was exciting to me, because it meant that while I was in Italy I felt closer to the planet of cars and everything they did. That our relatives owned an actual garage made me feel closer still.

While the grown-ups were busy, I climbed into the inspection pit where my uncles Marco and Giuseppe worked, and gazed up at the innards of Fiats and Citroëns. I sat on the hot leather seats of Alfa Romeos – which, even warmed by a fierce August sun, did not burn my bare legs anything like as painfully as the plastic ones in my parents' Marina – and brummed them in my mind all the way back to school, where I would pick up Taj Mukherjee

and Emma Buttons and my nan and drive them to Alton Towers theme park. I inhaled engine oil and exhaust, mixed with the smell of my aunt's pasta sauce being cooked with fresh tomatoes and other ingredients grown on the allotment behind the garage which everyone called The Land. Even the bad smells were good in Italy.

Just like last time we had come here, it took me an extraordinarily short amount of time to become an Italian child. I picked up bits of the language and was soon able to go and order myself gelato and granita and, once, even a salty pork cob from a stall on the market in town. After only four days, my skin had completely changed colour, which my mum said was because of my Mediterranean jeans, which, until she explained exactly what she meant, confused me, because since we'd arrived I had exclusively been wearing shorts made from a light synthetic fabric. At a festa we went to, which had a brass band and lots of bottles of wine in baskets, some women my almost-Italian aunt Grace and her sisters-in-law were talking to touched my cheek and said I was 'carino' and for a joke, my almost-Italian aunt Grace told them I was her nephew from Perugia, but then when they started asking me complicated questions in Italian I got very confused and ran off to find Donna and Frank.

Our Italian relatives were all very loud, and when we sat at the big table next to The Land with car and motorbike parts all around us and ate pasta that my almost-Italian aunt Grace tossed together with sauce in the biggest pan I'd ever seen, everyone seemed to be talking at the same time, and it was very hard to follow the conversation, even when people spoke in English. My dad, who was very loud at home, except in the times when he was very quiet, joined in, and seemed much more excited and happy than he was in Nottinghamshire. I impressed everyone by telling them that, until around 500 years ago, there were no tomatoes in Italy, but kept quiet that the reason I knew this was because Emma Buttons had told me about it one evening after school a few weeks ago. After we'd eaten, all the adults put a hand to their stomachs and groaned and my mum and my aunt Sue said they needed a siesta, although I wasn't sure if that was because of the food or because hearing everyone talk so loud had made them tired.

I noticed that Kev often left vegetables on his plate and seemed subdued, like he felt bewildered by it all. He and Donna had had what my uncle Jerry had described, to Donna's annoyance, as 'a lover's tiff', which I thought meant kissing or cuddling but in fact meant an argument. I couldn't tell what the tiff was about, but when we were at The Land, Donna had asked our cousin Rocco to pass messages across the kitchen between them. At one point I'd heard Donna say to Rocco 'the feeling is mutual', then seen Rocco walk over to Kev and say 'the feeling is beautiful', which was funny but probably didn't help anyone. I couldn't work out precisely what feeling was mutual, but the two of them didn't speak so much after that. Kev stopped coming to the swimming pool with us, instead staying in and around his tent reading football magazines or playing a game on his digital watch. His hair seemed to wilt in the heat, the straggly rebellious parts at the back plastering themselves to his neck. At night I could hear soft sobbing sounds coming from his tent. My mum told me he was upset because he was missing England and that we should all make sure we were extra-nice to him. But Donna and I didn't miss England at all. Most days I completely forgot it existed. I forgot about Lee Barrowcliffe and Colin and the aliens, who hadn't come for me like I'd thought they would in hospital after I slipped and put my arm through the window of our garage, and I forgot about school, and even about my arm, though it still hurt a bit, and had hurt a lot more on the day a big Italian wasp stung me inside the wound.

We went to a river and my uncle Jerry jumped into the water off some high rocks and then my dad did it afterwards, a bit less confidently, and Donna and I did it too, but off some rocks much lower down. I beat some Italian kids at table tennis and then some German kids and some French kids but got thrashed by a kid I thought was from China at first before he began to speak and told me he was from Barnsley. Donna and Rocco and Frank and I got to ride to the beach in the Mini Moke, which was a car Marco owned with no doors which could go on sand and grass as well as roads, then Donna and I dived into the sea again and again from a boat with pedals beneath it and complained when we were told it was time to go back to

the campsite. Marco and Giuseppe had once lived in Nottinghamshire, just like us, but I possessed no uncertainty about why they had decided to come back and live here instead. I didn't understand why we couldn't stay here forever, and get my nan and my other relatives and maybe two or three of my favourite schoolfriends to come over and live here too.

More photos that I love: really sharp and crisp ones, instinctively and thoughtfully framed. You can tell here that my parents were enjoying their camera, learning more about what they could do with it, my mum in particular. My uncle Giuseppe proudly holding a giant cucumber he had grown on The Land, even more massive than Mr and Mrs Chudley's biggest courgettes. Me and Donna and Frank all diving into the pool in unison. Me riding Rocco's little bike through a yard of sickly cars, nut brown, browner than my cousins, wearing a half-eaten necklace of sweets. Marco with his head poking out from under our Marina, the car that, even though it was in pain, looked after us and held on all the way across France and Switzerland and half of Italy until there was someone who could nurse it back to health. Me with Klaus and Nicklas, two blonde German boys I swam with for a week before they were replaced by other German blonde boys I also swam with. Tables covered with bright fruit and vegetables outside vine-drowned buildings on jumbled hillsides, being inspected with great seriousness by my mum, who always looks, in these photos taken by my dad, like she is caught in the gaze of someone who loves her extraordinarily deeply. My cousins' great-granddad, who everyone – even people in town who weren't related to him – just called Nonno, showing us a tree full of ripe plums, pipe in mouth, and then, later, teaching my mum and my aunt Sue how to spar with some vintage Tuscan swords. An extremely old man, even older than Nonno – my dad would paint him, when we were back home – in a checked shirt and apron, hunched over a basket that he was weaving.

Looking at all this, I do not feel I am looking at a holiday. I feel I am looking at a whole life; one that I slid into every summer, like olive oil into a pan. My tiny tent was all the home anyone could have ever needed. I walked the terraces of the campsite confidently, shoeless, the soles of my feet hardening like those of a feral child born to a hot land. Just like in my actual home, I lived under the shadow of two hills. Unlike home, the hills were not made of mining waste. They were made of dust and olives and wild dogs and boar and lizard. But like home, they seemed in a way like the end of everything: the vanishing point where the secrets were kept. They were the place where all the deeper, more primal sounds came from during the nights. Vast, short nights lit by stars and the flashing lights of what I now know were not spaceships but machines containing families who took a more impatient approach to foreign travel than mine. As tired as I was from my full, energetic days, I lay awake and tried to figure the sounds out, attempted to get to them via all the closer sounds, such as the tymbals of enthusiastic cicadas and the wings of bats and the laugher of my dad and the zips of tents and the half-stifled tears of Kev.

I clearly remember the village at the top of the tallest of the two hills, can still walk through its maze of cobbled streets in my mind, under the shadows of its hanging buildings; smell its tiny, haphazardly parked Fiat 500s and taste its roadside peaches. We went to watch a football match there on one of the hottest, driest days. Marco and Giuseppe and Frank and Rocco shouted excitably at the action, which made no sense to me, as all I could see was a big ball of dust moving from one end of the pitch to the other, the only details about what was going on inside it being what was filtered to us from the scoreboard directly to our left. There were few tourists in the village and even fewer people who weren't extremely old. I looked at the extremely old people, heard their cracked-chalk voices, noticed their folded skin, and asked my mum if they were unwell. She told me that, on the contrary, they were probably very well indeed because they ate fresh healthy food and had the good fortune of living in a great climate with all the sun's vitamins, and because of that they lived for long, long periods of time, sometimes stretching all the way back to the previous century. I had thought about death before, of course, especially when Ethel Troutlock died, although perhaps not in a way where it seemed quite as applicable to me, not even when the aliens came to get me by bursting my appendix. The extremely old people in the Italian village made me contemplate death in a different way, a way perhaps no less mystifying but more real. The fact began to occur to me that the human body was some-

thing that could only exist for a certain amount of time before it wore out, like the tyres on some of the Alfa Romeos and Citroëns and Lancias and Fiats at The Land. After the wearing out was all done, you wouldn't be here anymore – not as you, not as what you were. But how was that possible? How could that ever be possible for me, or Donna, or my mum, or my dad, or my uncle Jerry or my aunt Sue? How, when we were all so very, very here?

Alien

REPORT OF MISSION TO EARTH FROM THE PLANET VOZKOZ. 1983. PART I. (TRANSLATED FROM THE VOZKOZIAN.) Interview conducted with Commander Zzzz Trelazian by Communal Mainframe Intellect Gas.

GAS: Can you summarise the point of your mission?

TRELAZIAN: The point of our mission is to gather therapeutic intelligence.

GAS: Where is the mission taking place?

TRELAZIAN: The city of Nottingham. The country of the United Kingdom. Earth. Solar System. Southern Starbag. Orbit 96.

GAS: Why did you choose Earth, as opposed to other planets in Orbit 96?

TRELAZIAN: Because we were instructed to by Communal Mainframe Intellect Gas, aka you.

GAS: And, when you arrived at the instructed destination, why did you choose this country, 'the United Kingdom', and more specifically this place, 'Nottingham'?

TRELAZIAN: It appeared to be approximately in the middle of everything, which seemed pertinent to the mission's fundamental nature. Plus its climate seemed to be not too cold, but also not too hot.

GAS: And how can your initial findings be summarised?

TRELAZIAN: Subcommanders Ffff Trelunian and Rrrr Dodzz were dispatched in disguise to a building called 'Central Library' to gather background information.

GAS: And what were these disguises?

TRELAZIAN: Subcommander Ffff Trelunian morphed into a deputy department-store manager going by the name 'David White' and Subcommander Rrrr Dodzz morphed into his lone offspring, 'Lindsey', who was impatient for her parent to be done with his books and keen to go and see *Flashdance*, a motion entertainment recently constructed by the large, upbeat and violent nation 'America'.

GAS: Then what happened?

TRELAZIAN: Subcommander Ffff Trelunian erroneously entered a room intended for the disposal of personal body waste, believing it was an information portal. Here he encountered a male human, approximate age twenty-seven, who asked him, 'You looking at my dick, yoff? Worrarya, some kinda nancy boy or summat?' then placed Subcommander Ffff Trelunian in a neckhold, at which point Trelunian deactivated the male human, although only temporarily.

GAS: When the true information portal was finally located, what were the findings about 'Nottingham'?

TRELAZIAN: Settled in approximately 500 AD, by a commander known as Snotta, or Snot to his closer allies, around a river known as 'the Trent'. 920 AD: River is bridged. 1348 AD: 'Black Death' plague arrives, halving population from 3,000 to 1,500. The heroic 'Robin Hood' arrives shortly afterwards, stealing money to give to the underclass of the region, and as a result clashing with region's commander, who wishes the underclass to not have money and stay under. 1852: Man attempts to auction his wife for a 'florin' coin in the market square but gets no takers. Reputation for rioting grows in region. Themes of riots include police, bread, meat, poverty and dairy products. Industrial Revolution occurs. Best-known industries of the area become cigarettes, coal, pharmaceuticals, bikes, ale. Rumours increase that city has 'best-looking women in the country' and 'blokes who are best at fighting' (both unconfirmed). 1960s AD: Britain's tallest (unconfirmed) law enforcer Police Constable Geoffrey Haydn Baker patrols Market Square with steadfast companion Police Constable 'Tug' Wilson, and poses for 'amusing' publicity photo with Earth's best fighting man (confirmed) Cassius Clay. The music band 'Led Zeppelin' are paid £90 to make loud sounds near the river at nighttime at The Boat Club. Attractive heritage housing dismissed as 'slums' is destroyed by region's commanders to make way for block of 'concrete', by name of 'Broadmarsh Centre', containing ornamental fountains, ominous wooden play sculptures in the shape of animals and retail outlets including 'Stead & Simpson','Wimpy', 'Gentz', 'Decor Mecca' and – most intriguingly of all – 'Electricity'.

GAS: You will have to translate some of that more clearly to me later. And what about Trelunian and Dodzz's firsthand findings, as eyewitnesses to this 'Nottingham', or should that be 'Snottingham'?

TRELAZIAN: Humans are highly diverse in appearance. Many sizes and colours. This proves less to be the case upon diverting from population centre. An astoundingly beautiful grey bird with green on its neck, a similar shade to that of the light rocks from our magic Redaral Region, and a sonorous call full of impenetrable magic can be seen in great numbers in the population centre, but, bafflingly, is largely ignored, sometimes even actively scorned, by residents. Wives, it seems, are no longer available for purchase in the Market Square, but it is possible to get a 'tracksuit' from the nearby store 'Littlewoods' in the sale for just £3.99 (Trelunian procured two, using paper found in the pocket of the human he temporarily deactivated in the personal waste depository – let the report note I reprimanded him for this infraction of Communal Mainframe Intellect Gas surveillance guidelines). When it is cold, and night has fallen, and residents might be expected to cover their bodies in more fabric, they often tend to remove it instead. Mating calls are more often heard in the dark, especially around the 'Lower Parliament Street' area and are of an equally uninhibited character in both sexes. As the night intensifies, residents – males, largely – often deposit waste in alleys, sometimes from the holes in the middle of their bodies, and sometimes from holes further up, including – possibly in a ritual based on civic traditions – a thick green substance that shares the name of the city's original commander.

GAS: After you had gathered this information, did you begin to look for a potential target for your more central research, as commissioned?

TRELAZIAN: We did.

GAS: And where did you look for this target?

TRELAZIAN: Inner-city schools. The ones that small humans attended at no monetary cost to their parents.

GAS: And why was that?

TRELAZIAN: Being centres of information and learning, being distinctly outside the arena of human 'fame' and 'affluence', and containing selfless individuals working for little financial reward, they seemed particularly pertinent to the nature of our more central research.

GAS: And did you select one school in particular?

TRELAZIAN: We did.

GAS: And what was this school's name?

TRELAZIAN: Sandyhill Primary School.

GAS: Was the surveillance of this 'Sandyhill Primary School' a success?

TRELAZIAN: I believe so, yes.

GAS: And what was the method of surveillance?

TRELAZIAN: The Roundstone of Redara was placed on the roof above the staffroom and used for its conversation-trapping properties. Once returned to the starcraft, we were able to ascertain from the Roundstone that the regular school caretaker, name 'Mikolaj', was off work with a disease called 'pleurisy'. Using the superior morphology skills that we know her for, Subcommander Dodzz was deployed to infiltrate the school posing as a temporary replacement caretaker, name 'Stanislaw', height six foot one and a half, age fifty-one, city of birth 'Gdańsk'. It was believed that this identity was the one that would make Dodzz most 'invisible' to teachers and pupils at the school, especially as 'everyone would assume the replacement caretaker was authentic because everyone would assume someone else was responsible for hiring him'.

GAS: And, as briefly as possible, but with pith, can you summarise Dodzz's findings from her surveillance at this 'Sandyhill Primary School'?

TRELAZIAN: Dodzz reported that it appeared to be an accurate representative microcosm of the variety of humans found in the city as a whole. On her first day, she enjoyed listening to the happy singing in the weekly 'assembly', even though the verses to the song 'Parsley, Sage, Rosemary and Thyme' were undeniably off-key, and, through research conducted via shop 'His Master's Voice' 1.2 miles away, she had ascertained that the school commander Miss Wishbone's choice 'Yellow Submarine' was the least impressive song on the album *Revolver* by the group 'The Beatles'.

Dodzz's duties while posing as her alter-ego Stan-islaw included 'stoking the boiler', 'operating the lighting system', 'supervising cleaning staff', 'using a big key to lock up at night', 'shaking sawdust on top of puddles of vomit', 'arranging for repairs to the playground wall' and 'removing a child from a chair he had got trapped inside'. All of these duties were performed to the great satisfaction of School Commander Wishbone. It was in the aftermath of the latter that the target was selected. Afterwards, Trelunian, Dodzz and their commander, aka I, celebrated in the craft's conversation pit by eating some pakoras left over from the school's Eid al-Fitr festival, held to mark the end of Ramadan, the holy month of not eating any food. Trelunian then opened a bottle of 'Babycham' procured from a nearby off-licence, chosen because he liked the four-legged lady animal on the bottle, known as a 'deer' or, more specifically, 'faun'. This proved to be much less enjoyable than the pakoras, casting a slight pall on the evening. Dodzz also told us some jokes she had heard in the school.

GAS: Can you give me an example of one of these 'jokes'?

TRELAZIAN: A skeleton walks into a pub and says, 'Can I have a pint of bitter and a mop?'

GAS: I'm not sure that I get it.

TRELAZIAN: The skeleton is asking for the mop because – due to his lack of skin and internal organs – when he drinks the pint of bitter it will go straight through him onto the floor, causing a mess. The joke is additionally appealing because, with great economy of words, it paints the skeleton as a conscientious individual who prefers to clean up after himself and not create unnecessary jobs for others.

GAS: Hmm. I see. When the target had been selected what action did you take next?

TRELAZIAN: From a safe distance, we followed the target home approximately eleven and a half miles to the 'mining region'.

GAS: And what did you discover, once you were there?

TRELAZIAN: We were surprised to find it was the same place we'd been to a few weeks earlier, when we had first been culturally and ecologically acclimatising while scoping out and getting a feel for this place 'Nottinghamshire'. Its similarities to our own Zoxzog industrial region had piqued our curiosity. After tracking target to target's home, just like the earlier time, we landed behind a dark fake hill, inaccessible to the public. We covered the spaceship with branches, found nearby, and some old blankets that had been slung across half a sofa and some food cans, unused. Using her superior powers of morphology, Dodzz was able to smoothly join a family of alpacas – an animal known for its long neck, silly teeth and powers of observation – in a field approximately 0.8 miles distant, posing as one of the alpacas' relatives. Trelunian, using his inferior powers of morphology, was also able to join the family of alpacas, although less smoothly, sometimes clashing with other males in the group and spitting regurgitated grass and fruit at them in an attempt to show dominance.

GAS: What did you counsel at this point, as commander?

TRELAZIAN: I counselled less spitting. I also counselled patience. At night, both alpacas left their enclosures to embark on reconnaissance missions. The Roundstone of Redara was placed on the roof of target's home to gather further intelligence at regular intervals, before being returned to craft for recharging. It was at this point regretted by Subcommanders Trelunian and Dodzz that they had not morphed into a type of Earth animal more naturally disposed to climbing. Using her superior powers of morphology, Dodzz assumed a new identity in order to blend in – 'Jonathan', a 'poet' on a research trip from 'Henley-on-Thames' – and visited the mobile library and the newsagent and the public house and the shop 'A&E Electrical' to gather pertinent local information, which she passed on to us via her extensive and thorough notes.

GAS: Such as?

TRELAZIAN: Dodzz discovered that 'coal' is a black rock with a brownish tinge that cannot be used to listen to people through walls but can make people's homes warmer and generate electricity. Dodzz discovered that 'coal' came from 'mines' and that a great deal of these mines were to be found in the Nottinghamshire and nearby Derbyshire region, although many were now no longer operational. Dodzz discovered that the 'National Coal Board' had been set up under the 'Coal Industry Nationalisation Act' in 1946. Dodzz discovered that the new commander of the 'National Coal Board' was 'Ian MacGregor', originally from the country of 'Scotland' but more recently from the upbeat and violent country of America whose film *Flashdance* Dodzz still, to her disappointment, had not seen. Dodzz discovered that MacGregor's appointment as commander was down to 'Margaret Thatcher', the chief commander of the country. Dodzz discovered that Margaret Thatcher had once stolen some milk from small humans. Doddzz discovered – via the news being shown on one of the TVs being sold in the Ironfield shop 'A&E Electrical' – that Margaret Thatcher had a voice that made Dodzz want to put the Roundstone of Redara over her own head and deploy it as an auditory shield. Dodzz discovered that the commander of the 'National Union of Mineworkers', known more commonly simply as the 'NUM', was 'Arthur Scargill', born in 'West Riding' in the county of 'Yorkshire'. Dodzz discovered – also via the news being shown on one of the TVs for sale in A&E Electrical – that Commander Scargill had a voice like people in the Nottinghamshire coal region's voice, but sort of dialled up. Dodzz discovered that Commander Scargill had called Commander MacGregor an 'American butcher of British industry' and said that the policies of Commander Thatcher aimed to 'destroy the coal industry and the NUM'. Dodzz discovered that Commander MacGregor had replied by describing himself as a 'plastic surgeon' sent to 'rebuild damaged features'. Dodzz discovered that Scargill believed this statement to be 'a load of old flannel'. Dodzz discovered that 'flannel' was her new favourite word to describe the words of humans or other life forms who talk a lot without ever telling you what you want or need to know.

Dodzz discovered that on 28 June 1871, in Coppice Colliery, four men died from burns sustained after a controlled explosion in a tunnel failed to be properly controlled. Dodzz discovered that in 1888 at Naghill Colliery, Joseph Longhouse, age forty-six, had died when a box of slack had fallen down the shaft on him from above and that only several hours later it had been discovered that Archibald Noon, age twelve and three quarters, had died as a result of the same small avalanche. Dodzz discovered that in 1908, in the same colliery, two boys aged no more than thirteen, Thomas Babbington and Edward Wadston, and a pony were the victims of a roof fall, Babbington being trapped against a tram at the time and losing his arm in the process. Dodzz discovered the boys were only saved due to some frantic digging by two of their elders, as the roof was 'bitting', but the pony was not so lucky. Dodzz discovered that the descendants of the owners of the colliery still lived in a nine-bedroom house, in the woods, with mock lumps of coal as gateposts. Dodzz discovered that neighbouring Pastry Lane colliery (1821–1978) was now a Safeway supermarket, where you could buy a *Radio Times* and find out what time *Panorama* and reruns of *The Dick Emery Show* were being broadcast.

Dodzz discovered that she was morose and distracted many times upon reconvening with Trelunian and me at the craft. 'And have you heard this?' she asked, as we sat in the control room, with the photo of Commander Scargill she'd cut out of the newspaper, *The Daily Mirror*, staring down at us from where she had attached it to the wall, using Blu-tack purchased from the Safeway that was formerly the Pastry Lane colliery. 'It's from the diary of Samuel Hall, a miner from Pinxton, in Derbyshire: "Sunday 3 March, 1850. Arthur (brother) and I went to the funeral of Thomas Hall. He was not but thirteen years old and had fallen into the soft pit when he could hold the chain no longer. He could not be saved and that is life. Wind was biting when we came up over the ridge after." '

Dodzz was often late back to the alpaca enclosure and the craft, being waylaid in the village pub attempting to talk to workers from the mines while in her Jonathan the Poet disguise. Dodzz discovered that the workers were less concerned about the danger of their jobs and more concerned about the danger of their jobs ending because of Commander Thatcher and Commander MacGregor. Dodzz discovered that many of the workers were reluctant to talk to her in her Jonathan persona, especially when she announced his artistic vocation and that she came from Henley-on-Thames. Dodzz discovered that some of the workers' called Jonathan a 'fairy'. Dodzz discovered, upon returning to the library, that a fairy, also spelt 'faery', was 'a rather ancient being who could levitate, steal cattle in revenge, and often consorted with hags, dragons and bogles'. Dodzz discovered she rather liked this and was surprised it was locally viewed as an insult.

GAS: And how exactly did Dodzz believe this was relevant to your mission, and the target in question?

TRELAZIAN: Dodzz put it under the category of 'background', 'texture' and 'research'. Dodzz cited that the target had several non-blood relatives who had been miners nearby, two of whom had died in a pit explosion earlier this century. Dodzz cited that the target also had countless real blood ancestors who'd worked as miners. Dodzz's commander, aka I, replied that, yes, that was true, but reminded Dodzz that these had worked at Owl Hole Colliery and Brinsop Hall Colliery, which were both in Lancashire, over a hundred miles away, plus that had been over a century ago.

GAS: And what was then concluded by Commander Trelazian, aka you?

TRELAZIAN: After several weeks, it was concluded that Dodzz had slipped too far down a research rabbit hole, and been diverted from her reason for travelling to and finding herself on the planet Earth in the first place. It was concluded that Dodzz was sleep-deprived, obsessive, overemotional and prone to mistakes, especially when, at the end of a long day of research, she mislaid the Roundstone of Redara.

GAS: And has the Roundstone of Redara yet been recovered?

TRELAZIAN: Not thus far, no. But we remain hopeful.

GAS: So then what happened?

TRELAZIAN: I counselled no more patience. Actually, I counselled impatience. I counselled that it was time to do the job we came here for and gain the prize we required, for the benefit of our own kind. I counselled that the target should be apprehended as soon as was practical.

GAS: Was the rest of the mission then instantly smooth and successful?

TRELAZIAN: It was not.

GAS: Why not?

TRELAZIAN: Upon approaching the target's home, we realised that the target and the target's family were not
there, and the curtains were closed and that voices we
heard from the house emanated from a radio tuned to
medium-wave station 'Radio 4'. Upon looking into the
matter closely, the target and the target's family were
found to be 1,011 miles away, crossing the Swiss border
into Italy. Which surprised us all. Especially considering what we knew about the health of the landcraft
they travelled in.

GAS: Presumably you caught them up with no trouble
at all.

TRELAZIAN: We would have. But we had an unforeseen
issue.

GAS: Which was?

TRELAZIAN: Well, as you know, none of us are equipped
to survive in heat of over twenty-nine degrees. There
are so many dangers: peeling, melting, brainmist, sometimes even permanent deactivation. It was twenty-seven
that day and, according to the forecast, no sign of it letting up any time soon. So: a bit iffy.

GAS: And what was decided?

TRELAZIAN: What was decided was that more patience
would be counselled, and we would wait however long
we needed to.

GAS: So where are you all right now, precisely?

TRELAZIAN: We are in Tapley Woodhouse. Trelunian is in
the field, living as an alpaca. I believe he has grown to
quite like it there. Dodzz is back at the Central Library,
looking into the history of the Park Estate, on the edge
of the city; how it evolved from the personal hunting

forest of Henry II to a lavish urban region where famous architects, including Thomas Chambers Hines and Watson Fothergill, built grand houses for the Nottingham manufacturing bigwigs of the nineteenth century, such as Boots the Chemist founder Jesse Boot, the hosiery manufacturer turned Lib Dem Cabinet Minister Anthony Mundella and, later, the Nottingham police force commander Athelstan Popkess. It's a bit of a new obsession for her: it makes her less morose than all the mining stuff. She's also interested in the history of the caves nearby, cut into the sandstone. Some of them were still registered as domestic abodes until about thirty years ago. She said she would probably also pop into the shop 'Electricity' in the Broadmarsh Centre on her way back, being intrigued to find out whether it sells electricity, and, if so, what form the electricity takes, and whether people take it home in a bag. She would probably be the first to admit she's mostly killing time at this point. Oh, and me? I'm right here, typing this to you.

Colin

W hen was love invented? Was it when one dinosaur looked across an inlet in a great swamp and spotted another dinosaur, discerning an indefinable something in its walk and eyes that was suggestive to it of a mutual future that was exciting yet warm, mysterious yet safe. Did that dinosaur then successfully woo the other dinosaur? Did they then live alongside one another in harmony for a number of years, eating the same plants, structuring their life around a shared set of values and goals, living more for each other than they did for themselves? Did one of the dinosaur couple then, out of the blue, break all the trust that had been established between them, leaving the other dinosaur on the floor, with all four of its legs in the air, staring at the sky, reassessing the precise point of existence? Did the beleaguered dinosaur then turn itself back the right way up, dust the dead ferns and insects and crusty vegetable matter off itself and slowly hit upon methods to reassemble its life? Did that dinosaur then meet another dinosaur and try its best to trust again but unintentionally bring some of its paranoia and hurt into the new relationship and teach it to the third dinosaur? Did those dinosaurs then part ways and teach more hurt and mistrust to other dinosaurs? Did that hurt and mistrust grow exponentially, across species, for millions of years? Did it mutate into bitterness and wariness and cynicism and keep expanding until finally it seeped into some people's actual DNA, and they were sometimes born with it right there, pumping through their veins, ready so easily to heat up into outright hatred, until finally we were in the second half of the twentieth century and you had a furious man standing on a grass verge in a village in the East Midlands, poisoning some flowers, just because it briefly made him feel better about all the wretchedness that he fundamentally was and diverted him from dwelling on other things, such as his face in the mirror in the morning, with his life written indelibly upon it?

Barrowcliffe trashed my place, but I suppose it could have been worse. I suspect it was carried out with assistance and intended primarily as a warning. The 'Composted' on my hand-painted 'Trespassers Will Be Composted' sign had been crossed out and replaced with 'HERE'. Surprisingly witty, I thought. The living-room carpet was a write-off: paint thinner and baked beans and vinegar and at least three other liquids from bottles in the kitchen all over it. Rosa Bosom's left arm had been snapped off, but that would be easy enough to reattach. The tyres on my bicycle had been slashed and there was a little smouldering pile of ashes in the garden where magazines and books and notes had been incinerated, apparently at random. What I mostly felt was lucky. Lucky that I wasn't short on money, wasn't struggling, and this wasn't the final gust of wind which pushed me over the cliff edge. Many people might not have been so fortunate. Looking back, particularly at the political situation at that point, you see the inauguration of a certain attitude: every man for himself, do what you can to nip ahead. If you've got the dosh, you've got your cushion, ready to fall back on if the hard times come. If not, sod you, m'duck.

I opted not to call the police. I'd seen Barrowcliffe in the pub, drinking with at least one of the local bobbies. And what kind of spavined leg would I have to stand on, when they accused me of starting it by burgling his shed? Instead, I went to ground, further to it even than before. I wrote. I changed my walking routes, heading away from the village, over a BMX track, past an old gatehouse and more profoundly into the woods. I took my sketchpad and sketched a ruined priory I'd found a couple of miles away. I planned – but did not rush – my escape. I swallowed my original intentions and bought a car from a man at a chicken farm: just a Vauxhall Viva, three previous owners, 63,000 on the clock. I drove it into the city, tried to ignore a smell on the upholstery which put me in mind of straw and amniotic sac. I ate packed lunches in libraries, bit wincingly into thick-skinned apples and watched the goosebumps spread along my arms, bought carbide lamps and Victorian chisels from dingy antique shops on reticent streets. I overheard disparate conversations which soldered together in my mind: 'I've done sixteen fish today . . . I'd shoot the whole ruddy lot of 'em all if it were up to me.' I saw the clefts in the earth on the mound the city's oppressed had once climbed to set the old castle alight. I was serenaded by pigeons in a giant equine underpass carved through the sandstone and I wondered why people had not told me about it, wondered why they did not walk around raving enthusiastically about it every day. I witnessed disagreements – disagreements pulsating with little histories, disagreements that sounded to an outsider like uncrackable codes – between trios of men with not a full mouth of teeth between them, then realised that some of them were not men. At the end of the day, when the shops closed, the city felt like the bottom of a glass that too many people had been drinking from.

Back in the sixties, when I was attending a lot of Happenings at bookshops in Soho, there had been a Romanian girl named Irina who used to hang around with us all: a tall statuesque figure, very unvarnished in her opinions. She had this extraordinary way with language that I think a lot of the musicians heard then applied to, or even appropriated for, their lyrics, a turn of phrase all of her own for so many situations. 'I licked all ten of my fingers,' she'd say after a meal, or, upon watching some older guy drive his open-top sports car down Wardour Street or embarrass himself by trying to chat up some teenage girls, 'Oh dear. The gate is closing.' On the days she wasn't feeling so good about herself, she would announce, 'I look like washed shit,' although of course to everyone else she always looked drop-dead gorgeous. When I assessed myself in the bathroom mirror that had been smashed by my neighbour during those dog days in my stubborn adopted home a decade and a half later, I really did look like washed shit. It was as if my body was somehow mimicking the shrivelling, straggly vegetation outside. I was not eating as much or as well as I should have done. Every time I did, a broken molar I'd neglected to attend to caught on my gum and stoked the fire of a burning ulcer. The upper left part of my spine felt detached from the rest of me when I walked, just by a centimetre or so.

As the weeks went by, I felt the emptiness of the house directly to my right more acutely than I'd expected to; missed the happy cries of children ringing out from the garden and the two adult voices, one quiet, one loud, discussing the planting of a new vegetable crop or shrub. I hadn't seen Elaine McNulty for weeks. We always had plenty to talk about, but it just wasn't there for us in other ways: when we'd finally got physical, something felt oddly practical about it, like we were both working in the same locked supermarket and had been asked to team up to stack shelves in the same aisle. She checked in on me via the phone a few times and invited me out but I said I was fine, a bit too busy with work, then regretted it. Could it have been that the content, semi-voluntary loner was finally experiencing that elusive sensation, loneliness? I gathered the first apples from the garden, sliced them up and fed them to the alpacas in the field behind the woods. I moved slowly in every action I performed. I stared at the alpacas. I looked past my alpaca racism and began to see them as individuals. There was a petulant one, a more quiet and thoughtful-looking one, an unusually hungry one who was always first to the apples and looked a bit like a demented stag. An undeniable power structure was in evidence, even here.

When I saw the Mosses' car back in their drive, it was all I could do to stop myself from rushing straight over and enclosing each of them in my arms, but I managed to restrain myself. Nobody wants visitors immediately after they've driven halfway across Europe. They were probably tired and clammy from the road. So I gave it almost two whole days, turned up looking as nonchalant as I could with a bottle of petrol-station wine, four KitKats and an old Co-op bag full of early russet apples. My timing could not have been better. Pete had a huge pan of pasta sauce simmering away, the table was set, and they asked if I'd like to join them for lunch. A bottle of wine that had travelled all the way from Tuscany with them. All thoroughly delicious. I licked all ten of my fingers afterwards. I did mention the break-in but made light of their concerns for me, changing the subject to the project I had been working on and how they might all be able to be involved.

Catherine seemed a little more subdued than normal. Every time she left the room for any length of time, Pete shouted to her, 'I say, you all right, Cath?' He was always attentive, but had become much more so. His hand was constantly on her shoulder or back, although not in what I would have called a possessive way. None of it appeared to be related to my presence in the house. He just struck me as a man very much in love, maybe even a man recently shocked into renewed love, hyperaware of his fortunate predicament in the grand scheme of life.

Catherine lit a stick of incense and attempted to shoo a fly through an open window. A violent draught caused the kitchen door to slam and all three of us abruptly levitated, no more than an inch. Below us, on a planet far away a few feet to our left, Benji held a KitKat in one hand and, using his other, assisted a toy car in negotiating the contours of a rug; an aerodynamic continental vehicle which had clearly become his priority, usurping all other concerns for the time being. A few other toys lay around him, abandoned: a tiny lead representation of a dwarf wielding a club, a Lego astronaut and a plastic Brontosaurus, on its back, staring despondently at the place where the sky should have been.

Thug

Fuck me backwards, is tharra *woman's* bag? What do you keep in it? *Your books and lipstick*? Aye, I'm only kidding, yer big streak o' piss. Come over here, drink some more wi' me. Drink wi' me! Shut yer whittlin', it's been fuckin' yonks since we got wrecked together. Nah, fuck that. One more. ONE MORE. She'll be alreet. What yer worrying about? There's a word for what you are. It rhymes with Wussy Lipped. Ok, two words. Check my face for botheredness, like ah giya shit. You're like fuckin' Riggsy, who drives one of the forklifts down at our place. He says he went out an' bought a dishwasher t'other fuckin' weekend. I says to him, 'What d'yer need one of those fer? Yer already got one. It's called a wife and yer just need to fix it so it works proper.' Nah, though, I'm only kidding, yoff. She's all right, your 'Chelle. At least yer not sleeping in an empty bed. I 'ant 'ad my end away for months. Giy it a bit longer and I'll be whispering sweet nuffin in that fruit machine's ear. Not that it would work between us, long term, like. That slot at the front int big enough, for a start. Anyway listen. No, LISTEN. I've got summat to tell yer.

I were down London t'other week. Me an' Stumps and Other Lee and Onions got the coach for the Notts County match an' thought we'd mek a weekend of it, ay some tins. Not even England anymore down there, is it. Not bein' funny, but you go in the shops and there int any real English people in them. Yeah, I know your dad came from Trinibados or wherever it is, ALL RIGHT, Cuba, check my face for botheredness, but you know what I'm on about, right. Course yer do. An I get on all right wi' most of them. Don't ay a problem. But it's still got to be a country, 'ant it. It's still gorra look like England. ANYWAY, look, gerrin' back to me central fuckin' point, we were down London an' fuckin' 'ell you know what Onions is like. Fuckin' prize space cadet. You think you're wi' him then you realise he's wandered off somewhere. We was up Mansfield once, pissed out our 'eads, goin' dahn this street, and I looked behind me an he'd pissed off into some old biddy's front room. She'd had her door wide open and now it was him in there, an' this old biddy and this dog, this fuckin' Jack Russell which were about eighty itsen, just staring at Onions. 'Excuse me, but might you have any Rich Tea biscuits?' he says to her, in that voice he does. She woulder called t'fuzz if I ant dragged him out of there quicksharp.

Anyways, we was down Leicester Square and he'd fucked off, all the way to India for all we knew, which may as well be London nowadays. And then everything went pear-shaped an it's just me an meesen in this club, giyin' it some, and this blonde comes over, tall like, even though I can't see her face proper coz it's dark and she really seems like she wants it hard, so I'm fuckin' grinding against her, and then she drags me over to t'corner near t'bog and, fuck me, I realise she's really just some massive bloke, so I get t' fuck out of there, but it's wazzin' it down. Then I look down and I'm only wearing one shoe, looking like I wazzed meesen. Had a kip on a bench in St Pancreas, or worrever it's called. Not bein' funny, it were pretty fuckin' comfy. Might giy it a five-star review on TripAdvisor. Then I'm on the train, and it's heavin', everyone's got their ears in some other fucker's armpit and their elbows in his arsehole, an' guess who sits next to me. GUESS! Worra you mean, the Queen? Fuck off. Dean fuckin' Berry. You remember him? Nah, of course you do. Him an' his brother Wayne. Used to sit on the top of t'skips at the tip when they was piled up wi' old sofas an' that. Everyone knew their dad, he were always walkin' around town centre lookin' like he were covered head ter toe in pigshit. People said they went on holiday in Long Eaton, or Derby, if they were feeling really fuckin' fancy 'n' minted. They moved to Shirebook, didn't they. YOU REMEMBER. NO YOU FUCKIN' DO, YOU CUNT.

But listen to what I'm fuckin' sayin'. Now Dean's on this train wearing a suit, an' I'm sitting there, like a fuckin' drowned rat, wi' one trainer on and that ant got its laces anymore. Dean tells us – get this – he works as a fuckin' 'Marine Conservation Support Officer' now, whatever that is. I'm all fuckin' 'ark at you, I used to snap yer new pencil every Monday morning. Then I fell asleep, because, not bein' funny, I'm still fuckin' wrecked, and when I wake up I'm leaning on his shoulder and there's this little wet patch on his suit and I know it's coz I've gobbed on him in me sleep, but I reckon fuck it, coz he ant complained or twatted me for it an I nod back off an' then when I wake up again he's gone an' the train's pullin' into Pond Street Station in Sheffield, or worrever they call it now. I thought fuck this for a game of soldiers. Went straight to t'pub. They've got one in t'station there.

Ey, take that fucking big girl's coat off and sit down. TAKE IT OFF RIGHT NOW, YOU GREAT TOSSPOT. I told yer I 'ad summat to tell yer and that stuff about London and Dean weren't it, so listen. I'm telling yer this coz I wunt tell it to anyone else, and coz we been through a lot, you and me. Eyup, is that a bunch of fuckin' grey hair, sticking out from under that hat o' yourn? That's what happens when yer henpecked. Nah, sit down, I'm only fuckin' kiddin'. It's a fuckin' JOKE, yoff. I'm *playin'* wiv yer. At least yer still got some on top. Not like me. Giz a cuddle. I'm lonely and I need a big lad to keep me warm at night. GIZ A CUDDLE, YOU GREAT WANKSHAFT. Did that big orangutan-looking cunt just vom in his pint glass over there? No, not him. *Him.* Now come here and cuddle up and listen. I'm not sayin' this loud as I don't want that lot to hear. You ever been up t'twitchel, when you come off Naghill down Stringy Lane, near where t' Miners' Welfare used to be? Roundabout up the road on the playground that we wrote off. You know it. Course yer fuckin' do. Gob pile used to be right opposite. Still is, 'cept it's covered in all trees an' flowers an' bees an' other bollocks now, you wunt even know it were a gob pile. Used to be this little cunt who lived up the road, built little wendy houses on it, like he were playing families, rehearsing to be some big cunt's nice little wife, and me an' Darren Butcher kicked t'shit out of one of them, burnt t'fuck out of his little chair and teddy. Feel a bit bad about it sometimes, not bein' funny, but we was just kids. It's what kids do, innit.

Anyway, I were coming down twitchel there one day on me bike, I couldn'ta been more than nine at t' time, and then the sky went all dark blue an' shit an' all these crows flew up an' I looked up and there were this fucking massive flyin' saucer, 'overing over t'gob pile. A fuckin' proper UFO. Swear on my life, I int tekkin the piss. I fuckin' shit my pants twice over and got down reet flat on the ground. I dint get up 'til the light wa'nt blue anymore, but I kind of knew it were still there, so I climbed t'gob pile and I couln't see it anywhere at first an' then I saw the back end of it stickin' out from behind t'other gob pile, over by Tutley's farm. And then this hatch thing opened, one of them doors like the car in *Back t'Future*, but massive, wi' a ramp, and out walks this woman wi' permed hair, an' even though I were too far away to properly see, I knew it were the little twat's mum, Missuz Moss or whorrever she were called. She were wearing dungarees and she had all this paint on them and there were some bloke, this blonde streak o' piss, with her. And they just start walking back towards Tapley Woodhouse, normal as owt. And then I legged it home, and didn't see owt more. And I ant told anyone about it from that day to this. And if you tell anyone I did, I'll kick yer fuckin' 'ead in and I'll kick theirs in next.

Fucking hell, innit just gone cold in here, right this minute. Must be gettin' nesh in me old age. What fucker's round is it next? Ah, that's right, innit: it's yours. Guwahn then. Gerrem in. Bar's not open all night. Worrar yer waiting for?

Ey, come back here a minute. Yeah, back just here. Cuddle up. Ok. So listen. Now do yer believe I love yer?

Parents

'You and my mum and my sisters used to call it "the day Catherine disappeared into the compost". Do you remember that? It was because that's what I'd been doing, taking some food waste up there from the kitchen. I honestly don't remember much about it other than that, though.'

'Well, that's the point. I suppose you wouldn't. What was it the doctors called it? Global transient amnesia? You recognise places and people but don't know how you got there, or who you are. That's what you kept saying on the way to the hospital, "Please can you tell me who I am?"'

'I know I'd been taking the carpet up. Then the next thing I can remember, I was in the hospital and you and my mum and Sue were there, all staring at me, like I was some kind of exhibit. Then we were pulling into the drive, and I looked over at the lawn and thought, "Bloomin' 'eck, that convolvulus got really out of control while we were away: I need to sort that, pronto."'

'I remember it clear as yesterday. Always will, probably. We'd not even been back from Italy twenty-four hours. I'd covered the distance in no time, not much sleep for any of us. Normal people would have wanted a rest but you were straight into Action Woman mode, as usual. We'd been looking through all those open doorways in those Italian hill towns and seeing all those nice wood floors and you decided to take the carpet up in the back room and repaint the wall. You had your blue dungarees on, it was maybe just before one, and I know it was a Sunday because the *Archers* omnibus edition had been on the radio. You said you were going up to the compost heap at the top of the garden. Potato peel, that's what it was. You had it in that old blue colander that used to be your dad's, almost the exact same colour as your dungarees. I was painting from the photo you took of the Italian basket maker and I'd got a bit lost inside it, so it was actually the best part of an hour before I realised you hadn't come back. Benji was lost inside his own world too: I could hear him brumming his Alfa Romeo, doing these voices of mechanics speaking to each other, mostly in English, but with a bit of Italian too. I remember how happy it made me feel and that I felt much less anxious than I usually did at the end of a summer holiday, even though term was only a few days away from starting. I'd assumed you'd got involved in another garden job, or the tiredness had finally hit you and you were having a sleep in the sun, but then, after around the third time I'd checked every room in the house, and been back up to the top of the garden, I saw the colander on the ground, near the compost, and my heart turned over in my chest. I walked up the road, then up the pit road, starting to run. I don't know why I thought you might be up there. I knocked on Colin's door but he wasn't in. I called Sue and Jerry and they said they'd come straight over. I didn't call your mum because I thought about her heart and I didn't want to worry her. I knocked on the Chudleys' door and asked them if they'd seen you and they said they hadn't. I think they might have thought we'd had a row. Then Sue and Jerry and Tom and Sarah arrived, almost impossibly quickly, and Tom and Sarah walked down the street into the village and me and Sue and Jerry drove down every street we could think of, and then when we'd done that, we came back to call the police and there you were, sitting on the stool in the middle of the back room and the first thing you said was, "Excuse me, but please can you tell me where exactly this is? I think I'm lost." The whole thing must have lasted no more than three hours but to me it felt like thirteen. I somehow managed to keep everything from Benji. He was upstairs, lost in his cars and books the whole time. When we went to the hospital and left Donna to look after him, he just thought everyone had gone out to the garden centre to get some plants. After he finally came downstairs and you were still a bit dazed, we just told him you weren't feeling well. "Is it hangover?" he asked me.'

'I still feel awful to have put you through it, even now. Perhaps the blame was with that Italian wine we were still drinking. I knew it had something a bit unusual about it.'

'Yeah, that was it. Definitely. I was still in a big state of

worry – maybe a bigger one – even after we'd found you and we were in the hospital, and you'd remembered you were Cath, and long after that, too. While you were missing, I kept coming up with what I told myself were rational explanations: you'd gone over to some neighbours with some fruit or veg, even though we weren't really what you'd call friends with any of our neighbours apart from Colin and the Chudleys, and maybe the Figshaws at a push; you'd gone to pick some flowers and fallen asleep in a field; you'd remembered something we needed urgently from the shop. But in the days after I got you home I would come back in my mind again and again to my cousin Agnes, who'd had a stroke while she was riding her bike when she was nineteen. I kept worrying about something similar happening to you and felt sure it would. And all these years later it still hasn't.'

'It's funny, I think of that as the start of quite a good period for us. You were still doing the supply, which could be rough, but not long after that you got the job at Gowenlock Hall, doing the art for them.'

'Yeah, it was just bits and bobs, and it didn't pay well, but it was better than having some massive yob from Bulwell threaten to beat the shit out of you because you gave his lad an E minus for his essay on the emancipation proclamation. It was an amazing place, really – sadly underused. All those corridors, those grand walnut staircases, all those rooms filled with weird historical artefacts.'

'The teachers at Sandyhill *definitely* made the most of the resources at Gowenlock! Miss Buttons and Mr Stone and I would hang the drapes in the classroom, some of that nice geometric Heal's fabric, and we'd display the stuff on the table for the kids, and Miss Buttons or Mr Stone would base a lesson around it. It might be a model of a trebuchet or a Norman castle. One day you brought home a full-size Roman centurion's outfit. There'd be Indonesian shadow puppets, costume dolls from all different periods. You brought an Alaskan wolf home once, just stuck it right there, in the kitchen, with its face pointed at the cat-food dish, to surprise me.'

'Some interesting people worked there. Quite a strange variety. Taxidermists, and a caretaker who was also an amazing artist who liked to print on old rags. Colin came over to have a look around a couple of times. I showed him this room on the top floor which was pretty much entirely devoted to the reconstruction of a Victorian cigar factory, and another one which had all this old radar equipment salvaged from Orford Ness in Suffolk from when it was used for secret military tests in the Second World War, and you could see the cogs in his brain turning over, him thinking, 'What could I create from this?' And of course he loved all the taxidermy. Brian, who was in charge of everything, seemed very interested in him and tried to buy one of his robots. I think the council had given Brian quite a bit of money to spend but I don't think much of it went to his employees. He was always buying quite inappropriate things, including this collection of art from some Victorian artist who was probably a total paedophile and liked to paint nude young boys. Brian was a bit drunk a lot of the time, I think. One time me and Mike Dobwalls, who was the driver who took all the stuff to and from the schools, went around making all the paintings wonky before Brian arrived. Another time I cut some newspaper into the shape of tiny shorts and we stuck the shorts on the nude boys in the paintings. Brian didn't notice. And then Mike Dobwalls' pet guinea pig snuffed it and Rob, the in-house taxidermist, offered to preserve it for posterity and Mike seemed a bit torn but said yes. And then months later, he was looking for some ice and he opened Rob's chest freezer, not realising it was the taxidermy freezer, and there was his guinea pig, looking up at him, and he burst into tears. We called the freezer 'the coffin'. There was some nice woodland you could see through the window behind it, but when it thinned out in winter, you could see the tower block that Deborah Fennel's cousin's mate jumped out the top of in 1980. Mike Dobwalls makes UPVC fascias and soffits now. He lives over in Tibshelf with an iguana.'

'I think I might need a lie down.'

'Is it the weather?'

Alpaca

It didn't take us long to learn the language, to pick up the nuances of it, grasp the humour, the occasions where something was being said but actually the precise opposite of what was being said was intended to be conveyed. Well, I say 'us'; what I really mean is 'me'. Trelunian? I liked him well enough but, let's face it, the guy hadn't got four complete thoughts in his entire head; he was like a heathen from a simpler age who went on an extended wander while trying to satisfy one of his primitive urges and fell through a rip in time by mistake. Trelazian, meanwhile, was no different to every government-affiliated commander I've ever known: most of the time he talked a big load of flannel. His main skill was steering around a subject, dodging the point like it was an asteroid in the slaggfield a couple of thousand miles above Vozkoz. I don't think I'm being too bumptious if I tell you that it's best if you hear the story from me. There will probably always be some language gaps, but I've got most of it nailed now. I'm not saying that it's the only story, nor that there aren't other totally valid angles it can be viewed from. I'm just saying that if you get it from another source, you might not get such an undiluted version.

The central point is: our planet had not been going through a great time. This is what our journey was all about, why the three of us were on the Nottinghamshire-Derbyshire border and not light years from there, respectively relaxing with our history books or our lifesize punchdroids or at an exclusive café with our fellow starcraft commanders. But when is a planet going through a 'great time'? I'll tell you when: probably when it isn't a planet. But you can't just be seen to accept that and give up trying, so the powers that be, noting the escalation of certain aspects of behaviour vis-à-vis the population of Vozkoz, decided it was time to dig into the planetary budget and take some action. It's hard to explain precisely what that behaviour was, or exactly what seed it sprouted from, without giving you the entire history of our culture, stretching back millions of years, but I suppose you might describe it as a sort of 'mass uselessness'. The root of this uselessness was complex: a mixture of self-punishment, narcissism, and unwillingness to spend time on any activity that would not potentially lead to high praise or be perceived as 'prestige'. At one time not so long in the past, the Vozkozians were a practical and self-effacing race, but more recently many of us had begun to lose such basic skills as cooking our own meals, washing our own clothes and working the lock mechanisms on the front hatches to our homes. Yet at the same time our breed were, in part, more advanced than ever. Some of us could consume vast amounts of information phenomenally quickly, perform remarkable feats of morphology, fly between starbags in machines we'd made ourselves, or effortlessly deactivate adversaries from other planets. But many of those who could not perform morphology, make or fly a starcraft, demonstrate great and perfect success in relationships or become renowned as a famous Vozkozwide genius had started to view themselves as worthless. So extreme was their focus on their success, or lack of it, in these advanced fields, they had begun to view more basic parts of day-to-day survival as 'not worth bothering with'. As a result, our population was not only ailing; it was decreasingly, rapidly.

I have learned that, for you on the planet Earth, suicide is not a simple action to perform. There are some ways of doing it that are more straightforward and potentially less pain than others, but even these involve severe risks if they do not go through to their intended conclusion. On Vozkoz, it's not like that. If you choose to end your life, you go to one place, a ledge whose name would probably translate to English as something along the lines of 'the Happy Cliff Above the Water Cloud'. The process, they say – although I'm not sure how anybody would be able to report back and state it as a fact – doesn't involve the tiniest fraction of pain: you merely step off the ledge and, as your life force is siphoned into the void below, you experience only the gentlest of sensations, as if falling into a set of large floor cushions that are also somehow bubbles. Forty years ago it was rare to see more than a dozen citizens per week on the Happy Cliff Above the Water Cloud, but now on the average afternoon it is not uncommon to see queues of well over a hundred Vozkozians crammed on the steps carved into the rock below it. And why are they there? They are all individuals, but the core reason is almost always the same: they have decided life is pointless because they have not been decreed 'esteemed' or 'renowned' by their peers. Of course, their choices are their own – suicide has not been illegal on Vozkoz for centuries – but the aggregate result is a worrying population crisis for the planet as a whole.

As I pointed out, this is not the time or place to tell the entire history of Vozkoz, nor of the many religions that have variously blighted and inspired it. I will say this, though: that suicide rate was not the same before our citizens started standing under the fizzboxes once a day. What is a fizzbox? I suppose you might compare it to some of your own electrical systems, connecting the wires above your towns. For many years, there was a fully functioning one in every village, containing a vast store of power, but then, around a century ago, Vozkoz's best scientists discovered that there was a healthier and even more powerful source of energy to be found in the rocks in our most mountain-ous regions. For around forty years after that, the fizzboxes remained semi-dormant, left there like the sky relics of a failed civilisation. But then along came a self-styled guru and ex-homeopath called Jjjjj Tugrefsian. Tugrefsian declared that, far from being useless, the fizzboxes in fact still contained magic and true wisdom, since if you stood directly beneath them and told them something about your recent achievements in life, and they approved of it, they'd fizz and pop and crackle. To pro-vide what he believed was 'proof' of their mystical qualities, he proceeded to write an 800-page book and called it *The Manual of Light*, detailing within it all the immutable moral powers of the fizzboxes, and listing ways we, as Vozkozians, could 'please' them. Some dismissed him as a crackpot at first but, slowly, curiosity grew. Citizens began to stand under the fizzbox in their town or village and show it the diplomas they had received, awards they'd won, photographs they had taken they were espe-cially proud of. Some went further, bringing their partners to stand beneath the fizzbox with them, and believing that if the fizzbox fizzed, popped or crackled, then they had received the ultimate vindication regarding their romantic choice. And who exactly was this Tugrefsian, you might ask? I will tell you: the Vozkozian equivalent of what you on Earth would call 'just some guy'. Who decided all this. In his head. One day. Probably while he was bored and feeling a little hollow about his life.

Yet still the mania grew. More of our citizens visited their local fizzbox once a week, then once a day, as advised by

Tugrefsian's bestselling follow-up to *The Manual of Light*, named – in what for him must have been a real moment of once-in-a-lifetime inspiration – *The Second Manual of Light*. Can you imagine the pressure? Having to have something special and impressive to say about yourself and be judged on it *that often*? But it was kind of ok, because at that point – for a reason that might or might not have had something to do with the residual power that had stayed in the fizzboxes from their former function, decades before – the fizzboxes nearly always crackled or popped or fizzed approvingly when anyone was beneath them. But then they started to not crackle and pop and fizz so often. And then did fewer people ritually visit them? Quite the contrary. Hundreds of thousands flocked to them, in every corner of the planet. They also seemed to try harder to seek the fizzboxes' approval, setting the standards of their own life ever more unreasonably high, feeling relentlessly perceived as they did so. Then, pretty soon, what do you know: big queues at the Happy Cliff Above the Water Cloud. Coincidence, or what?

By now you might be sitting there thinking there was a simple solution to our planet's problem: take down the fizzboxes. Rip them apart. Show the people the emperor has no clothes. But if you are thinking that, it will probably be because you have never been to Vozkoz, or met a Vozkozian, or have no concept of the maddening ways governments manage their infrastructures. I am not immune to planetary pride, and I'm none too keen on outsiders traducing my birthrock, but I also am not going to be so deluded and partisan as to deny glaring facts about its flaws, such as that it is a place of extremes. One of the main extremes is this: Vozkoz contains both the galaxy's most intelligent beings and its most stupid ones. Many of those beings – I will refrain from saying which kind – began to pay some of the little money they possessed to be permitted to stand beneath a soulless box of metal and wires and let it make them feel awful about themselves once every day. What might be viewed as another flaw is this: a lot of that money had started to be funnelled to our government, due to a complex trade deal set up with the corporate estate of Tugrefsian after his death in the year 30288 (1977 by your calendar). And here is another flaw: like all planetary directorates I have ever known, Vozkoz's does not place the health of its citizens above the health of its own bank balance. I suppose the way they see it, there will always be citizens who are unhealthy and unhappy, and that's just a fact, but there are a lot of things money can do for a planet, such as fund research trips to other planets.

So there we were, Trelazian, Trelunian and me, feeling a little uncomfortable – some of us more than others – about travelling on rocket fuel paid for by a mass cult of self-harm. But that was the decision made by the molecular parliament of no fixed shape which rules us, and our mission was not created entirely without the collective good of our people in mind. Some planets suffering a bad patch might go out and shoot holes in some other planets to let off steam, but not ours. We prefer the more cerebral approach. Our aim is to learn, not invade. We had been finding out much about the social character of Earth for a long time, via the listening rocks we sometimes sent to it. We knew it was a complex and – compared to Vozkoz – large planet with infinite problems of its own, containing many individuals brimming over their own psychic rim with self-love, especially within its film and media industries, but also that it was a planet capable of much humility, whose residents mostly just 'got on with it' without expecting the moon on a stick as a prize (which was fortunate, as Earth only has one, in stark contrast to, for example, Jupiter, which we know has ninety-five). Since our listening rocks contain some of the constituent fragments of many of our wisest ancient dead, it could be argued that Vozkozians had already visited Earth several times. However, we would be the first living ones to do so. We would not be alone, forming part of a fleet of eleven starcraft intending to land in scattered regions with climates unlikely to stray above the Vozkozian survival threshold. Nonetheless, it was a historic occasion and I felt special. Also, as everyone knows, travel can only broaden the mind.

You know how people's skin can sometimes change condition for the worse when the seasons shift, or they arrive in a new country? Passing into the atmosphere of a new planet is like that, only significantly magnified. You need to wait around, let your body acclimatise, slowly permit your skin and olfactory receptors and breathing patterns to adjust to the air. Vozkozians are widely known as a patient race but even we got a little bored at first. To feel a little better, I reminded myself that at least we weren't on Saturn, where years last 29.5 times longer. Once that period of adjustment was done, we started making little forays down onto solid ground, having a scout around here and there. We initially sent down underpods to take pictures of potentially interesting locations. Trelunian was reprimanded by Trelazian for using the underpods to knock on the doors of people's homes, then – to Trelunian's own tireless amusement – quickly withdraw them, leaving residents looking out onto the street, confused.

In our first human guises we sampled a variety of foods. Probably the worst was called a 'doner kebab', which only Trelunian, of the trio of us, enjoyed, eventually consuming seven in one night. Mainframe Gas had permitted us plenty of time to achieve our goals, so it was all nicely relaxed. We were able to gather intelligence on popular music and fashions and forms of transport, using the Roundstone of Redara and the underpods. I morphed into a nineteen-year-old female, Sadie, purchased a form of spraying glue from the chemist, coated my hair heavily in it to increase my height, then, unaccompanied, took a train to London, on the pretext of attending a concert by the similarly

tall-haired popular music band Depeche Mode. I was repre-
hended for this by Trelazian, who saw it as unneccesarily
excessive morphing that might drain my energy, but I was feeling good.

In the capital, I saw a profusion of tiny boxy landcraft and
learned they were referred to as 'cars' or, by others, 'Mini
Metros'. Everything was much busier and angrier and faster
than I'd expected it to be. I wondered where the gentle humble
planet of my relentlessly hypothesising imagination could be
found. I purchased a sandwich called a 'ploughman's' from a
shop and asked another customer in the shop, female, with hair
far less tall than mine that looked like it could cut you if you
touched it, why it was called that. She seemed alarmed that I had
found the boldness to address her, but explained that the name
came from many centuries ago, when it was the preferred meal
of agricultural labourers. I thought it seemed like a curious food
to sell in an area where agricultural labour was obviously scarce,
but I very nearly enjoyed the taste of it.

While I ate, I sat on a bench beneath a semi-mountainous
monument: a long pole with a stone representation of a man on
top of it in a wide hat, holding a sharp weapon. Two of my
fellow females, around my age, possibly marginally younger,
with hair even taller than mine, made themselves comfortable
on the other end of the bench. 'Denise, I am telling you, you
would not soddin' believe the things I would do to him if I got
the chance,' one said to the other, pointing to a poster on a
building opposite, depicting an attractive waistcoated male, esti-
mated age thirty, holding a large black gun. 'I'd probably get
arrested for them.' On the opposite side of the plaza where we
sat, I noticed a member of the London constabulary and feared
for the girl's safety, but he walked on, possibly having been
urgently called to break up a political demonstration or intimi-
date a Black or homeless person. Soon the girls left and were

replaced by a man, approximate age thirty-seven, and his son, approximate age nine. 'Did you know that John Noakes climbed right to the top of that, in his flares, without safety gear?' the man said to the boy, pointing to the monument. Before returning to our base 140 miles north, I repaired to a large library, to find out more information about this brave individual 'Noakes', who was clearly a great hero to the people of Earth. I discovered he was an abnormally attractive man, considerably more attractive than the man pictured in his waistcoat holding a gun in the poster on the side of the building. I discovered that flares were a form of trouser, wide at the bottom, also quite attractive but rarely seen in the capital. I liked the black-and-white dog that appeared with Noakes in most photographs I found of him. I learned that 'Get down, Shep!' was something John Noakes said to the dog a lot, and it made people laugh. Together, it seemed, he and the dog had presented several television programmes.

You will know some of the rest, if you've read Trelazian's rather stiff and dusty report. I returned to Nottingham and morphed into an arthritic middle-aged school caretaker, which was initially jarring, after being inside two light and flexible bodies free of wear and tear. I very quickly, instinctively learned what was expected of me, and enjoyed the job more than I anticipated, with the exception of the dog faeces and chewing gum that I had to clean off the carpets after the children brought it in off the streets on the soles of their shoes. I even liked the smell of old fire that permeated much of the building. Although I was only there for four weeks, I assimilated well. I loved being in a place of learning and in that short time got to know most of the teachers and many of the children well. I was constantly eloping to the large library in the city centre after work and learning all sorts of facts every day, and thousands of new phrases, such as 'socio-economic backgrounds' and 'Marxist Sandinista government of Nicaragua'. The children at the school seemed to come from a range of socio-economic backgrounds. I noticed that the children from the less affluent socio-economic backgrounds were the ones who still wore flared trousers and the children from the more affluent socio-economic backgrounds sometimes laughed at them because of it, although not with any genuine malice. A similar pattern occurred amongst the teachers. In this case the laughing by the teachers without the flares at the teachers with the flares was done in private, although, again, without genuine malice.

There was a sweet, inquisitive little girl, the daughter of one of the teachers at the school, who followed me around, asking me lots of questions such as 'How does a central-heating system work?', 'Why does your boiler suit have to be blue?' and 'If you could choose one planet in the entire solar system to go to, which one would it be, and why?' She carried around a small optical instrument with her everywhere which, when you looked into it, due to a collection of tiny tilted mirrors, created amazing patterns, such as the ones we had seen on first emerging out past the slaggfield and into the starbag after departing Vozkoz. I asked her where she had obtained this instrument and she told me her mum had bought it for her on a trip to the Science Museum in London.

I was by this point noticing something curious about Earth: its children talked constantly about outer space and other planets and the creatures you might find on them. They watched films about it and flew small models of the starcraft from the films around their classrooms using their hands. Yet Earth itself had thus far made only made the most pitiful forays into space, barely getting further than its own moon. One night when I was mopping the assembly hall and listening to the radio, I heard one of the planet's most famous commanders, Ronald Reagan of the upbeat and violent country America, talking about a 'strategic defense initiative' called 'Star Wars', but it turned out it had nothing to do with stars at all; the defense initiative related to a part of his own planet, not an alien one. All this was pretty much the antithesis of Vozkoz, which, despite being much more youthful than Earth, had forged many billions of miles into space on exploratory missions, and possessed a population which rarely talked about anything going on beyond the air more than a few dozen feet above their own heads.

All the teachers at the school worked hard and displayed avid commitment to their jobs, but I noticed that two of them, Mrs Moss and Miss Buttons – the mother of the little girl with the amazing psychedelic mirror tube – often stayed an especially long time after the children had left, cutting old magazines up in the shape of letters, stapling photos and drawings to walls or pinning them to fishing lines strung across the big metal beams high above the classroom floors, decorating and transforming the classrooms so they'd be whole new exciting universes for the kids to travel through the following morning. I soon came to consider both of them friends and they were able to answer various questions I had about life in Nottinghamshire, which, as a known recent immigrant, I felt I could ask without being suspected of being from a different planet. Satisfyingly, Mrs Moss was able to render me finally enlightened regarding what the strange rough metal plate was which I'd seen on the back seats of city buses during my trips to the library. 'They're for people to stub out their fags on,' she explained. By 'fag', I realised, from other conversations I'd overheard around the city, she meant one of the 'cigarettes' that many of Nottingham's residents enjoyed inhaling from as a pleasant accompaniment to their meals.

Mrs Moss's job at the school was to help the children whose parents had only recently moved to the United Kingdom and were only just beginning to learn the language, but she was involved in so many other aspects of the curriculum: teaching the cooking and hardening of clay, speaking placatingly to children who were upset or were suffering from the common hair illness 'nits', painting colourful hopping games on the floor of the concrete playground, arranging concerts and trips, making exciting food as rewards for children who'd done particularly good work and children who hadn't, and going to the main hall and setting up a machine called a Betamax so it played sad films about painted rabbits. If a colleague was struggling with the completion of a task due to time constraints or lack of expertise, it was always, 'Let me take care of that.' There appeared to be no end to her talents, nor to the lengths she would go to to help others, and she never demanded praise or recognition for it. I noticed that sometimes large ceramic items with elaborate and innovative patterns would appear in the classrooms. One looked so professional, it would not have appeared out of place in Habitat, an expensive and fragrant shop I had visited in the city centre during some much-needed downtime from cleaning up chewing-gum-coated dogshit and maintaining a thirty-one-room building's heating and lighting system. Paintings, too. Even a wooden chair. All her own work, carried out in who could guess what window of time between her actual job and her home life (I still had no idea how industrious *that* was at this point). But did she tell anyone about any of it or blow a little trumpet to herald its arrival? No. All of it was produced with no more fanfare than most people would apply to the pouring of a glass of water from a nearby tap.

'I am telling you, m'duck,' I said to Trelazian (I was really starting to ease into the speech patterns of the Nottinghamshire people now). 'If most Vozkozians had crafted anything even an eighth as good as these, they'd be off to the fizzbox like a bat out of hell.'

The bond I had established with Mrs Moss after gently extracting her son from a classroom chair whose innards he'd become mystifyingly trapped inside had also established a greater intimacy between us, which in turn offered me deeper insights into her character and background. 'Do you ever find this place spooky?' I asked her one night, when only the two of us remained, floating around the school's empty corridors. 'I've never really thought about it,' she replied. 'I doubt ghosts exist and if they did, I don't think they'd be interested in me.' On my final day as stand-in caretaker, she brought me a lemon drizzle cake she'd made at home the previous night. I was touched, and did my best to apply the emotional gravity appropriate to a last goodbye, even though I knew that was unlikely to be what it was for us.

Discussions between Trelazian, Trelunian and me were subsequently held in our starcraft's conference room. Trelazian did not require much convincing, upon being presented with my findings. Trelunian, whose speech function had been rendered temporarily inactive by a doner kebab, held a thumb aloft in assent. Our decision was made.

A few words about this whole morphology business: it can be tiring. You need to give yourself plenty of downtime in between morphings. People have called me an 'advanced morphologist' and, on occasions, 'a genius' due to my abilities, but it's really mostly about practice. You need to be able to centre your mind and shut out interfering visions. When Trelunian and I morphed into young Nottinghamshire alpacas, I was extremely calm and focused on the task, soaked in thoughts that were wholly 'alpaca', whereas Trelunian was rather distracted, obsessing over the marketing logo for an alcoholic drink featuring a drawing of a young deer, so when we became alpacas my alpaca was quite convincing, whereas Trelunian's looked a little bit off, especially around the eyelashes.

I found myself having to cover for Trelunian more and more in front of Trelazian. During one of our reconnaissance missions to the area around the Moss house, he vanished for considerably more than an hour. I eventually found him beside a pond on the opposite side of the road, sniffing from a tub of industrial-strength glue which he had appropriated from the shed of a neighbour of the Mosses, a prolific racist by the name of Barrowcliffe. I discovered his speech to be slurred and took from his comments about a giant weasel, sitting on the distant headstocks of the mine, that he had passed into a hallucinatory state of consciousness. 'I'm going to let you sleep that off,' I said to him, returning to the starcaft. Here I made a mistake, entrusting Trelunian to bring back the Roundstone of Redara in his altered condition. After he misplaced the Roundstone and our hunt for it in the pre-dawn hours proved fruitless, I took the blame, being aware of the thin ice Trelunian was standing on with the Vozkozian authorities and the fact that he was only here on our mission to Earth due to a kind of community service outreach programme: a gesture extended to him after he'd been found brawling over meat in the kitchen of the canteen at our largest starport and, later, been allegedly responsible for the vandalisation of a famous Vozkozian statue. A 'three strikes and you're out' situation, as it were.

'Subcommander Dodzz, I would expect better from you,' Trelazian told me. 'And who do you think will have to shoulder the blame for this, on our return to Vozkoz? Yours truly, of course. The only consolation is that it has happened now, when our mission is close to complete and we have gathered most of the data we require.'

'I cannot apologise enough,' I said. 'I have not been myself recently.'

'Now go back to your meadow and think about what you've done,' said Trelazian who, despite being an authoritarian who spent too much time talking to machines, was also not immune to absorbing some of the local sayings and catchphrases.

In all honesty, there hadn't been much obvious point to us becoming alpacas. Our nocturnal trips to the house to affix the Roundstone of Redara onto its roof could have been carried out in the guise of any number of creatures, many of them possessing a far more convenient physiology, and, being over a mile from the house, in a quiet spot, our enclosure gave us limited opportunities to gather research. There was the potential wool, of course, which could perhaps have been used as a form of currency, but we'd morphed in freshly sheared form, so by the time our personal supplies of that were replenished, we'd be long gone from this place. In truth, the morph was largely an archetypal Vozkozian act of patience, based around the bigger picture. Alpacas don't do much apart from spit and eat grass and chopped apples and break wind, so being them would give us plenty of time to calmly gather our strength. Sure enough, when it was time for my next morph, into a poet from the south of the country with the name of Jonathan and a physique reminiscent of one of the sunflowers that were starting to appear in the Mosses' garden, I found it uncannily easy.

By now, I had begun to contentedly pickle myself in Nottinghamshire life and history; much more so than Trelunian, and especially Trelazian, who seemed to view such pickling as beneath him. I read about the way industries – bikes, ale and especially coal – had shaped the area since the Industrial Revolution. I went to the closest public house, the Nag's Head, and further absorbed the Nottinghamshire character, especially the male version, which I learned was long on the qualities of pugnacity, aridity and mordant observation. I heard some of the wet-lipped locals talk about the bar lady, Kazza, amongst themselves, then, to my puzzlement, glance down at their own trousers and exclaim 'Get down, Shep!' even though the dog belonging to the statue-climbing hero John Noakes was not present.

I expanded my learning to Britain as a whole, discovering the legend of the brave King Arthur and scaring myself by studying the drawings of the green-haired Victorian artist Aubrey Beardsley. I moved onto other countries, such as Japan and the upbeat and violent nation of America, curious over the roots of its upbeat violence. I took some of my findings back with me to the Nag's Head. 'One of the things I have realised about Ieyasu, the first Japanese shogun, is that he was quite easily swayed in some of his beliefs, switching alliances when he believed he might benefit from it,' I told a mineworker known amongst his peers as 'Flinty', while I waited for Kazza to pour my drink. But Flinty just stared at me, open-mouthed, rolled his eyes and twisted one finger in his ear, as if pretending it was a tiny screwdriver, then relocated to the other side of the bar. Later, when I announced the fascinating material I'd learned about Andrew Carnegie and his astounding personal journey from a teenage immigrant working in a bobbin factory to one of the most prominent philanthropists in America, I was pelted unexpectedly with a storm of dry-roasted peanuts and pickled eggs by a group of men including the prolific racist Dave Barrowcliffe, until finally forced to retreat to the relative comfort of the rainy beer garden. After that, I slipped more into the role of Observer than Observed on my visits to the public house. I was still the subject of derision, but when it became clear to my deriders that their jeers and aerial assaults would not cause me to cease my visits, they soon petered out, and I became largely ignored.

I had been increasingly noticing something about humans, which was that displaying deep interest about other humans and their amazing lives and art and achievements was a trait widely and bafflingly looked down upon. 'Weirdo' was a word I heard frequently, which I took to mean 'possessing imagination and curiosity and a resistance to being force-fed culture by capitalism' but more often than not it was uttered with a dismissive, disapproving smirk or snarl. 'Fookin' right weirdos, that lot up top bit of Stringy Lane,' I heard Dave Barrowcliffe say to his peers on a couple of occasions, making no disguise of the fact that he was referring to Mr and Mrs Moss, Benji and their immediate neighbour, Colin, a man of unspecific occupation who owned some robots not dissimilar to those employed in factories on Vozkoz three or four thousand years ago. Colin, whom I'd observed from a distance and found to be 'weird' in many fine and admirable ways, was often on the receiving end of the group's most barbed ridicule.

One night in the final scruffy days of summer I overheard Barrowcliffe boasting to some of his friends, including a member of the local police force, that he'd broken into Colin's house. Far from being shocked by this, the group seemed energised and approving upon hearing details of the damage he'd caused, including the dismemberment of Colin's most antediluvian-looking she-robot. That night, from a safe distance, I followed Barrowcliffe home, via an unlit twitchel. Once in the twitchel, with my southern poet's floral silk neck scarf pulled up to cover my face, I moved forward all my reserves of speed, deftness and stealth and temporarily deactivated him.

Had I become overassimilated? Perhaps a more fitting question would be, 'How on Earth could I not become that, in the circumstances?' I liked Nottinghamshire. I liked its libraries, and its shopping-centre water sculptures, and its headstocks, and its towering piles of colliery waste pretending to be hills, and the haberdashery sections of its department stores, and its caves, and a not inconsiderable percentage of its inhabitants. 'I used to think you were a bit of a robot, but you seem different here,' Trelunian told me one afternoon in the alpaca field, in what for him was a rare moment of perception. 'I don't mean because of the fleece. It's more than that. It's like somebody shook you awake then lit a little fire in your chest.' Through my time working alongside our target, and listening to her domestic life via the Roundstone of Redara, I had begun to feel a closeness to her, and her family, and even their friends: a closeness I had not prepared for when I'd strapped myself into our starcraft and readied myself to leave Vozkoz's atmosphere. Because of the clandestine mystical properties of a piece of mineral matter transported from the other side of a starry abyss, I knew the songs she liked to sing to herself while she was making jam or sanding down an old table or feeding some towels into the hinged mouth of a machine that removed sweat and hair and lint from them. I knew that she had lost her dad when she was not long out of her teens. I knew – from my observations while working as the school caretaker – that she gave money to the homeless, and I knew that she didn't tell anyone about it. I knew that her mum was often ill and lived alone and how much she worried about it. I knew that Benji had come within twenty minutes of losing his life when he was four and how agonising that had been for all of them and how much they worried about something like it happening again. I knew the perilous state of their bank balance. I knew that Mr Moss sometimes claimed to Benji and Benji's friends that he'd fought in the Boer War (1899–1902). I knew that both Mosses often shouted, 'Oh, bloody sod off!' at an entertainment show on the radio called *The Archers* but still listened to it. I knew that Benji wanted a ZX Spectrum computer with soft rubber keys and I knew how sad they felt that they couldn't buy it for him. I knew that Mr Moss experienced nightmares about schools and milk and giant fish and knives and I knew Mrs Moss was skilled at soothing him in their aftermath. I knew that if Mrs Moss was in the bath for longer than twenty minutes, Mr Moss always knocked on the door, to check that she hadn't drowned. I knew a few more personal details that I probably shouldn't have known. But nothing I knew made me like any of them any less and nothing I knew made me feel any less that Mrs Moss's essence was precisely what my planet had sent me and my compatriots here to find, and nothing about that would stem the tide of guilt and unease that was rapidly coming in and washing up against me.

One morning, from a safe distance, by bus, I followed the Mosses' car into the city. It was a misty morning, but around half-way through the journey, the strong and decisive sun broke through the haze above the new Aspley branch of Video Magic. I arrived in the metropolis several minutes later than the Mosses but soon located them by lingering around two of their favourite haunts, J. E. Wright's art supplies, behind the Victoria Centre, and the Mushroom Bookshop in the area of the city formerly famous for the manufacture of lace. Keeping a safe distance, I followed them from the Victoria Centre across town to the less favoured Broadmarsh Centre, with its terrifying giant wooden playfrog and ornamental waterwheel and surprisingly attractive earthen-ware tiles and dimly lit colour scheme that made you feel slightly like you were inside an ashtray. Here, Mrs Moss and Mr Moss prevented Benji's attempts to swim in the shallow water beneath the waterwheel, handed him a Jacob's Club biscuit as a distraction and talked amongst themselves about the logistics of doing some-thing called 'nadging' later that day. Mrs Moss met Miss Buttons, said goodbye to Mr Moss, and the two teachers, with Benji and Emma in their wake, headed back to the market square, then climbed Mansfield Road to the health shop, where they purchased rice and lentils, then entered a small shop stuffed with leaves where Miss Buttons purchased a snake plant, also known as a 'mother-in-law's tongue'. Here I left them and refound Mr Moss at WHSmith, where he bought a pack of six blank cassettes for forty-nine pence, then from a distance accompanied him to the Central Library, from which he borrowed the long-playing records *Heartattack and Vine* by Tom Waits and *Dark Magus* by

Miles Davis. I then followed him past a car showroom, at whose window he stopped to stare at three extremely clean Ford Sierras, to the Victoria Centre's New Vic public house, which he walked directly through, exiting via its rear door without purchasing any alcohol, and heading in the direction of the market, at whose flower stall he bought a large mixture of roses, tulips and anemones in a bouquet which, nine minutes later, he presented to Mrs Moss in the Children's section of Sissons Bookshop. Here the Mosses said goodbye to Miss Buttons and Emma and proceeded to the house of their friends, the Fennels, stopping once again at WHSmith on the way to buy a set of pens. Near the Fennels' house, they stopped to say hello to an acquaintance in the company of a man who appeared to be limping in a way that suggested an injury around the top of his legs where they joined his torso. Here, I left the Mosses and made my way back to the bus station, where in error I boarded the number 53 in the direction of Daybrook, leaving at the next stop and then returning to the station to board the 357 in the direction of Mansfield.

On the bus ride, I absentmindedly rubbed the cigarette stubber on the back of the seat in front of me, striving to understand myself. What had I been hoping to find, during the morning's stalking exercise? Did I want to give myself the illusion that I was part of the family outing too? Or was I looking for some defect to use to shatter the picture I wanted to be close to, then use that defect to assuage some of my guilt about the operation I was about to carry out? Whatever the case, I was unsuccessful. My fond feelings for the Mosses and their ilk had only grown and, with them, my misgivings about the mission I was part of. Trelazian had assured me there would be no long-term risk to our target's health. The whole procedure would last a maximum of three hours. After seizing our target, spraying her with knockout gas and taking her back to the starcraft, we would extract the elements from her bloodstream that would create the serum that we needed: the one containing the essence of unshowy brilliance and doggedness that would supposedly aid our planet. She would neither know about nor remember any of it. Upon being redelivered home, all she would feel would be some temporary residual amnesia. But how could anyone be sure? I'd already used my voice-morphing powers, a red telephone box and three ten-pence coins to mimic the target's voice and place reassuring telephone calls to her and her sisters (I chose not to call her mum, owing to what I knew about the condition of her heart). It was a risky move, a flouting of the chain of command, executed without Trelazian's knowledge or consent, but I had not been able to prevent myself from speculating about the effects of our mission on the family: I had felt strongly that I must do something, give them something to cling to in the event of distress or problems. Now, with the day of the deed imminent, I worried even more. It came as a relief to me when our mission was postponed, due to the family's sudden trip to the other side of Europe and the perils of the temperature there (had Trelunian not misplaced the Roundstone of Redara, we would have known about the holiday in advance).

The next day, to kill time, the three of us went to America: Pennsylvania, not one of the hotter parts, and unseasonably cool on this particular day. Pittsburgh, if you want to be more specific. I worked out from the starcraft's navigation console that it would take only eleven minutes to fly there, and we had plenty of time to kill, so I thought, 'Why not?' Trelazian was convinced Mainframe Gas would somehow find out about it, so he just stayed in the starcraft the whole time and sulked nervously. Trelunian and I had quite the craziest day. Trelunian, who'd morphed into an attractive floppy-haired man not dissimilar to the singer Hall from the popular music group Hall & Oates, spent most of the time living it up at a busy suburban water park, trying on sunglasses and being chased down the nearby streets and alleyways by a diverse age range of American women. Meanwhile I visited the site of Andrew Carnegie's childhood home and the museum named after him, got to step inside a model of an original Pullman railway sleeper carriage from the 1860s and stand under the reconstructed bones of the Diplodocus dinosaur whose 1899 excavation Carnegie made possible with his immense, generously distributed wealth. I found myself thinking how much Benji Moss and Emma Buttons would have liked the last part and discovered I was already missing being in their tiny orbit.

I noticed that Americans were different to Nottingham people: louder, and keener to pass on information about their private lives. Most were friendly, apart from a couple of men in big peaked caps who, to my befuddlement, called me a cigarette. In the early part of the evening I went to the cinema, where I finally got to see Jennifer Beales turn in a stunning performance as a lowly steel-mill worker determined to dance her way to the top. I was back in the bar of the Nag's Head by 8 p.m., listening to the bitter xenophobic chatter of Barrowcliffe and his cronies (this was a few days before I temporarily deactivated him), and feeling like a true Vozkozian of the World.

The days dragged on as we awaited the return of the Mosses, but I found much to occupy myself: reading, tuning in to the radio news via our starcraft's console to hear reports about rioting in Chile in protest of Augusto Pinochet's military government and what the weather forecast was like for people boating around the United Kingdom's coast, then morphing back into my alpaca form when I craved a less cerebral life. I walked several miles to Newstead Abbey, a priory founded by King Henry II at around the time Vozkozians were making their first forays into space. Here, I entertained myself by carrying out brass rubbings of heraldic symbols, in imitation of those I'd seen in Miss Buttons' classroom, and visiting the needlessly large tomb of Boatswain, a dog belonging the Abbey's former resident, the famed poet Lord Byron. Courtesy of information boards, I learned more about Byron, such as that he lived with many diverse animals and was almost as good at swimming as Headmistress Wishbone.

On my way back through one of the isolated tree clumps some locals optimistically still called 'Sherwood Forest', I spotted Colin with his ear pressed to the ground, but chose not to introduce myself, taking the view that he probably would not welcome intrusion to his studies and that I did not want to socially complicate my life in this alien place more than I already had. I passed the newsagent, where a sexual organ had recently been drawn by a profuse local artist. I passed the house on the opposite side of Colin's to the Mosses', where I took a long green vegetable in a not dissimilar shape to the sexual organ from a cardboard box with the word 'FREE!' written on it, but upon biting into it concluded that it probably required seasoning. I stroked the Jack Russell terrier belonging to the Figshaws, who lived across the road, moderately confident that it did not have rabies.

My walks gave me ample time to reflect on our mission. Strangely, even after so many months away, I discovered that I did not especially miss Vozkoz, nor my prestige status there as a known genius of morphology, science, martial arts and information absorption. I contemplated what I'd learned about all the vastness of Earth, and what a tiny speck I was within it, whether I was an alpaca, or a tall-haired teenager called Sadie or a slightly younger, less tall-haired teenager called Lindsey or a persecuted poet warming up before scrabbling around for his first publishing deal.

As soon as we discovered that the Mosses had returned from Italy, Trelazian wished to waste no time in getting down to business. The plan stood as before. We knew from our research that Mrs Moss spent a lot of time attending to the compost heap. It also provided a secluded spot, with good access from the rear. Upon her arrival, I stepped from my hiding spot and administered the gas to her ears quickly. As I did, Trelunian, back to his alpaca form now and standing on his hind legs, applied a mud-caked hoof to her mouth to prevent her screaming in the four seconds she would have been able to. Due to the gas's properties, she would remember none of this later, but perhaps, in those four seconds, I didn't totally imagine the recognition and hurt in those eyes as they gazed upon me. I noticed the colander at her feet, and was struck by its resemblance in shape and texture to our starcraft, although it was a different shade of blue. And then we were off: Trelunian galloping over the gob pile back to the starcraft with Mrs Moss slung effortlessly over his back, and me jogging close behind.

After that, everything went very simply and smoothly. Trelazian, for all his Mainframe Gas-ordained authority and starbag-navigating abilities, didn't know a great deal about science. And, as for Trelunian, he could barely distinguish a test tube from a wine glass. They were happy to leave most of the job to me. Once we'd placed Mrs Moss on the operating table and extracted the necessary liquid from her veins, then mixed it with the preservatory solution we'd carried with us across the galaxy, I sealed it and, unaccompanied, carried it to the starcraft's hull. I placed it in the cooling chamber where it would stay until reaching Vozkoz, where it would be microdiluted and injected into our citizens. After that, I tuned into the news and reluctantly consumed a glass of Babycham, which had been offered to me as a reward by Trelunian. Trelazian fired up the starcraft and took it round the block, partly to prevent the engines cooling and partly, apparently, just because he felt like it. It didn't take much more than another hour for Mrs Moss to begin to come around and, once she was able to stand, I walked her back across the gob pile to the compost. I noticed that some of the white paint on her dungarees, being still damp, had rubbed off onto my own trousers.

Her eyes were fully open by the time I sailed her over the fence, from where I trusted that even in her disorientated state she would be able to navigate her way back to the house, and now she looked directly at me – directly at my poet self – for the first time.

'Where am I? Who are you?' she asked.

'You're in your garden, behind your house on Stringy Lane. And I am your new good friend,' I replied.

Benji

S quizard were coming, and everyone was struggling to stop
themselves spontaneously combusting from the pure excite-
ment of it.

I'd heard the news first thing on Monday morning from Danny
McNulty, who made it clear that he was only telling Emma Buttons, Taj Mukherjee and me because we were in the privileged
position of being his closest friends. By midday, it was all over the
school. Every corridor and room seemed hot with the word, as if
it was a thick electric current passing through those big old metal
pipes that ran along the walls: 'Squizard. Squizard. Squizard.
Squizard? Squizard.' We were all thinking the same thing: Could
it be true? Squizard? Actually here? On the north western edge of
Nottingham city centre, in Sandyhill Primary School?

'Mr Stone, are we allowed to bring cameras to school to
photograph Squizard when they come?' Emma Buttons asked
Mr Stone during lunch break.

'It's possible,' said Mr Stone. 'But first someone will have to
tell me what Squizard is.'

We were rocked by his ignorance. Most of us viewed Mr Stone as the school's grooviest teacher: he was the one who had the best games in his classroom, the one who encouraged us in our Dungeons & Dragons adventures, the one with the most hair on and around his face, the one who'd given us our first copies of *The Forest of Doom* and *The Warlock of Firetop Mountain* to read. How could he not know about Squizard? Yet, simultaneously, many of us, without revealing it to our peers, were asking ourselves a question not dissimilar to his. The facts I held in my grasp were these and only these: Ian, Danny McNulty's thirteen-year-old brother, was probably the most impressive human being I'd ever met, who, as well as being able to do karate and fit three snooker balls in his mouth and having acted on telly via the Central Junior TV Drama Workshop, had been – according to Danny – the first person in the whole of Nottingham to own a Dungeons & Dragons *Monster Manual*, and could properly play the guitar, including all of 'Purple Haze' by Jimi Hendrix. Squizard was the rock band he was in with two of his schoolfriends. Ian had decided on the name during a car journey with his grandparents, after he and Danny had seen a strangely green and sinewy squirrel run across the road on Wollaton Vale, not far from the Hemlock Stone pub, and this squirrel-lizard creature had looked back at them with a wise expression on its face. That aside, I was more or less in the dark, especially never having seen a concert by a rock band. What happened at a rock concert, and what precisely were you supposed to do while you watched it? What songs would Squizard play? If I asked nicely, would they sing 'She Blinded Me With Scientist' by the amazing genius scientist singer Thomas Dolby or the song whose name I couldn't remember that I'd seen Wonder Woman sing on *The Muppet Show*? How loud would they be and would it hurt my ears? In the end, however, all that was beside the point. Squizard were coming!

It would happen in the gym, Danny had told me, although exactly when was yet to be confirmed. That week, singing assembly was held there, and as we sang songs we had sung so many times before, all we could think about was the infinitely more exciting music that the auditorium would soon be filled with, even though most of us had never heard any of it.

As usual, singing assembly gave me what we called 'Lego legs' from sitting on the floor for too long and featured a mixture of material that was approximately 65 per cent terrible to 35 per cent decent, providing me with my earliest education in what it meant to cringe. I could cope with 'Lord of the Dance', which had a slight Dungeons & Dragons feel to it, but 'Lily the Pink' could be relied on to set my teeth on edge every time. Perhaps even worse was 'Ob-La-Di, Ob-La-Da', especially the bit where Molly hears Desmond say that he likes her face, which I could only ever bring myself to half-heartedly mime as every constituent part of my innards attempted to twist itself back to front. I was scandalised to be informed by my dad that this had been written by Paul McCartney, the same person responsible for such classics as 'We Can Work It Out' and 'Paperback Writer', which I had danced around the living room in joyous circles to on countless occasions since I had been able to walk. My dad added, however, that this more rubbish and soppy Paul McCartney was a fake Paul McCartney who'd arrived after the other one had been in a car crash and been abducted by aliens. He said one of the reasons that you could tell he wasn't a real human was because he'd gone on to form the band Wings, who, along with Margaret Thatcher, were one of the main things responsible for the downfall of British society since the 1970s. I told my dad that that was silly, because even though I'd once believed aliens were real, I knew they weren't now, because I was more grown up and starting to become what my nan called 'a man of the world'. It was, I said, one of lots of things I didn't believe that I used to believe when I was smaller, such as that wasps made marmalade in the same way that bees made honey and that the black market wasn't a real market in a town, just something called 'a concept' (I was still a bit shaky on this last one, which had been outlined to me by Emma Buttons).

In demonstrating my new maturity to my dad, I was sure to emphasise that it did not make me any less keen to get hold of one of the *Star Wars* action figures I'd seen when I'd been to Paul Hashimoto's birthday party, preferably Lando Calrissian or the bounty hunter Boba Fett who, with his green-helmeted face, put me in mind of the shield bugs I sometimes encountered in our garden.

I'd missed *Return of the Jedi* on its original release in late summer, something I'd been reminding my mum and dad of ever since at more or less daily intervals. Fortunately, that autumn the ABC Cinema showed a triple bill of the entire *Star Wars* trilogy. My mum and I were joined for it by Emma Buttons and her mum, and Taj Mukherjee, and Mandy and Kate Figshaw from across the road, but not by Danny McNulty, who'd already seen it three times. We were in the cinema for more than six hours but it didn't seem anything like that long at all. I could tell Taj Mukherjee was excited because during the trailers he started making these really fast percussive sounds with his mouth, which was one of his great skills and one which went a long way to relieving some of the tedium of school singing assemblies. He could do cymbals and maracas as well as drums and was in the process of generously passing on some of his expertise to me. Everyone was always impressed, but when he got carried away and beatboxed a bit too loud during *Return of the Jedi*'s climactic battle scene on the planet Endor and the people in the seats ahead of us turned around to look, my mum and Miss Buttons instructed him to shush.

My mum told me after the final film had finished that she liked it but thought the Ewoks were unrealistic, which I accepted as a fair criticism, although not one I agreed with. It was unusual for my mum, instead of my dad, to take me to the cinema, but she'd seemed keen to see the films. It represented part of a broadening I'd noticed in her science-fiction interests since our return from Italy. She often sat on the sofa at home with me and watched reruns of *Blake's 7* and *Buck Rogers in the 25th Century*, and seemed extraordinarily involved when we saw an episode of the magazine show *Tomorrow's World* about how one day in the future people would consume food entirely via small pills, a little like the sweet junior aspirin I looked forward to eating when I was poorly.

The ABC Cinema was in the city centre, across the road from the library my dad borrowed books from and sometimes took them back to, and my visit to it to watch the *Star Wars* trilogy had been my first. All my previous cinema experiences had taken place at the Savoy, where tickets were much cheaper and which was just outside the city centre, near the house where my granddad had died and the school where my dad used to teach and get physically threatened by the parents of pupils and the house where my mum and dad had lived before I existed.

One time when my dad and I were walking along the corridor of the Savoy, on the way to watch *BMX Bandits*, a tall youth of around eighteen had come running around the corner at high speed, straight into me, and knocked me several feet into the air, so I landed quite heavily on the ground. It hadn't hurt as much as a lot of times I'd been injured, such as when I put my arm through the window of the asbestos garage, but my dad had instantly disappeared in pursuit of the youth. A few seconds later he had returned with a certain look in his eyes that I had never seen before, gripping the youth by the collar of his shirt, and made him apologise to me, before adding, 'Now in future don't be such a bloody great PILLOCK.' The youth had appeared deeply frightened of my dad, even though my dad was at least four inches shorter than him, and it had been the first time that it had occurred to me that, if it came to the crunch, my dad would probably be quite willing to kill someone if my or my mum's personal safety necessitated it.

I remember there was a road my dad avoided when we were heading home from that part of the city: part of a route that I knew, because of my burgeoning interest in all things navigational and automotive, would have been the most logical one back to Tapley Woodhouse. I asked him why he didn't drive down it and he just said it was grotty and he didn't like it.

Some days, that autumn, we'd take a much longer detour over to Gowenlock Hall, the educational resource centre where he'd started working part-time. It had a scale model of Concorde, all sorts of dead animals with stuffing inside them and real army helmets that I liked to try on, imagining I was Boba Fett or an Imperial Stormtrooper. As we drove home, my dad pointed out all the things flashing by that could potentially kill you. 'Don't ever dive off the high board in there,' he said, as we passed Beech-dale Swimming Baths. 'You'll get concussion . . . See those railings over there by that wall? Bloody lethal.' He pointed out a hedge he'd been thrown into as a kid on the day President Kennedy was assassinated. 'Everyone remembers what they were doing when they heard about it,' he told me. 'So I'll always remember: I was being thrown into a big hedge by Doggy Fletcher.'

Sometimes, when it was just the two of us in the car, he would forget that he was the person at the wheel and that I was me, not my mum, advising me, 'Check your mirror,' or, 'Watch out for this plonker in the left lane; he doesn't know what the bloody hell he's doing, probably pissed from the pub.' My mum was a driver now, too, having received a course of lessons solely from my dad. She'd passed her test on the first attempt. Her success had been inevitable after being schooled so thoroughly by him on every possible negative eventuality and how to avoid it.

One day we returned from one of the early journeys she took on a full licence, to my nan's, and heard my dad in the back room, shouting, 'Help! Quick! I'm being eaten!' and found him on his back on the newly sanded floor, using his hands to shield himself from a large inanimate wolf attached to a wooden stand. But my dad wasn't really scared of wolves eating him during the course of day-to-day life in Nottingham. He was more concerned about the Barrowcliffes' German shepherd, Rex, being let loose on Stringy Lane while almost certainly contaminated with rabies.

'It hasn't got rabies,' my mum said. 'You'd know. It would be far more slobbery. Also they've almost eradicated it in this country now.'

'I wouldn't be so sure,' said my dad. 'Lord Byron's dog had it and died.'

'That was in 1808.'

'Look, I'm just saying: you can never be too careful.'

My childhood world was one where people were deemed to be largely trustworthy but animals, architecture, machines and even furniture were all potentially out to do you harm. On TV, I repeatedly watched children die from 66,000-volt shocks after trying to retrieve their frisbees and kites from electricity sub-stations and pylons, and a sensible yet slightly unhinged animated cat who told me not to play with matches or fall into water. I sat in chairs with increasing caution, switched lights on and off with only the driest hands. In the shopping centres in the city, I stepped with great care onto the escalators, remembering a story I'd heard about a man being sucked into one's inner workings and swiftly dismembered. 'Don't go near the entrance to the mine and fall in!' my dad said, as I set off in the direction of the pit road on my bike. When I started spending more time playing across the road at the Figshaws with Mandy and Kate and their Christian friends Brett and Philip Diltree, he appeared to relax slightly. Yes, they had a barn with a rickety ladder leading up to a perilously high ledge, which we sometimes jumped from into deep hay that could potentially be concealing an upturned pitchfork. Yes, their Jack Russell terrier did look suspiciously wet around the chin. But it was better than me being up at the colliery, or near the asbestos garage, or over in Petalford at the semi-derelict playground with the iffy swings and the roundabout that looked like it had been written off by drunk joyriders. Better even than being at Colin's, whose robots had some dangerously sharp and rusty bits on them.

The Figshaws and the Diltrees were different from the kids I knew at school, but also different from the other children I'd met in and around Tapley Woodhouse: they were polite and gentle and inquisitive and made orange squash and sold plastic cups of it from a stall at the end of their drive. Their mums fed me as many tinned frankfurters as I could eat. They handwrote a village magazine and stapled it together. They talked about flowers and knew the names of different kinds of sheep. They read Enid Blyton books and, in imitation of some of them, had formed their own Famous Five Gang, the only issue being that they were missing a member. The Jack Russell being unwilling to sign up for the Timmy position, I came along and filled the gap. They made me see myself, even at eight, as citified and sophisticated but also marginally feral. Soon we were all going to be in a play together in the village, directed by Colin. It was going to be the first proper acting I'd ever done and I was excited about it because it meant I would get to spend more time with Mandy.

I showed her some drawings I'd been working on since the summer, about a caveman I'd imagined living in the Mont Blanc Tunnel in the Alps, which separates France from Italy. She helped me turn them into a comic strip, changing his name from Monty to Alf of the Alps, which we both preferred, and helped me add words to his adventures. The day Alf found the broken-down car of a distressed family from Nottinghamshire in the tunnel and used his phenomenal strength to push it through to the daylight on the other side. The day he washed his all-over body hair in a mountain waterfall. The day he fell in love with a cavewoman, Amanda of the Alps. Mandy sowed the seed of something amorous, to the extent anything can be amorous when you are eight years old. She dotted her 'i's with big circles. She said she wanted to be a writer when she grew up. I said I'd prefer to be a racer in the Tour de France or a cartoonist or librarian. We talked about the house we'd have together, by the sea, where Kate would live too, in our garage. 'I like the sea in Italy best. Can the house be there?' I asked. 'Ok,' she said. I asked her if she had ever heard of Squizard and she said she hadn't. 'Don't worry, you will soon,' I reassured her.

'Is Mandy your girlfriend?' teased Donna.

'No!' I replied.

'It's funny, I always thought Emma Buttons would be the one you got married to. Or Wonder Woman.'

One day when he was staying over for the weekend, I took Danny McNulty to the Figshaws to meet Mandy and Kate and Brett and Philip, but it didn't quite work: he was much quieter than usual, and refused to jump off the high ledge with us into the hay. He overheard Brett, who, being ten, was the oldest amongst us, talking about the choir practice he attended a couple of villages away, and told him that God didn't exist and if more people realised that, there'd be a lot fewer problems for everyone. The following day Donna came over with her friend Sharon and they and Danny and I rode our bikes up to see the alpacas who lived up the road and which I now knew were not aliens. A small bit of rain came out of the sky, like it was raining just on us, and not on the rest of the world, and the temperature dropped just slightly, like it did when somebody turned on a cold tap in a room. As Sharon and Donna fed the alpacas, Danny and I sat on the wall with our plimsolled feet swinging back and forth.

'Elaine says Enid Blyton is a racist,' said Danny, who had recently started calling his mum 'Elaine' instead of 'my mum'.

'I already know,' I said. 'My mum and dad told me. I haven't read a book by her. I just said I had so I could be in Mandy and Kate and Brett and Philip's gang.'

'Elaine said Roald Dahl has racist tendencies too.'

'I don't believe her. His books are the best books in the whole world and nobody who is a racist would write the best books in the whole world.'

I changed the subject, keen to get Danny back on my side. 'I told my nan and my mum that I think Maggie Thatcher is the biggest stupid idiot in the whole world, but my nan and my mum said that part of the problem is actually that she isn't a stupid idiot, and is really clever and devious. But I don't think my nan and my mum are right, because why would you stop people having jobs and make missiles to kill people and have a stupid annoying voice unless you were a stupid idiot?'

But Danny was staring up the lane to our left and seemed distracted. In the distance I could make out a familiar figure coming towards us, holding a lead attached to a large Holstein cow.

'What is THAT?' said Danny.

'That's Mr Staythorpe and Daisy,' I explained.

'The countryside is WEIRD,' said Danny.

I sometimes heard my mum and dad talk about moving closer to the city, which my mum seemed particularly keen on and said might be beneficial to me, in a few years, but I wasn't sure why. My dad said he would prefer to move to a farmhouse in Italy, but my mum said that probably wouldn't be practical, what with her mum and her sisters and work all being here, plus the language barrier to consider, and our new pet cat, Edwina. I discovered that I did not have strong feelings on the situation. I liked Tapley Woodhouse – especially now I'd joined Mandy and Kate's gang – and I liked school and Nottingham and had no problem living with one foot in each place. I could not imagine living in one of the houses my schoolfriends lived in and there still being robots next door or a barn nearby with hay I could jump into. I would also be further from my nan, meaning Donna and our baby cousin Andy got to spend more time with her than I did. But if I transferred to a school nearer home, I would miss my schoolfriends so so much. I also couldn't imagine one of those schools letting me play Dungeons & Dragons or holding a concert featuring a band as exciting and brilliant as Squizard.

I had been enjoying school more than ever recently, especially after the flutter of fame by association that I'd felt following the news about Squizard had been doubled up on with the arrival of our new teacher, Mrs Lofthouse. Mrs Lofthouse was a supply teacher, like my dad, who worked at schools all over Nottingham and was only going to be here until our new proper teacher arrived, but, as she told us during her first day at Sandy-hill, her husband, Gordon, was a brave and famous mountaineer who had even climbed Mount Everest, the best and most famous mountain of all. After we asked her more about Gordon and the mountains he climbed, she brought in some slides of his adventures. These confused me, because some of them looked like they had been taken in a country where the weather was extremely hot, maybe even hotter than Italy, and I'd thought mountains were only in snowy countries. Mrs Lofthouse said Gordon had once crawled all the way down a mountain from the top after breaking both ankles. I asked her how much bigger the mountains Gordon had climbed were than the hills in the Peak District that I sometimes climbed with my mum and dad at the weekends, and she made my head hurt in that 'where is the end of outer space and what will happen when I die' way, but not quite as much, by saying they were hundreds of times bigger, although in fact Gordon's passion for climbing had first been ignited by climbing those same hills in the Peak District when he was around my age, so maybe I could be a mountain climber one day. I told her I would like that and asked her what 'ignited' meant.

'It's when you cause a spark, and something catches fire,' said Mrs Lofthouse. 'Like when you light a match.'

I thought again of Charlie, the rule-abiding but unhinged cat in the public-information films, and imagined him saying 'Charlie says don't ignite passions' in his demented cat voice.

'Did Mr Lofthouse decide to climb mountains because his name is Lofthouse and he thought he could build a lofty house on one of the mountains?' asked Emma Buttons.

'Haha, it's not impossible that you might be on to something there,' said Mrs Lofthouse. 'Do you know what you call it when somebody's name sounds a bit like their profession or something else about who they are?'

'I do,' said Emma Buttons. 'It's called nominative determinism.'

I thought the class about mountaineering was one of the best classes the school had probably ever had and Taj Mukherjee and

Paul Hashimito and Emma Buttons all agreed. Danny McNulty was off sick that week and I was sad to know he'd missed the lesson. He didn't reappear in school until midway through the following week and seemed sad and quiet. At lunchtime, when we were outside, Mr Stone, who was on playground duty, asked him if there was anything wrong.

'Yes there is,' said Danny. 'It's something very bad. One of the worst things ever.' He paused, as if summoning the strength to convey the true gravity of what was coming. 'It's Squizard. They have broken up.'

'Oh, I'm truly sorry to hear that,' said Mr Stone. 'What was the problem?'

'Cree-cree . . .' We waited with bated breath, as he finally choked the words out. 'Cree-ative differences.'

And then the story all flooded out and, with it, a torrent of tears no smaller. It had all come to a head around a week ago, we heard. Squizard's bassist Matt and drummer Warren had come to Danny's brother Ian to explain they were tired of the name Squizard and thought it would be best for all concerned if the band name was changed to Your Mum. Ian had explained he didn't think this was wise, owing to the reputation and following Squizard had built up around his school and Nottingham as a whole, despite them not having played a gig yet. He said that it was his right to overrule the suggestion of changing the band's name to Your Mum, being lead singer and guitarist. Matt and Warren argued that it was actually their right to overrule his overruling, since there were two of them and only one of him. A compromise was briefly put forward by Warren to rename the band Squizard Mother instead, but this too was overruled, the meeting ending in raised voices and a kicked guitar. According to Danny, Ian had not spoken to Matt and Warren since.

'Maybe they just need a bit of time and they'll work it out,' suggested Mr Stone.

'I don't think so,' said Danny. 'It's well and truly over.'

Taj Mukherjee, who had told me he'd been secretly hoping to play mouth maracas for the band at their debut performance, and I put a comforting arm each around Danny's shoulders. As we did, a few fat raindrops began to fall on the playground, as if God, too, could not hide his sadness about Squizard, even though his existence, like theirs, had been blotted out, after being quite dubious in the first place.

'Typical,' said Taj.

'Oh how fluctuating are all earthly things,' said Emma Buttons.

Headmistress

The windy days always made the children a bit crazy, I will always remember that. The back of the playground was very exposed – we were quite high above the city – and you sometimes got a strong north easterly coming through there. Combine that with a full moon and you knew you had to be ready. You'd often end up with a line of kids standing against the wall by late morning; kids who'd been caught running through the corridors wailing like banshees, or pulling down somebody's trousers, or swearing at one of the dinner ladies, pupils who on any other day would be impeccably behaved. As for the children who were already a bit high-spirited on a normal day, well . . . Do you know that the word 'lunatic' comes from 'lunar'? But nobody was ever yelled at or caned or smacked. My girls always handled it calmly and order was restored – our own peculiar kind of order, anyway.

Oh, look at me with my sweeping generalisations: 'my girls'. We did have male teachers at the school, too. There was Mr Stone, who probably had enough facial hair to count as three

male teachers. And, earlier on, Mr Crowhurst. Then later, Mr Dodds, although there was something quite ethereal and feminine about him. I remember a letter I once received from a former pupil, one of our first wave of children, a boy called James, who probably left for secondary school in 1981 or 1982 and went on, eventually, I believe, to become a social worker, and there was something he said in the letter that really stuck with me. He said his time at Sandyhill was a kind of template for his view of women as the supergender, that it made him assume all women were wonderful. He said that in adult life that had led to some problems and disappointments, as I imagine it might, but that he wouldn't change it for anything. I'd been told similar things before, but how touching for a male pupil to say that! Of course, how could he have thought anything different? I attempted to maintain as professional a relationship as possible with my staff, but they were such a uniquely interesting and warm and genial bunch, it was hard not to want to be friends with every one of them.

I did go to Cath Moss's house once. I can't remember the

exact reason – I think it might have been something to do with an exhibition her husband, Pete, was helping us with – but I remember the visit. I hadn't explored that part of the county much, being generally more socially linked to and familiar with the east side. What little I knew about it was from a quite politicised friend of Malcolm's and mine called Oliver who used to sometimes go over there at weekends and agitate organised gatherings of fascists. I remember that it had been this perfect golden day in the city; one of those that sometimes comes along out of nowhere in early November to remind you that everything is not dying forever and give you a shot of hope in the narrowing days. But then when I got within a mile or two of Tapley Woodhouse, the gold got hidden from me. It was as if I'd driven into a teabag. I remember a lot of metal on the horizon and a curious profusion of horse-head gateposts. Here in Cornwall it often feels like what you see above ground is shaped by what's below, the long subterranean industry of the place, but it was possibly even more like that there. Some of the houses were visibly diagonal, like quarter-sunk ships. Catherine was waiting for me at the door with tile dust on her trousers, holding a wooden basket of thick socks she'd knitted. She said she offered them to everyone who visited. The weather was unseasonably mild but she said I'd be surprised how cold my feet got in the living room. It was, she said, because of the void beneath it.

Pete was in the back garden. He was layering orange paint on a giant wooden panel, which he said was a sign he'd been commissioned to illustrate for a pub just outside of Sheffield. The top of the wooden panel was still blank but on the bottom was half a fox, some unruly grass and the beginnings of a pair of human legs. We chatted for a while but he seemed a little lost in concentration and said he wanted to make the last of the daylight but would be inside in a moment. 'Sorry about the mess in there,' he said. 'Catherine didn't tell you we lived in a factory, did she.' I knew from the couple of other times I'd met him that he could be quite withdrawn and shy. I wondered if that side of him was connected to something that I'd heard from Miss Buttons, who knew the Mosses well: that a few years ago he'd witnessed a murder in Nottingham city centre. I might not have got that totally right. But there was something. I never asked Cath about it. I didn't want to pry. I remember thinking how much sense they made, though, as a couple. A creative power-house, coming out of left field.

We returned to the living room. A few tools were on the floor and a book about the moon landings in one of those see-through protective wrappers that libraries always put on books. Two fireplaces were standing loose: one of those 1970s electric ones with the fake plastic coal, and a tiled Victorian one with cast-iron reeded panels, which Cath said she'd bought recently from a scrapyard for a budget price that made my jaw drop when she specified it. After a few minutes Benji came downstairs wearing a black apron and cotton cap. He had black charcoal rubbed across his cheek and was holding an old burnt frying pan. 'What do you think?' he said.

'He's rehearsing,' explained Catherine.

'I'm the ghost of a juvenile colliery worker!' said Benji.

'He's a minor miner,' added Pete, entering the room.

They told me about the play that Benji was poised to be in, which was being directed by their next-door neighbour, Colin. Catherine said it was going to be shown in the Miners' Welfare a few miles away, in the town where her mum and sisters lived, and that it was quite strange and experimental: set in the 1800s, but with some science fiction and supernatural elements. She was a little sceptical about how well it would go down with the locals. 'It has robots in it,' Benji added. 'Real ones.'

I asked if it might be something Colin and his cast might be interested in bringing to Sandyhill. 'I'm warning you: it's quite surreal and bonkers,' Catherine said.

'You've known me six years,' I replied. 'Have I ever seemed like a person to be put off by that?'

We said we'd chat about it more soon, after she'd talked to Colin. Benji said he was going to ride his bike and Catherine told him to go no further than the pit road and back, because it was getting dark. By this point the temperature had dropped and I was glad of the extra pair of socks. The whole house, with its hospitality and its fireplaces and its knitwear and its recent jam smells and its burgundy door, seemed like a busy shrine to warmth, but as soon as you stepped onto the street, that was obliterated. The weather? I imagine it didn't have much bearing on the situation. The building, the inside of it anyway, was palliative to the terrain. I was familiar with eerie places, odd, lonely places. How could I not be? I'd grown up in north Lincolnshire. But there was something else going on here: a brutalist ghostliness, a quiet sorrow in the gravel and grit, a metallic funereal otherness presiding over it all. It, and what I knew about the leeway Pete and Catherine gave Benji to explore on his own, made me understand more about why he was precisely the kind of child he was, always seemingly half in one world and half in another spectral one of his own creation. Kids have such an instinctive sense for the hidden, the stuff under the icing on top of everything. It's one of the reasons we should let them wander a little, permit them to discover danger and magic firsthand. It's what so many of the old fairy tales are about. It will help form them and they will most likely thrive on it. But for an adult, that kind of ambience can land differently on the nervous system. A lot of us spend our life arranging ways to run from it.

At the junction at the top of the hill, my car's engine cut out and I felt a chill pass through me, then a flood of relief when it restarted. I indicated right, watched by the long, sad stone faces in the shadows, towards the city, away from the saturating desolations of the lane and the one house there that didn't seem to know it was Sunday.

Daffodils

'We go down further than you think; way down, every summer. It's a right bloomin' journey, I can tell you. No bugger really notices us vanishing because we've blended into t'crowd by then, been drowned out by all t'show offs, primroses and brambles and what ave yer. Everyone's out enjoying t'weather and there's us, down there. All we feel is the rain, seeping down into us. 'Narcissus', they call us. That's a bloody laugh. No mirrors where we go.'

'One time they slung an old tyre on top of me. As if I wasn't even there. I wanted to shout, "Watch it, you ungrateful sod! Who do you think put in that conservatory that you enjoy every day?".'

'You will never stop goin' on about that, will yer. It could 'ave been worse. At least they're not one of that lot with the plastic grass. They could easily have been. There's a lot of them buggers around these days, I can tell yer. Doesn't bear thinking about. Anyway, point is, it's bloomin' dark down there. And we're there for a lot of it, every year. And even though you're not as far down as the mine, you can feel it all. Everything that's happened. All the layers, all the crust, soaking you up. And a lot of it int pretty. And you need to feel it all, every bit of it, because that's what it's all about. And when you have, that's when you start to grow again, and it's all in you, and you've got your colour back. And then when you come up again, you might look like any other daffodil, but you're not.'

'No. You're a Tapley Woodhouse daffodil.'

Alpaca

The three of us stuck around. To my mind, there was no need to rush matters: Vozkoz wasn't going anywhere, apart from around its bright emerald sun for all of eternity. Trelazian brooded and fidgeted in the starcraft, for the time being desiring no company aside from his contraptions. Trelunian appeared content to eat his grass and spit at his contemporaries between regular journeys to the communal dung pile. I spent little time in my original form, morphing back and forth between the other two and tending to favour the less hirsute, bipedal one. I continued to visit the Nag's Head and all the region's libraries easily accessible by foot or bus.

One day, I was on my way for what had become my customary lunchtime pint and ploughman's and could not help noticing that the Mosses' front door was wide open, even though all other signs suggested they were not at home. On my way back to the starcraft, a couple of hours later, the door had still not been closed. I took the status of the door to be an error, probably made by the Mosses in their haste to get to their respective jobs on time. Having heard about several burglaries in the area, I felt it my duty as a good citizen, part-time neighbour and possibly friend, to shut the door, which I noticed was the automatically locking kind known as a 'Yale'. But before I did, I also decided it was my additional duty to quickly assess the house for signs of invasion.

It was strange to realise, after all our time listening to the goings-on in it via the Roundstone of Redara, that this was actually the first time I'd set foot in the home of the Mosses, but it was every bit as comforting as I'd imagined: arranged but not too arranged, tidy but not too tidy. A bustling and inquisitive life was being lived here. The front room had a clean smell, not dissimilar to that of our starcraft a few months ago when Trelazian had decorated its atrium in preparation for our mission. On the kitchen counter, alongside a packet of a powdered food called Instant Whip and an unopened envelope with the words 'East Midlands Electricity Board' and 'FINAL NOTICE' on it, I found a book all about the first time that humans had landed on their moon. On the top of the book was a library ticket featuring the name 'Catherine Moss'. It was at this point that I noticed a small black cat watching me from the vantage point of one of the cabinets to my left, as if in severe judgement. Feeling penetrated to my core by this judgement, I searched in several cupboards until locating a tin displaying an illustration of two other cats and the phrases 'Kattomeat VIP' and 'WITH BEEF'. I then located an opening device for the tin and transferred its contents to a small plate, where it sat, rigid and ignored, like a daunting jellied replica of the tin itself, while the cat sauntered out of the room in the direction of the house's upper floor. Making small beseeching noises that stripped me of my dignity, I followed it up the stairs, where it settled down on a towel that had been left on the floor in the smaller of the two bedrooms. Through the half-open window, I could see Colin watering his roses and hear him singing to himself in a voice that managed to be simultaneously wobbly, passionate and tuneless.

I returned to the living room, sank into a dark pink shell-backed two-seater sofa, and began to flick through the pages of the book about the 1969 moon landing. I learned that one of the astronauts, Neil Armstrong, liked to cook pizza and smoked one cigar a month ('but I sometimes forget to'). I learned about the Reverend Ralph Abernathy, a close friend of the civil rights leader Martin Luther King, who had led a group of protestors at ground control, questioning the fact that America had spent many billions of dollars on the trip, in preference to concentrating on the many unsolved problems remaining on Earth, such as poverty and racial segregation and the rise of bacterial weapons of genocide that were rapidly destroying the planet's organic matter. I could not help pondering our own mission, whose exact cost I will not detail here, for fear of frightening anyone, aside from saying that by comparison it made the budget for America's famed lunar excursion of 1969 seem like that of the modest domestic camping holiday of a small family. I thought about the problems on Vozkoz which, I felt in my heart of hearts, would still remain after our return, or at least be replaced by other ones that were no less thorny.

Upon returning to the kitchen with the glass I'd used to drink an unpleasantly sweet liquid called Ribena – which I would soon learn tastes slightly better when diluted with water – I noticed half a vole near the doormat, presumably a casualty of the cat, an animal kept by earlier humans to keep such rodents out of domestic buildings but kept by the Mosses presumably because it was attractive, intermittently affectionate and made a satisfying activation noise when you found it asleep and gently pressed its torso. Looking at the rodent, and thinking about the moon landings, and our own missions, upon returning to the sofa I found myself pondering what is meant by 'nature' – both here, and on Vozkoz. Where are its borders? How can we say for certain when it is definitely being interfered with and overruled, and when it is not?

Maybe it was because thinking about the complexity of such an issue was tiring, or it was the strength of my lunchtime pint of lager combined with the meagre nature of that day's serving of ploughman's from Kazza in the Nag's Head, but the next thing I knew I was waking up to a room devoid of light, it being the time of year that, in my time as a school caretaker, I'd heard the children refer to as 'Dark Before Blue Peter'. I could not instantly tell how long I'd slept for, but I knew it was possible that, unless they'd planned any post-work tasks or social activities, the Mosses could be back at any time. Yet I found myself unwilling to leave.

I switched on the TV set, where I saw crowds, including Commander Thatcher's new opponent Commander Kinnock, in London protesting the placing of cruise missiles in Britain by America. I turned the dial to the right and was pleased to find the popular music band The Beatles running around and having fun and playing their guitars. I laughed when I saw The Beatles go through four different front doors which led to the same front room and soon realised that, although they were being The Beatles, they were probably playing at being another version of The Beatles, different to the one you might have seen if you'd met them when nobody was pointing a camera at them: a bit like how the version of Trelazian who reported back to Communal Mainframe Intellect Gas was different to the Trelazian who spoke to me and Trelunian. The weirdest thing of all was that after a few minutes, at one of the points George Harrison, my favourite Beatle, was on screen, a familiar man appeared in a waistcoat and bucket hat using some chattering teeth to cut an indoor lawn next to George's bed. It took me a moment to place him but I soon realised that the reason he looked familiar was that, although younger and having darker and thicker hair, he looked a lot like Colin, who I'd just seen attending to his roses in his own garden. Not much later, he appeared again, playing the flute part in a song performed by The Beatles called 'You've Got to Hide Your Love Away'. The resemblance was so uncanny that it made me wonder for a while if I'd properly understood what television sets did and if, despite it being black and white and having very poor picture quality, this one was far more advanced than I'd realised. Intrigued, and somewhat gripped, I followed the film, which I found out was called *Help!*, through from its promising beginning to its rather messy and unsatisfying conclusion.

After I'd left the Mosses' house, being careful to fully close the front door, the image of the man in the gardening clothes continued to play on my mind, so I took a long bus ride to what I'd discovered was one of the most extensive and relaxing Nottinghamshire libraries, in West Bridgford, on the opposite side of the wide river where Commander Snot had once amassed his tribes. Here I found a large book called *Halliwell's Film Guide*, publication date 1977, which informed me that the name of the actor who hung around with George Harrison and cut his indoor lawn was Bruce Lacey. Deeper research, with the help of the library's microfiche archive machine, told me that early in his adult life Lacey had been one of the 1950s comedy musicians The Alberts, had once brought a functioning robot to a major poetry event, and had been subject of the song 'Mr Lacey', by the folk rock band Fairport Convention. Even deeper research uncovered a photograph of the top half of Lacey, unclothed, and even more recognisably Colinlike, at the Rougham Fair not much more than a year ago, in an edition of the Bury St Edmunds *Mercury* newspaper.

In my in-depth research regarding human behaviour, I had learned a lot about famous people, or at least I thought I had.

Sometimes they kept their money to themselves or, if they gave some of it to people less fortunate than themselves, it appeared that they often made sure the general public knew about it. They often gravitated to major cities or rural areas of outstanding natural beauty. They found the pressure of lots of strangers looking at them and analysing them too intense and stressful, but also seemed slightly lost without it in a way that suggested, if it stopped, they believed they might vanish in a puff of smoke.

I had met Colin/Mr Lacey – if they were indeed the same person – only in my less observant, although actually surprisingly observant, alpaca form, but I had observed him comprehensively enough from a distance in my Jonathan the Poet form to know that none of these usual 'Fame Rules' applied to him. Granted, he was not famous in a significant worldwide way, or even the way that the climbing hero John Noakes and his dog Shep were famous, but he had experienced a life close to many significant cultural events, brushing shoulders with household names in music and theatre and art, yet he had chosen to live in a way antithetical to his position. 'Why was he in Tapley Woodhouse?' I couldn't help wonder. If our mission had not been essentially complete, I might have suggested him as an excellent further target study for the Vozkozian government. I rushed home from the library that day, keen to tell Trelazian and Trelunian my findings, However, upon entering the starcraft, I became cognisant of an immediate atmosphere of tension. Trelazian was at the console, frowning at a complex matrix on the screen in front of him. Trelunian, who was still in his alpaca form, was sitting on the ground, staring dolefully at a half-eaten Braeburn.

'Is something wrong?' I asked.

'It's over,' said Trelunian. 'No more fresh air and freedom. We're being sold.'

'In what sense?'

'He means the alpacas,' said Trelazian.

'It's some bloke from just outside Rotherham,' said Trelunian. 'He wants to use us for trekking and weddings. I wouldn't even bother morphing back if I were you. He's coming down next Tuesday with a trailer. It's a fucking travesty. He wants us to wear these wreaths and veils and bow ties. There's talk of us being ring bearers for total strangers. I want no part of it. It's an assault on our collective dignity. Also I was just starting to properly get somewhere with Sophie. Yesterday she let me groom her tail for the first time.'

Trelazian began to say something then, but I was too busy reeling from the strange experience of hearing Trelunian use a phrase like 'an assault on our collective dignity' and had to ask our commander to repeat his sentence.

'So . . .' he began again. 'I was thinking that in view of this latest turn of events, and the fact that we've done what we came here to do, it might be time to turn the page, much as I know that might be difficult for you with some of the . . . bonds you have forged here.'

'Turn the page in what sense?' I asked. When did we all start talking so much like humans, I wondered.

'What I'm saying,' said Trelazian. 'Is it's time to go back to Vozkoz.'

Parents

'She's out in the garden right now so I will quickly tell you this: she wrote a nature journal while we lived there. *Cuckoo Spit* was what she called it. Everyone's doing that sort of thing these days; the bookshops have got entire sections devoted to it: all those memoirs with the pretty linoprints, the ones that start in January and end in December, and the others about how somebody was sad then they befriended a trout in their local river but realised it was just a trout, who had no expectations about anything, then they saw all the beauty in life and everything was ok forever. She was ahead of her time. Listen to this: "3 June 1980: A wood pigeon appears in the air above a tree in the garden like a piece of crumpled paper shot from a cannon." "11 December 1979: Walk from Ambergate to Cromford. Pete lost in thought, somewhere far away, painting it all in his head. I watch him forge ahead, into the vast lichenous disarray." Yep, that was me all right: far away. So wrapped up in my own problems I didn't even realise I was married to Henrietta David Thoreau. I'll get it published one day, if she'll let me, which she probably won't.

We were – are – both romantics, dreaming about the sancti-fied green places we were not fortunate enough to have a 24-7 VIP pass to. The difference was, back then I complained about not having those places on my doorstep while she did her best to find them between the cracks of what we had. In early adulthood I was already romanticising the spacious 1950s, especially the tatty countryside close to the council estate where I grew up. It was a place of infinite mystery for me. There were old cottages in the woods with gaping holes in their roofs and ponies tied to stakes outside. The people who lived there placed a great deal of importance on the kind of knives they owned. I joined a gang, built fires, had fights with kids from other gangs, not for any reason other than that the kids came from somewhere else, half a mile away. I started getting the bus into Notts to buy jazz records, thought I was a bit better than everyone else because of it. I'd have asked you outside if you'd slagged off a Mingus album.

That was me when she met me: a snot-nosed lad, not fully housebroken, ready to fight the world, a collection of angles in a mohair suit. We were both seventeen. I weighed not a lot over eight stone. Her family fed me like I'd never been fed before. I ate everything they'd give me. Her mum and dad and sisters opened their arms, treated me as one of them from day one, even though I spoke with my mouth full at the dinner table and took their Rod Stewart LPs off the record player and replaced them with ones by Sun Ra.

What you can see in the first photo of the two of us after Benji was born is that, in the six years since we met, one of us has grown up. Look at me, in my vest and cords, the nervous smile. What it says is "I'm not ready for this". I was still strutting about the place, gauging every bloke I met for his fighting prowess, telling anyone who would listen, plus a lot of people who wouldn't, that I'd once had a slash next to Dizzy Gillespie in the bogs at Ronnie Scott's. Teaching secondary in one of the roughest parts of the city centre brought me down a peg, but only one, at first. Then one night me and Richard Fennel went to the flicks. *Marathon Man*, it was. Dustin Hoffman and Laurence Olivier, the Nazi dentist, torturing him – a bit, now I come to think of it, like one in Basford that Cath came back from in the mid-nineties with a mouth full of blood. It was showing at the Savoy. I said bye to Richard on the corner of Lenton Boulevard and turned down Welby Avenue and just happened to look in the phone box there, and there was this bloke sitting on the floor, covered in blood. I opened the door and asked him what happened, but all that came out of him was this dry rasping sound. It was almost as if I was still in the cinema but there was this tsunami of adrenaline rising in me. I knew instantly it was bad. I couldn't get to the phone to put a coin in, because it would have meant stepping on him, so I vaulted the front wall of the nearest house and banged on the door. A woman who must have been at least eighty answered it, looking like she was expecting me to break into her house, but by that time I'd vaulted the wall of the house next door too, and was banging on their door, just standing there, spinning in circles, shouting to the whole of the city to fucking call an ambulance, please.

Every image from the hour directly after that tumbles into another in my mind: the empty look in the bloke's eyes as they loaded him into the ambulance, the blood on his patchy beard, the pristine cigarette in his hand, the smoky-green interior of the police station, Cath's transforming face as she opens the door, Benji in his cot, me taking off my white shirt and noticing the brown blood drying on the cuff.

Not long after that, we moved out of the city.

I found out he'd only been nineteen: an usher at the same cinema Richard and I had been at that exact night. 'Mugging gone awry' was the theory. Just a young lad, like me, from Notts – the UK city where you're statistically most likely to be

assaulted by a stranger — who'd gone to school only a mile away from me, probably been in a gang a bit like mine, but who'd just been minding his own business, stopping to light a fag on his way home, and was now dead as punishment for having the temerity not to hand over a wallet to a stranger. I remember he was wearing black plimsolls; they were the kind kids wore for PE. I doubt they let him wear them in the cinema. He'd probably slipped them on just for the walk home. No laces. Pumps, we used to call them. It's weird, the things that stick in the brain. Choice doesn't play much of a part in it.

And then in the days and months that followed I saw it: the terrible risky truth behind everything. You could take the most care possible while you were driving your car, but that didn't prevent a potential catastrophe if you just happened to pull out on a semi-blind bend on the same day a pissed knobhead was driving home. Planes didn't crash often, but they crashed sometimes, and when they did, parts of them had to land somewhere, and who was to say that somewhere wouldn't be your house. Sometimes people lost their grip on sharp knives while they were preparing food or washing up – there was nothing to be done about that. And sometimes children and animals might be directly beneath the flight path of the knives. I left the house and thought about the stray toy or glass on the stairs that would trip Catherine or Benji up and send them plummeting to their death.

I stayed in the house and thought about the gunmen holding up the bank, the bus driver fresh from an argument who didn't see the red light on the pedestrian crossing. I sampled the suspect anti-depressants of the time. I did not discuss my predicament. I retreated into my black fears. They made me absent at times when I should have been present.

When Benji was around three, the house got burgled, and I remember when we got home and found the mess my feeling was, 'Ok, yes, I was expecting that.' I became good in a crisis. The flipside was I also became a crisis in good. Although what it also meant was when I saw my own child beginning to die before my eyes after a misdiagnosis from a GP, I acted quickly. It's one thing I can thank depression for. Twenty minutes is what the doctors told us. Maybe a few minutes more, at most. That much later, and it would have been too late. The poison from the burst appendix would have done too much damage to his tiny system. He was so light as I ran with him from the car park into the hospital, but it wouldn't have mattered if he'd been the weight of a tank: I would not have moved less quickly.

Other images I remember from those twenty-four hours: the brown files, so many of them, in the doctor's waiting room, all those histories and bodily secrets. The disinfectant smell in the hospital corridors. The tall nurse who Benji thought was scary then thought was nice, and the small nurse Benji thought was nice then thought wasn't quite as nice as the tall nurse. Wonder Woman, on the *Muppets*, doing the song that Benji liked, with the Rubber Band creatures, the one originally by the soul band who, like so many soul bands, had gone disco. Again, it's strange what sticks to the memory pad. But one thing sticks hardest of all: my revelation, upon seeing Benji there on the hospital bed, all frail and weak, grinning at me, despite the tubes sticking out of every part of him, and Catherine sitting to his left, that I was the father of this child and the husband of this woman. And the revelation that came with it that I had been wrong about everything for a long time: I was not one of the unlucky ones, but the exact opposite. Probably one of the luckiest of all.

That was stage one, for me: the first part of me swimming out of the black cloud. The second was when Cath vanished into the compost. The actual scariest four hours of my life: two in and around that hospital, and, three and bit years later, two searching the roads and twitchels of Tapley Woodhouse for the only person who had ever truly understood me, the person who made everything ok, always. I was different after that. The same but different. That was when I began to see the *real* terrible risky truth of everything, and why it was risky, and why it would always be worthwhile.

I've often wondered where I'd be without her. Cardboard box is one theory. Dank bridge beside the Trent: that's another. It's a rum world, I can tell you that much. We can't all be Dizzy Gillespie.'

'Ok, I'm back. What have I missed?'

'Nothing exciting, yoff. I was just talking about wood pigeons, and how underrated they are.'

Review

The Hidden Mothers – *Intergalactic Hagstone*
(Selkie Records, 2016)

4/5 stars

It might just be possible that we are entering a bold new dawn in face-melting psychedelic rock, quite possibly the boldest since the late sixties, when bands such as Blue Cheer, Leaf Hound and Sir Lord Baltimore first hit upon the idea of taking flower power to the blacksmith's and forging some heavier shoes on its behalf. Right at the forefront of the movement, perhaps a little unexpectedly, are this power trio of Derbyshire professors, who despite their insubstantial bespectacled appearance can probably make more claim to true rockosity than any of their peers (two out of the three members' chosen field of academic expertise is geology). Their debut LP Intergalactic Hagstone, *released via the rejuvenated Selkie Records, is not without its missteps. Side two of the LP is entirely filled with 'Borehole/Stabilisation', a Hammond organ-led song suite which could have happily been trimmed to a third of its* length – and there is nothing here quite as stupendous and other-worldly as their debut single 'Squizard' (also the name of a less successful band once fronted by singer Ian Porterdale) – but the title track, 'Praisegod Fairbones' and 'You Can't Sue For Vibes' are herby, mud-caked cavedude anthems whose potent fumes anyone who enjoyed Wolf People's Steeple album will not be able to resist getting high on. The band's name comes from a type of photo collected by drummer James Franks, the one non-geologist of the group: Victorian child pictures where the child's mother is present, usually to calm the child or keep them still, but cropped, not always successfully, from the daguerreotype. As for the title of the LP itself, that is a reference to a very real solid mass of mineraloid matter. 'It's this weird stone that my friend Mandy has in her garden,' explains Porterdale. 'We always used to reckon it looked like it came from outer space. It's really light to pick up, has a hole in the centre and seems to glow this weird blue-green colour at night. Mandy is actually a big influence on the album. The line about "the good banshee of the shaft" in the song "Pit Witch" is inspired in part by her, too. I felt nervous writing this stuff because she's an author, a proper one who does it full time and has won awards and everything. Not just somebody pissing about on a free weekend here and there, like us.' But perhaps he and his fellow matriarchs shouldn't be quite so concealed and self-effacing. Academia's loss would most certainly be the gain of intelligent proto-swamp metal.

Steve Pages, Mojo magazine

Colin

I left on a high. It was my high. Nobody else could be the arbiter of it. That was the point. That had always been the point. It always has to be, otherwise you're just lost in somebody else's game. I'd done my best work, although it's unlikely there's any trace of it now: no grainy Super 8 film on YouTube, no old newspaper reviews. Photos? Perhaps they exist, but if so, they'll probably stay where they are, in some old album, buried at the bottom of a trunk in somebody's attic. They won't make it out into the public eye, because why would they? But does that make something that's been enjoyed by the people involved in it any less valid? Discuss in no more than 2,000 words.

Before I left, around the time I was doing the last of my packing, I received a surprising package from Dave Barrowcliffe: a polythene bag containing seven screwdrivers of wildly varying oxidation and vintage. I assumed it was from him, anyway, because the bag had been left outside my front door with 'FROM DAVE' scrawled on it in black marker pen. I'd not seen him much since the break-in, save for a couple of sightings on the lane, walking his large, aggressive dog. He appeared diminished, as if recently pressed a few inches further into the ground by some force from above. I wondered initially if the bag and its contents represented some kind of coded further threat to my welfare but upon re-evaluation realised it was probably his idea of a conciliatory offering. I imagined him looking around his house and shed and garage, wondering 'What objects can I find here that represents some kind of common ground between me and the oddball up the road?' Of course, a more evolved human would have handed me the bag in person, maybe with the addition of an apology, but I suspected that would never be his style, even in his new form, humbled by whatever had humbled him.

The more I looked at the bag, the more I began to see it as a piece of art: the thing that Dave Barrowcliffe assembled and left behind, to try to make Tapley Woodhouse a better place. And who was to say it wasn't? Who was to say it was any less art than anything else? If the media got whiff of it, people would probably end up calling him The Screwdriver Guy.

When I am no longer of this planet, which will be quite soon, what will they call me? The Robot Guy? The Naked Pagan Dancing Guy? The Space Guy? Almost certainly not The Surreal Nottinghamshire Mining Play Guy. Contrary to popular belief, it doesn't matter, because I won't be here. And while I still am, I don't expect to be comprehended; it would be terribly obnoxious and puffed up of me to expect anyone to be paying that much attention. I made my commitment to being misunderstood a long long time ago.

Something you are reminded of, working with children, is that it's the process that's the important part. Often it's while a person is dreaming about doing or being something that a lot of the real magic happens, not later, when the world has legitimised their right to do or be it and constructed a box for them in the shape of it. Perhaps because we're all so scared of not being here anymore, we place far too much importance on what will be written about us. We are chronic believers in the falsehood that people are paying more attention to us than they really are. Ultimately, we'll all just be a platitude on a headstone, not hugely dissimilar to the platitudes on the other headstones around us. That, and a big transient jumble sale of memory. We try to clean up after ourselves, which is admirable and right, but there will always be a futility to it.

Everything is just passing through everything, always, and that's the gospel truth. A skeleton walks into a pub and says, 'Can I have a pint of bitter and a mop?' because it's all he can say, forever.

Alien

REPORT OF MISSION TO EARTH FROM THE PLANET VOZKOZ.
1983. PART II. (TRANSLATED FROM THE VOZKOZIAN.)
Interview conducted with Commander Zzzz Trelazian by
Communal Mainframe Intellect Gas.

GAS: Is your mission now complete?

TRELAZIAN: It is. Or at least it will be once we've got safely
home. Ideally I'll be able to stop halfway and get the
starcraft's subengine looked at, but it should be fine.

GAS: And can you consider your mission a success?

TRELAZIAN: My belief is that we can.

GAS: What are the aspects of it that you would say define
it as a success?

TRELAZIAN: We are returning to Vozkoz with the
requested serum that will assist our planet. It might also
be argued we have learned a lot and grown intellectually.
Additionally I am bringing back an excellent recipe for
pakoras.

GAS: This is pleasing news. I am sure the three of you, plus your successful contemporaries who were sent to other parts of Earth, will be greeted as heroes upon returning. There may be bunting. Although don't quote me on that.

TRELAZIAN: Both of us will look forward to that.

GAS: This word you use, 'both', is confusing to Mainframe Gas. Am I right in believing the original members of the mission were Subcommander Rrrr Dodzz, Subcommander Ffff Trelunian and Commander Zzzz Trelazian, aka you?

TRELAZIAN: You are.

GAS: And am I right in believing Subcommander Rrrr Dodzz, Subcommander Ffff Trelunian and Commander Zzzz Trelazian, aka you, are currently making your way back towards our starbag with all possible haste?

TRELAZIAN: Yes and no.

GAS: Please elucidate the 'no' part of that answer.

TRELAZIAN: Subcommander Trelunian and Commander Trelazian, aka I, are making our way back towards our starbag with all possible haste. Subcommander Dodzz had what she described as 'a change of heart'.

GAS: Can you explain what this 'change of heart' entailed?

TRELAZIAN: During final preparations for our journey home Subcommander Dodzz explained that she had become attached to many of the people she had met on Earth, particularly in the Nottinghamshire region. She

237

also expressed misgivings about her life back on Vozkoz and her status there as a 'known genius' and 'vital government employee'. She then detailed the contrasting pluses of the new semi-anonymous life she had been leading as Jonathan, a struggling poet who doesn't appear to write any poetry.

GAS: What did you counsel at this point?

TRELAZIAN: I counselled that she could be about to make the biggest mistake of her life and should go off and have a hard think about it for an hour or so, perhaps while taking the air. Even though the air was quite foggy that day.

GAS: Then what happened?

TRELAZIAN: After two hours, she still hadn't returned to the starcraft. Subcommander Trelunian was then dispatched, in the alpaca form he seemed reluctant to abandon, to look for her and bring her back to the starcraft. His mission proved unsuccessful, although he said, before losing track of Dodzz's whereabouts, he had spotted her in the distance, sitting on top of the smaller of the two gob piles, staring out into the fog below her, in a way that reminded him of a painting he'd seen. I asked him what the painting was, to which he only replied 'some old one by some old dead bloke'. I informed him that this was far too vague. We then flicked through some of the art-history books Dodzz had collected from the region's libraries and left in the starcraft, until we arrived at Caspar David Friedrich's 1818 work *Wanderer Above the Sea of Fog*, at which point Trelunian exclaimed, 'Yes, that's it! That one! That one!'

GAS: Did you eventually locate Subcommander Dodzz?

TRELAZIAN: We did, although not for another nine days.

GAS: Where was she located?

TRELAZIAN: She was located, still in her lanky fair-haired 'Jonathan' form, in a house in a road opposite the target's school. We learned that here she was renting a loft room from Richard Fennel, occupation 'draughtsman for Trent Water' and Deborah Fennel, occupation 'special-needs teacher'. At this point, I morphed into the guise of 'Gerhardt', a German immigrant whose interests include walking and Georgian art, who had befriended Jonathan at a poetry workshop. I called for Jonathan at the Fennels', the door being answered by their twelve-year-old daughter, Jane, who explained, 'I'll get him now. He's upstairs. We have been drawing and listening to *Porcupine* by Echo & the Bunnymen. I think it might be their most complete and assured album yet.'

GAS: What was Dodzz/Jonathan's reaction when she saw you?

TRELAZIAN: I would characterise it as 'a sighing combination of irritation and bored inevitability'.

GAS: Did Gerhardt, aka you, then attempt to knock some sense into Jonathan, aka Dodzz?

TRELAZIAN: I did.

GAS: Where did you do this?

TRELAZIAN: Over the duration of a long walk around the periphery of Nottingham city centre.

GAS: And how did this go?

TRELAZIAN: Rancorously, for the first part.

GAS: Can you elaborate?

TRELAZIAN: I told Dodzz she had become attached to her surroundings in an unprofessional way and had let her emotions get in the way of rational decision-making. Dodzz said this was bullshit. Dodzz then talked about Commander Thatcher, citing the fact that a lot of people said that she was the only woman who could ever be commander of the United Kingdom because, unlike other women, she wouldn't let emotions get involved in her decision-making. Dodzz said this was bullshit too, and implored me sarcastically to look at what good that was currently doing the country. Dodzz said that the country, and by extension the planet, and by extension Orbit 96, and by extension the galaxy, and by extension the starbag, and by extension all of space, could benefit from more emotion. Raising her voice uncharacteristically at this point, Dodzz expressed the opinion that, if extra emotional maturity occurred, and people truly got in touch with their feelings and expressed them openly, there would be a lot less war. By this time we'd reached the news kiosk in the pedestrian underpass on Maid Marian Way and a crowd of seven or eight people had gathered nearby and were pointing at us. 'Fight!' one of them, a man in a hard hat carrying a foil-wrapped sandwich, was heard to shout.

GAS: And where was Trelunian during all of this?

TRELAZIAN: He'd taken advantage of the free time by taking the starcraft back to the mining region and saying a final goodbye to his friends in the alpaca enclosure before they were transported to a field five miles south of Rotherham.

GAS: Did you and Dodzz accede to the hard-hatted stranger's demand for physical conflict?

TRELAZIAN: We did not. But matters remained tense. I asked Dodzz what on Earth she was planning to do now. She produced from the pocket of her trenchcoat a forged diploma from a local teacher-training college, and a letter from Headmistress Commander Wishbone welcoming Jonathan, aka Dodzz, ahead of his first day of work at Sandyhill Primary School.

GAS: What did you do then?

TRELAZIAN: By now we were in the Park Tunnel, under Derby Road, which leads to the Park Estate. We didn't say anything for a number of minutes. I was quite tired and, I have to confess, somewhat emotional. Everything was very quiet and atmospheric in there, generally, and nobody else was around. It was as if the ninth-largest city in the UK wasn't really above us at all. The only sound we could hear was those beautiful native birds with the green on their necks, sitting on ledges in the sandstone, cooing. There must have been over a hundred of them. 'Do you know who built this?' Dodzz asked me. 'Yes, it was Thomas Chambers Hine,' I replied. 'He built it so the wealthy people who lived on the estate and owned horse-drawn carriages could have easier access to it, but he miscalculated the gradient, so it was actually too steep for the horses. You told me all that months ago.' 'Wow,' said Dodzz. 'I can't believe you remembered.' 'I *listen*,' I said. 'You might not think I do, but I do.'

This significantly thawed the atmosphere between us and, at Dodzz's suggestion, we walked back down the hill to Ye Olde Trip To Jerusalem, where we ordered two pints of Shipstones Ale.

GAS: And can you summarise the effects that this Shipstones Ale had on the two of you?

TRELAZIAN: I quickly felt more relaxed than I had at any point in our mission. I enjoyed listening to Dodzz fill me in on the life of her new landlords and on the hectic nature of her social life since we'd last seen each other. She said she had been to see a 'play' at the Ironfield Miners' Welfare. She said the play was called *The Boy Who Heard the Earth Speak* and featured numerous child actors, including our target's son and some of his friends, posing as the ghosts of juvenile miners. Other characters in the play included several adult miners (these were played by actual miners from nearby villages), a robot with large red lips, the Angry Earth – played by the play's director, 'Colin Bruce', disguised quite convincingly as some soil – and the spectre of Lord Byron, plus the spectres of some of Lord Byron's many housepets, including a crow, ten horses, an eagle, eight dogs, three monkeys and a bear.

GAS: And what was the play about?

TRELAZIAN: Dodzz said its theme was the exploitation of the Earth for private gain and the fact that every day, without really being aware of it, we walk on top of a palimpsest. Although she mostly knew the latter fact due to the line opening the play, read by the ghost of a miner's widow, which said, 'Every day, without really being aware of it, we walk on top of a palimpsest.'

GAS: What is a palimpsest?

TRELAZIAN: I asked the same question. Dodzz told me it meant something that had been altered but still bore traces of its earlier form, and that the word came from ancient Greece, a place where people wrote on tablets then scraped and smoothed off the writing in order for them to be reused. I was impressed with her eloquence in describing this to me, at what must have by that point been, for both of us, at least four pints in.

GAS: So she found the play informative and rewarding?

TRELAZIAN: She said it was the confusing and chaotic product of a belligerent and cluttered non-conformist mind, and that it didn't always make much sense, but was no less enjoyable for that.

GAS: How else had she been filling her time?

TRELAZIAN: Dodzz said she had greatly enjoyed, in the company of the Fennels, attending 'Family Night' at a leisure centre across town, posing as the half-brother of Deborah Fennel. Here, Dodzz had, for the first time, played table tennis, badminton, squash and slid down a flume in some borrowed swimming trunks.

GAS: And did she morph again to adopt this disguise?

TRELAZIAN: No, she said there wasn't much point, and it would be a waste of valuable energy. She stayed in her Jonathan form. After all, it wasn't as if the leisure-centre employees knew who Jonathan was, or would be any wiser, or cared that much anyway.

GAS: And how was she feeling about her new job?

TRELAZIAN: Extraordinarily positive. She said she had been visiting the Central Library regularly, making lesson plans, and the enormous variety of stationery available at her new digs was proving hugely beneficial to her preparation. She said that, while life would have been easier if the house had been fitted with more than one bathroom, she liked the home of the Fennels and that it had a comforting smell which, while being not specifically of towels, made you unavoidably think of towels.

GAS: And when you had heard and evaluated all of this information, what did you counsel?

TRELAZIAN: Feeling the ale somewhat, I counselled that Dodzz should do exactly what the fuck her heart told her to do. I then told her that I loved her and that she would always be my best mate. We subsequently embraced for several seconds, until, realising I quite urgently required one of the establishment's four urinals, I broke off the embrace.

GAS: Then what happened?

TRELAZIAN: It seems that I fell asleep on my own arm while standing over the urinal, only to be woken by Dodzz, who, saying a final goodbye, helped me into the rear seat of a black-and-white vehicle – a Ford Cortina, I believe – handed the driver some coins, and directed him towards Tapley Woodhouse. I asked him to drop me at the house three or four doors up from the Figshaws', with the horse's-head gateposts, as I thought that would be most surreptitious. I then walked back to the gob pile, although I initially mistook the small gob pile for the large gob pile because it was dark and the effects of the ale were yet to wear off.

GAS: And had you collected Subcommander Trelunian by this point?

TRELAZIAN: I had not.

GAS: Why was this?

TRELAZIAN: During the course of my journey from the smaller gob pile to the quiet rear part of the larger gob pile I had ascertained, thanks to some noises I'd heard in the undergrowth, and then the evidence I saw with my own eyes, that he was mating with a fellow alpaca named 'Sophie'.

GAS: What kind of noises?

TRELAZIAN: Ones like none I'd quite heard before. I would compare them most closely to those we frequently heard coming from vehicles owned by humans during the early winter mornings of our mission when the vehicles were reluctant to start.

GAS: Did Trelunian then return to the starcraft of his own volition the following morning, and did you then set off for Vozkoz without being detected?

TRELAZIAN: He did, and we did, although I decided to leave it until around 11 a.m., as I wanted to make sure I was fully sober.

GAS: Finally, did you hear any more good jokes during the last part of your mission?

TRELAZIAN: Why did the chicken cross the road?

GAS: I'll answer that, but answer my question first.

TRELAZIAN: No, that's the first part of the joke: Why did the chicken cross the road?

GAS: I don't know.

TRELAZIAN: To get to the Other Side.

GAS: I'm not sure that I get it.

TRELAZIAN: 'The Other Side' is what many humans call the state that occurs after death. The implication is that

the chicken has walked out into the road solely to end its own life. It's quite dark. But the joke works on two levels. It can also be taken more literally. The fact that the answer is so straightforward and banal, with no 'comedy' actually present, becomes for some the joke itself.

GAS: I see . . . I think. Any others?

TRELAZIAN: Why did the chewing gum cross the road?

GAS: I don't know. Why *did* the chewing gum cross the road?

TRELAZIAN: It was stuck to the chicken's foot.

GAS: Oh, very good; I do like that one.

Benji

'Do you know what it will be soon?' said my mum as we climbed the hill – a real one this time – in the minibus and the engine cried out in pain beneath her. She always left it in second gear a little too long.

There were eleven of us in total, travelling in the minibus. My mum was in the driver's seat, with Miss Buttons beside her. I was in the back with Mandy Figshaw, Kate Figshaw, Taj Mukherjee, Holly Potter, Danny McNulty, Emma Buttons, Errol Watts and Paul Hashimoto, and Mr Dodds. Through the windows we could see Derbyshire gradually getting taller and emptier.

'Let me guess,' said Miss Buttons. 'Will it be time to change gear?'

'I know!' said Errol Watts. 'It will be Christmas.'

'That's right, it will,' said my mum. 'But I am thinking of something else that comes just after that.'

'1984?' said Holly Potter.

'Yes!' said my mum. 'And do you know why that's significant?'

'Because it will be a different year to this one,' said Errol Watts.

'Well, yes,' said my mum. 'But it's also significant because there is a very famous book about it. It's quite a frightening book which was written a long time ago, before even Miss Buttons and I were born, about what the author thought the world might be like by now, but luckily it doesn't look like the world is actually going to be like that in the real 1984. You should all definitely read the book one day, but it's a grown-up book and quite hard to understand in places, so perhaps not for quite a few years.'

'I've dipped into it,' said Emma Buttons.

'Me too,' said Mandy Figshaw.

'Typical,' Taj Mukherjee and I said, in perfect unison.

'When we will be at the moon?' asked Errol Watts.

'I hope it's soon because I need a wee,' said Paul Hashimoto.

'Not long at all now,' said Miss Buttons. 'Try to hold on.'

'Will it be made out of cheese when we get there?' asked Errol Watts.

'And will a cow jump over it?' asked Holly Potter.

'There will definitely be cows there, but I think it would be difficult for them to jump all the way over it, unless they are really big cows. Would anyone care for a pakora?' asked Miss Buttons.

'That all depends on how much care the pakora needs,' said Mr Dodds, and all of us laughed.

The trip we were all on had been Mr Dodds' idea, although it had sort of been my idea too, before that. In school, Mr Dodds had been teaching us all about the first ever moon landing, which had happened in 1969, after a lunar module called *Eagle* had flown there from America. We had learned ever such a lot, including that the moon was a bit like a desert to walk on, and something else not a lot of people knew, which was that actually *Eagle* wasn't the first spaceship to touch the moon because another spaceship called *Luna 2*, sent there by the Soviet Union, had crashed into the moon almost ten years earlier. Danny McNulty said that none of it had happened, and it had all been faked in a TV studio as part of a giant conspiracy to make America look powerful, but we didn't believe him because we all knew by now that Mr Dodds knew everything.

The weekend after we'd been learning about the landings, I heard my dad talking to my uncle Jerry about a place called Kinder Scout in Derbyshire, which he said was very very high and 'looked just like the surface of the moon'. The next day at school I told Mr Dodds about it. Paul Hashimoto and Taj Mukherjee and I talked about how cool it would be to walk on something that was like the surface of the moon. Then, without telling us, Mr Dodds talked to Miss Buttons and my mum and hired a minibus using his own money, although they all agreed my mum and Miss Buttons would have to take turns with the driving, because Mr Dodds didn't have a driving licence. I asked if Mandy and Kate Figshaw could come too and he said that would be fine, if they were well-behaved, as it wasn't really an official school trip anyway. I said I thought they would definitely be well-behaved because they always were and that was one of the main reasons my mum and dad approved of me being friends with them.

In the two months that he'd been teaching us, as the permanent replacement for Mrs Lofthouse, Mr Dodds had already probably become my favourite teacher ever, and when he'd said he would take us to see what the surface of the moon was like, his place in the top slot was sealed. I knew that a lot of my friends felt the same. Mr Dodds was good at listening to you and had this brilliant way of making you feel like you were just playing all day, but then when you went home you realised you knew lots of new stuff too, such as when the first dog was sent into space or how long the first Transatlantic flight took John Alcock and Arthur Brown to complete. Because of all the stuff he taught us about outer space, and how clearly he explained it all, I now knew that it was unlikely that any of us would ever travel into another galaxy, and that aliens probably didn't even exist or, if they did, they were so far away that we would never see them. His classroom didn't have a ZX Spectrum like Mr Stone's but it did have a *Millennium Falcon*, all the best books and lots of Lego, including a model of the Apollo 11's Lunar Module *Eagle* itself. He also liked good music, and when I told him I thought 'Streets of London' and 'Lily the Pink' were rubbish and I didn't like singing them in assembly, he said that he agreed with me but told me not to tell Miss Wishbone, and I promised I wouldn't.

Because he had started living in a room one floor above Jane Fennel, I had got to know him a little more quickly than I normally got to know teachers. One time when my mum and dad took me and Paul Hashimoto, who was my brother for that week, to Family Night with the Fennels, I even got to play and beat Mr Dodds at table tennis, although afterwards, when I watched him beat Richard Fennel 21–3, I wondered if he might have been letting me off a bit lightly. He seemed happier than other adults I knew, even when he thought he was alone, such as one time when Emma Buttons and I arrived to school early and saw him through the little square windows of the double door to the classroom, dancing around the pouffes to a song on his tape player. Later in class we heard him singing the same song. Emma Buttons asked him what it was and he said it was called 'Maniac' and told us it was from a film he liked which was about a welder who wanted to be a dancer. He said that we should keep it under our hats for now, but next year he might direct a special Sandyhill Primary School version of the film in the gym. I told him I didn't have a hat anymore because I'd lost it in the playground down Ironfield and Emma Buttons said it was just a figure of speech and Mr Dodds didn't mean an actual hat. I said that was ok then. I told Mr Dodds that I'd like to act in the school version of the film because I had acting experience, having played the bartender in *Bugsy Malone* and more recently been in a play where I was a ghost in a mine and actually had to say two whole sentences, which were 'I am so tired' and 'I wish I knew what it was like to have a suntan'. Mr Dodds said he already knew that because, although I hadn't realised, he'd been in the audience at one of the performances of the play where I was a ghost, and that made me feel slightly famous, a bit like I did when I thought I was going to meet Squizard.

I liked the song Emma Buttons and I had seen Mr Dodds dancing to, but I liked some of the songs on the cassette he brought with him on our trip to Kinder Scout even more. My favourite was the one which was about burning down a house and had lots of weird noises on it and was really exciting, even though I couldn't work out what most of the other words in it were. What made me laugh to myself was that it started playing just when my mum drove the minibus past the house which had been burned down and which my dad had said was 'semi-dethatched' when we passed it at the start of the year. As the song played, Taj Mukherjee played percussion with his mouth in tune with its weird noises and I found it hard to tell what was from Taj's mouth and what was from the tape. We passed sights that were familiar to me from weekends stretching as far back as I could remember, such Riber Castle, and the aquatic centre at Tansley. I told Danny McNulty and Mr Dodds about the piranhas that were in one of the big tanks at the aquatic centre, some of whom had missing eyes and other fish parts. 'Maybe they just need to be refurbfished,' suggested Mr Dodds, who was often funny in the same way my dad was funny. On and on the minibus went, until the hills became much bigger and I didn't recognise anything, and finally we pulled into a car park at the bottom of the biggest cliff I'd ever seen. The sky looked dark and frightening and I was glad I'd brought my anorak.

There was one other minibus and a couple of cars in the car park and some men in hard hats with ropes and hooks. I asked if we would need ropes and hooks too while we were on the moon and Miss Buttons said that we wouldn't, because we weren't going to the same part as the people who had them, and also they were actual climbers. 'Are they really going to climb all the way to the moon?' Errol Watts asked, while examining some stones on the ground.

My mum said to Miss Buttons and Mr Dodds that she was worried about the lack of daylight and the weather and the fact that most of us only had little legs. She told us that we wouldn't be able to go right to the top of the moon but we'd probably be able to get far enough to properly feel what the moon was like under our feet. I noticed that Mr Dodds had already changed from his white trainers into some old brown leather boots, possibly even older than the ones my granddad who was still alive wore on walks in Derbyshire. 'Got 'em from a jumble sale down

Basford, 75p,' he said to my mum, sticking a thumb up. I thought about how strange his accent sounded, like he was from Nottingham, but also somewhere far away, although not Japan, like Paul Hashimoto's dad, or India, like Taj Mukherjee's grandparents; somewhere a little metallic and cold. In his walking boots and dark green anorak, with his bright, tall hair, he looked like a thin wobbly giant or an overexcited sunflower, and his height gave the impression that he was straining for the top of the dark cliff before we'd even set off. When we did, he was soon many yards ahead of us.

'Don't try to walk as quickly as Mr Dodds,' said Miss Buttons to us all. 'He's probably got a lot of hiking and climbing experience and he's much bigger and stronger than all of you.'

Disappointed noises emerged from Paul Hashimoto, Errol Brown and Taj Mukherjee.

'Now stay close together,' said my mum. 'Keep your cagoules zipped up, and if your legs start to hurt, don't be afraid to tell me or Miss Buttons.'

I stared at that dark ridge above us. I couldn't imagine anything ever being higher or darker. Some of the clouds were actually below it, which was something I'd seen when my dad was driving us through the Alps, but never in Britain. All I could imagine over that ridge was the darkness of space itself: something impossibly huge and dense yet impossibly empty too. And there was Mr Dodds, forging towards it. For every tiny bit of progress we made, he made three times as much, until finally he was just a speck disappearing over the craggy rim far above us, into the unknowable weather. I asked my mum where he was going and she said he was just excited, as it was his first time in the Peak District.

I dropped back a little, and walked with Mandy and Kate. Kate had a sheep jumper on, a different one to the one she normally wore. I noticed, as I often did, that Kate acted bossily, like an older sister, even though Mandy was now nine and Kate was still only seven. Kate told Mandy off for wearing her gingham dress and getting it muddy. I noticed that it still had a rip in the bottom, sustained a couple of weeks ago when Mandy got it caught in the wooden frog in the Broadmarsh Centre. Behind us, Taj continued to play drums and cymbals and maracas with his mouth to the song about the burning house, even though it wasn't playing anymore. 'What is he doing?' asked Mandy. I told her it was called beatboxing and that I could do it really well now too. She asked me to demonstrate and I said that I'd wait until later to show her as I needed time to warm up, but promised her that, when I had, I was almost as good as he was.

As we reached a section of higher ground, the earth became blacker and the puddles had a skin on them which reminded me a little of the one my rice pudding at home had when I left it too long before I ate it, although this skin was icy and cold, not warm. Paul Hashimoto and Errol Brown enjoyed cracking the icy skin with their heels, while Danny McNulty talked to Miss Buttons about something which once happened here called the Kinder Scout Trespass, which Danny said his mum said was a big riot where walkers beat lots of wealthy landowners up with their fists. 'I don't think it quite happened like that, Danny,' said Miss Buttons. 'It was much more peaceful. But it was a good thing. It means we can all walk in more beautiful places now.'

Holly Potter complained about being cold and my mum suggested to Miss Buttons that now was probably the most sensible time to turn around and retrace our steps, especially since the sky was getting blacker. Then lots of hard bits of hail started bouncing on the ground and our anoraks and Holly Potter complained that they hurt, but I thought she was being a wimp, which was something she was the opposite of when she was in school or even in the playground outside it. Soon the hail turned to rain and got heavier and heavier until I could feel it going through the gaps in my anorak and down my chest, but I was happy because I was with everyone. Being with everyone always made me happy, even if 'everyone' didn't quite technically mean absolutely everyone. Ideally, I probably would have grown up in a commune.

'What about Mr Dodds?' asked Emma Buttons.

'He'll be fine,' said my mum, not sounding totally convinced by her own statement. 'If it wasn't raining so hard, you'd probably still be able to see him up there, in the distance.'

I winced, instinctively ready for my cousin Donna to raise a piercing protest, but then remembered she wasn't there.

When we arrived back in the car park, we were all surprised – especially Holly Potter – to find Holly Potter's dad there, waiting in his Austin Princess, which he'd parked next to the minibus. He told my mum and Miss Buttons that he'd seen the weather forecast on the TV, thought it looked 'a bit black over Bill's mother's', so driven out to check we were all ok. My mum told him we were fine, and I remembered a story I'd heard my dad telling Errol Watts' stepdad about Holly Potter's dad getting scratched by a cat then going to the vet instead of the doctor by mistake to get the scratch seen to. Holly Potter's dad said he'd take Holly Potter home, and also Paul Hashimoto and Errol Watts, then the rest of us walked into the village to the pub, which allowed children, unlike some pubs, and, even better, had a set of dominoes in its lounge. As we all drank Cokes and lemonades and ate cheese-and-onion crisps bought for us by Miss Buttons, a few more walkers came down off the top of the moon, looking even wetter than we had been. Some of them had walking sticks. I told Mandy and Kate Figshaw about a special walking stick my dad had showed me at Gowenlock Hall with a secret top that you could flick off and turn into a gun. Taj Mukherjee and Danny McNulty speculated about who would inherit Mr Dodds' *Millennium Falcon* if Mr Dodds didn't come back and Emma Buttons told them to be nicer and think about how kind Mr Dodds was to us all, always, and how he'd paid for today's trip himself. After our third Coca-Colas and lemonades, the man behind the bar at the pub said he had to close it for a few hours, and we would have to wait for our friend outside. It was only when we stepped out the door that I realised just how dark it was.

I was not sure precisely what I'd expected from the day, but I knew it had not been what was happening right now. I remembered Mr Dodds telling us that the most famous astronaut to land on the moon, Neil Armstrong, had said that its surface was soft and fine, like the sand on a desert, but what we'd walked on hadn't been like at all. It had been black and treacley and felt like it could suck your wellies off your feet. The walk we'd done didn't feel like much of a walk at all, as half of it had been just a reverse of what we'd already done, and it had never really felt like we'd got to the proper bit of what we were there to see. Now I felt cold and nesh and very far from home. My mum and Miss Buttons did their best to act like they knew exactly where Mr Dodds was, but I had heard Miss Buttons whisper some words to my mum which, even though I couldn't hear most of them, definitely included 'rescue' and 'helicopter'. It was so dark now that you couldn't even see that big bony ridge so high above us nor the several smaller ridges below it. The wind was like the frightened cry of a weird horse and part of all the smudged greys in front of us was a sort of swirling, tunnelling grey, angry and big and intangible. I looked into it and came to the abrupt realisation that all those orcs I'd fought with so many times on the spoil heaps and forest floors and wastelands around Tapley Woodhouse were not the real danger. The truly frightening monster, the one that woke you up in the night and made you glad you were living in Nottinghamshire with your mum and dad and not out in the woods on a cold black night, would come out of something like what we were looking at, at this very second. And just as I realised that very thing, Emma Buttons, with a scream that was swiftly echoed first by Mandy Figshaw and then by Kate Figshaw and then by Taj Mukherjee, pointed to a formidable hooded figure racing out of the gloom directly towards us, and I realised it was here and soon all of this would be over; all these things that, although I was only eight, had already made me me, would be gone, extinguished, leaving just the unknowable head-twisting abyss beyond. I had only enough time to wonder, in that fragment of a second, what it would look like, what nightmare face the last sight I ever saw would wear. But then, even in that foulest of light, we caught sight of just enough of it: the smile. The same smile Emma Buttons and I had seen through the windows of the classroom, above the

dancing feet that did not know they were being watched. A fresh smile, like our own. The face wearing it was not one of the innumerable ones we imagined coming to end us, in the darkest visions of our kaleidoscopic and generously nurtured young minds. It could not be. That was impossible. It could only be that of Mr Dodds, our new good friend, fresh from a bracing walk, all set to accompany us home.

Acknowledgements

The first people for an author to thank, at the end of a book inspired by his childhood in this particular way, are some of the people who are part of the long-ago-world it pays tribute to: specifically, the staff of Claremont Primary School in the early 1980s. I doubt I'd be precisely in the place I'm in today, writing novels like this one, if not for the inspirational environment of child-centred learning created there. Sandyhill isn't Claremont, but it owes a considerable debt to it, it wouldn't exist without it, without my fond memories of it, without what it quietly tried to achieve. Claremont was all for encouraging kids to follow their own interests and passions and I feel, in a way, that's what my publishers, Unbound, are doing with me now, as an adult. Writing is, more than ever, a kind of learning for me, and I am lucky to have people – in my editor Imogen Denny, my publisher Mathew Clayton, Unbound co-founder John Mitchinson and my agent Ed Wilson – who, when I tell them, each time I write a book, 'I think this one is probably going to be quite weird, and very different to the last one,' say, 'Fantastic!' rather than, 'Oh dear, the sales team isn't going to like that' or, 'OK, but instead could you write a safer book that's a bit like a book that's already been written?' Then when it's done and I think I've tightened the screws as far as they'll go, they pass it to copy editor Hayley Shepherd, who always turns out to have fingers that crucial bit stronger than mine, and Joe McLaren, who comes up with the perfect cover art, as directed by Mark Ecob.

1983 plus *Villager* plus *Notebook* plus *Ring the Hill* plus *Help the Witch* plus *21st-Century Yokel* makes six for Unbound, the first long-term relationship of my publishing life. Those books constitute a stubborn path, and an individual one, but one that, like Claremont, centres around an individualism that also feels a bit like being part of a wyrd little club. A few brambles on that path are always beaten back on my behalf by others: my readers, whose support and trust in these projects during their gestation makes them real; the friends I walk with and talk to; and my partner Ellie, my soulmate in the pursuit of being only interested in everything, whose unquenchable curiosity and Emma Buttons-like passion for random facts have inevitably flavoured the universe I have created in the first book she's witnessed me write from beginning to end. Bruce Lacey (RIP) was kind enough to invite me to his house in 2012 and it's the conversation that took place between us there that inspired this fictionalised version of his early eighties self. I hope the future will contain more artists who prioritise mucking about in a similar way to him. As ever, I also want to thank my inspiring and supportive parents Jo and Mick (whose 2011 book *A Grisly History of Nottinghamshire* helped me with a few facts about the city of my birth), especially for indulging me on those early 1980s school nights when it was getting late and there were endless jobs to do, and I asked, 'Just one more story . . . *pllllleaaaaase.*'

Unbound is the world's first crowdfunding publisher, established in 2011.

We believe that wonderful things can happen when you clear a path for people who share a passion. That's why we've built a platform that brings together readers and authors to crowdfund books they believe in – and give fresh ideas that don't fit the traditional mould the chance they deserve.

This book is in your hands because readers made it possible. Everyone who pledged their support is listed below. Join them by visiting unbound.com and supporting a book today.

Tamsin Abbott
Natasha Aburrow-Jones
Kathleen Ahearn
Adrian Ainsworth
Claire Alcock
Catherine Allen
Chris Allen
Kelly Allen
Andrew Allerton
Elizabeth Allison
Ariane Amann
John Anderson
Alexandra Andersson
Laura Anger
Anna, Mollie & Teddy
Kirk Annett
Richard Ansell
Teresa Ansell
Eleanor Anstruther

Darlene Antonich
Izzy Archer
Claire Armitt
Diana Arseneau-Powell and
    Alun Wyburn-Powell
Sue Arthur
Christine Asbury
Lindsay Ashford
Dawn Ashford and Andy
    Steele
Louise Ashton
Carl Ashworth
Kate Aspinall
Ian Atkin
James Aust
Nick Avery
Ann Avouris
Gary Bailey
Julie Bailey

Ed Baines
Katharine Baird
Susan Bakalar Wright
Bill Baker
Emma Ball
Kim Barbrie
G. B. Bard
Diane Bark
Deborah Barker
Naomi Barkevich
Andrea Barlien
Annette Barnes
Stuart Barnes
Loretta Barnett
Raquel Anta Barragan
Sara Barratt, Emma Graham
Louisa Barrett, Julian Barrett
Jess Bartlett
Sarah Bartlett
Sophie Basbayon
Laura Baughman
Gisele Baxter
Lisa Bayford
Emma Bayliss
Bob Beaupre
Bethany Beavan Pinches
Kate Beazley
Sarah Beesley
Donna Bell
Iain Bellis
Anita Benson
Julie Benson
Roni Benson
Christopher Bergedahl

Steve Besley
Jen Best
Mary Bettuchy
Karen Beynon
Mel Bhavsar
Heather Binsch
Maggie Birchall
Graham Blenkin
John Blythe
Alex Boon
Sean Boon
Jeannie Borsch
Sarah Boswell
Michelle Bourg
Jan-Joost Bouwman
Joanna Susan Bowe
Lynda Bowen
Kate Bowgett
Mary Ann Boyd
Darren Boyden
Alex Boylin
Elizabeth Bradley
Rachel Bradley
Susan Bradley
Hugo and Vicki Brailsford
Donal Brannigan
Gillian Brennan
Gill Brennand
Sophie Brewer
Hannah Brickner
Gemma Bridges
Mark Bridgman
Rhiannon Brislee-Young
Samantha Broadhurst

Karon Brown
Katharine Brown
Melanie Brown
Sharon L Brown
Steph Brown
Brian Browne
Sam Browne
Sally Browning
James Bryan
Leslie Buck
Elaine Buckley
Alison Bunce
Diana Bunnell-Remillard
Rachel Burch
Julie Burling
Donna-Marie Burnell
Arwen Burns
Joanne Burrows
Alex Burton-Keeble
Heather Bury
Mark Butler
Michelle Calka
Jon Callas
Joseph Camilleri
Donatella Campbell
Jeffrey Cannell
Elizabeth Card
Catherine Cargill
Susan Caroline
Caroline Carpenter
Juls Carr
Victoria Carr
Claire Carruthers
Lorrie Carse-wilen

Suzy Carver
Susan Catley
Heather Cawte
Kate Chabarek
Jayne Chalk
Barbara Challender
Tamasine Chamberlain
Laura Chambers
Caroline Champin
Matthew Champkin
Christy Chanslor Mangini
Liz Chantler
Heather Chappelle
Ailsa Charlton
Gill Chedgey
Eliska Cheeseman
Paul Cheney
Diane Chiacchio
Nigel Denise Chichester
Daniel Chisham
Andrew Chitty
Lesley Christensen
Gemma Church
Janet Clapton
Clare & Dan
Adrian Clark
Deborah Clark
Jennifer Clark
Heather Clark-Evans
Jenny Clarke
Jillian M Clarke (Australia)
Clawdius, Mina, Keith and
    Brooke
Katie Clay

Mathew Clayton
Lisa Bernadette Clegg
Robert Clements
Gill Clifford
Waving Cloud
Billy Clough
Gina Collia
Wendy Collier
Marguerite Collins
Michael Connell
Allan Conner
Susanne Convery
Peter Cooke
Bryan Cooklock
Clare Coombes
Sarah Coomer
Fiona Cooper
Jackie Copping
Liz Cormell
Rachael Corn
Ellie Cornell
Amanda Corp
Andrew Cosgriff
K Coutts
Ann Crabbe
Charlotte Crerar
WAAAAAaaaaanky Crisps
Tessa Crocker
Nancy Crosby
Alasdair Cross
Rachel Cross
Vivienne Crossley
Neil Crosswell
Jim Croxford

Leah Culver-Whitcomb
Dave Curtis
Matthew d'Ancona
Elizabeth Daggar
Beth Dallam
Jackie Daly
Claire Daniells
Polly Daniels, Cwytch
Ronald Yaffle Englebright
Evelyn Danson
Andrea Darbyshire
Claire Davidson
Rob Davidson
Alex(andra) C Davies
Andrea Davies
Meryl Davies
Nicki Davies
Penny Davies
Ariella Davis
Catherine Davis
E R Andrew Davis
Laura Davis
Lucy Davis
Patrick Davis
Jeannie Davison
Red Daykin
Annie de Bhal
Celia Deakin
Alison Deane
Michael DeCataldo
Joanne Deeming
Vicky Deighton
Laura Dempster
Pamela Denison

Albert Depetrillo
Emma Dermott
Heather Desserud
Stephen Deuters
Claire Dickson
Andie Differ
Max Dighton
Laura Dobie
Rebecca Dodman Wainwright
Zoë Donaldson
Sue Doran
Linda Doughty
Leigh Dowell
Laurence Downes
Rosalyn Downie
Rose Doyle
Eleanor Driscoll
Jill Drury
Eileen Ducksbury
Claudie Dungey
Julie Dunne
Sue Dunne
Jane Dunster
Lindsey Dyke
Robert Eardley
Andrea Ebnet
Sarah Eden
Jean Edwards
Sharon Edwards
Eirlys Edwards-Behi
June Ellerby
Tom Ellett
Debbie Elliott

Stephen Elrick
Alli Ennis
Mark Enser
Jeanette Esau
Carol Evans
Rachel Evans
Natasha Everard
Rachael Ewing
Sarah Faragher, Ryan King
Joanna Fenna-Brown
Lori Ferens
Peter Fermoy
Debra Ferreday
Adele Finch
Pamela Findlay
Mel Finney
Colin Fisher
Dave Fisher
Jo Fitz-Henry & Ruby Powell
Nick Fitzsimons
Poppy Flaxman
Sorella Fleer
Rachel Fleet
Joanne Fletcher
Andy, Jo and Django Flint
Maria Flynn
Sue Forber
Joanna Forbes
Chris Foster
Catherine Fowler
Jane France
Joanne Frankland
Nancy Franklin
Christine Fraser

Jacqueline Freeman
Anne Fucaloro
Sarah Fuller
Richard Furniss
Deborah Fyrth
Mel Gambier-Taylor
Richard Paul Gamblin
Emma Gardner
Elizabeth Garner
Christine Garretson-Persans
Annabel Gaskell
Simon Gebbett
Sally Geisel
Lorna Gibbs
Claire Gibney
Hanna Gibson
Joanne Gillam
Jane Gilligan
Craig Gilmour
Stephanie Gilmour
Jayne Globe
Dave Goddard
Jennifer Godman
Sue Godwin
Lucy Gomes
Rich Goodall, Paula Anne
    Goodall
Tim Goode
Katey Goodwin
Mandy Gordon
Emily Goss
Fred Gough
Toby Gould
Nancy Grace

Natalie Graeff
Nicole Grant
Andy Green
Darrell Green
Hayley Green
Leo Greene
Amy Gregson
Louise Griffiths
Helen Grimster
Martin Grocock
Veronika Groke
Michelle Grose
Rebecca Groves
Zabet Groznaya
Juliana Grundy
Mark Gudgeon
Jennifer Gundersen
Martin Gunnarsson
David Guy
Sara Habein
Julie Hadley
Karen Hagan
Sam Hailstone
Helen Hall
Laurence Hall
Niki Hall
Mal Hallard and Chris
    Harrison
Marie Halova
Stuart Hamilton
Sharon Hammond
Russ Hancock
Samantha Handebo
Kate Hannaby

Cathy Hanson
Hilary Harley
Lynda Harpe
Rachel Harrington
Charlotte Harris, Eileen
    Williams
Ruby Harrison
Sharon Ptraci Harrison
Greg Harrop
Paula Haselup
Shelli Haswell
Luke Hatton
Rachel Hawes
Emily Hawkins
Jessica Hayden
Michelle Hayes
Philip Hayes
Sue and Julian Hayley
Rebecca Haywood
Bethan Healey
Gillian Heaslip
Katherine Heathcote
Emma Heggie
Helen The Hedgerow Hag
Lynne Henderson
Cole Henley
Elizabeth Henwood
Diane Heward
Jo Hewitt
Kat Hewlett
Alice Heywood
Martin Hickman
Jan Hicks
Max Higgins

Jeremy Hill
Joe Hill
Rich Hill
Ann Hiloski-Fowler
Joeri Hilte
Beth Hiscock
Tony Histed
Frida Hjelm
Kahana Ho
Jackie Hobbs
Amy Hoddinott
Caroline Hodge
Becky Hodges
Marie Hodgson
Chris Hofstetter
Jason Holdcroft
Paige Holland
Samantha Holland
Sarah Holland
Tony Holland
Fran Hollinrake
Holly Holmes
Rae Holmes
Monet Holmquist
Ceil Hook
Martin Horlock
Clare Horne
Andy Horton
Jacki Howard
Paul Howard
Sandra Howgate
Carolyn Howitt
Sara Howland
Chris Huecksteadt

Crystal Hughes
Jennifer Hughes
Richard Hughes
Yvette Huijsman
Alison Hull
Charly Hunt
Ian F Hunter
Claire Hutchinson
Melanie Hutchinson
Liz Hyder
iestyn&corinne
benjamin ilany
Philippa Illsley
Christine Ince
Nigel Ince
Simon Inchley
Edd Ingham
Hazel Ireland
Judith Jackson
Lindsey Jackson-Kay
Briony Jackson-Newbold
Kasturi Jadhav
David James
Kellie James
Sophie James
Marieke Jansen
Sarah Jarvis
Luke Jeffery
Nik Jeffries
Christine Jenner
Lucy Jiwa
Vicky Johns
Andrea Johnson
Helen Johnston

John Jones
Meghan Jones
Sandra Jones
Suzi Jones
Alice Jorgensen
Melissa Joulwan
Vickie Kakia
Karla Kane
Katie
Annette Katiforis
Ardala Katzfuss
Paul Kay
Jo Keeley
Jacob Keenan
Lisa Kehoe
Ursula Kehoe
Minna Kelland
Steve Keller
Gill Kelly
Kelsey Kittle, Ty Kittle
Charlotte Kelshiker
Helen Kemp
Hilary Kemp
Rebecca Kemp
Joanne Kennedy
Mary Kersey
Helen Kershaw
Rebecca Kershaw
Gemma Khawaja
Dan Kieran
Caitlin Kight
Deborah King
Georgina King
Janet T King

Sue King

Simone Kinnert

Jon Kiphart

Rachel Knightley

Echo Knott, Patricia Knott

Chris Knowles

Laurie Koerber

Sandra Kohls

Teppo Koivula

Cathy Kompfner

Helene Kreysa

Brian Kumanchik

Laurie Kutoroff

Emily Kyne

Dawn Lacey

Kevin Lack

Leslie Lambert

Emma Lamerton

Gary Lamont

Ben Lancaster

Paige Landers

Aoife Lane

Jane Langan

Teresa Langston

Simon Lankester

Richard Lansdall-Welfare

Joelle Lardi

Phil Latham

Heidi Latzan

Ronni Laurie

Vanessa Laurin

Janice Lavelle

Terry Lavender

Jessica Law

Kim Le Patourel

Cynthia Leathers

Claire Lee

Gavin Lees

Scott Leger

Janet Lemon

Kathryn Leng

Alison Levey

Beth Lewis

Caroline Lewis

Helen Lewis

Katherine J. Lewis

Marian Lewis

Lidbert

Ian Lipthorpe

David Livingston

Siân Lloyd-Pennell

Benjamin Logan

Ellen Logstein

Michele Lohry

Madeline Long

Katy Love & Mike Rankin

Jane Lovell

Jennifer Lowe

Pat Lowe

Helen Luker

Nick Lupton

Katherine Lynn

Adam Lyzniak

Josh M

Margo MacDonald

Karen Mace

Sophie Macgregor

Helen Mackenzie-Burrows

Ian Mackintosh
Nick Madge
Laura-Jane Maher
Sue Mahon
Catt★★ Makin
Darren Manion
Alice Mannering
Steve Manners
Keith Mantell
Laurence Manton
Katie Marshall
Victoria Martin
Catherine Mason
Jo Mason
L. M. Master
Louise Matchett
Suzanne Matrosov-Vruggink
Lisa Matthews
Becca Mattingley
Shannon Matzke
Vicky Maull
Shirley mawer
Molly Mayfield
Mark Maynard
Ollie McAndrews
Melanie McBlain
Wendie McBurnie
Trevor McCarthy
Yvonne Carol McCombie
Kate McCormack
Megan McCormick
Helen McElwee
Jane McEwan
Peter McGinn

Ann McGregor
Holly McGuire
Sue McIntosh
Ellie Mckechnie
Fiona McKechnie
Lesley McLarnon
Vanessa McLaughlin
Cate Mclaurin
Cate Mclaurin, Kate
    Shakespeare
Paul McLeman
Mandy Mclernon
Fi McLoughlin
Amanda McMillan
Claire McMullen
Leanna McPherson
Geoff McQueen
Melanie McVey
Laura Mellor
Kate Menzies
John Mercer
Stacy Merrick
Michie
Elgiva Middleton
Judith Mighall
Jackie Miller
Scott Millington
Chris Mills
John Mitchinson
Kathryn Moffat
Sebastian Moitzheim
Jennifer Montgomery
Annabelle Mooney
David Moore

Kristine Moore

Natalie Moore

Sarah Moore

Sarah Mooring

Mercy Morris

Leigh Morse

Katrina Moseley

Scott Mowbray

@Mr_Spoon

Florentina Mudshark

Donna Mugavero

Alison Murphy

Ian Murphy

Hugh N

Vanda Naden

Laura Nardelli

Carlo Navato

Fiona Naylor

Joanne Needle

Lisa Neel

Kelly Neeley-Brown

Elinor Neville

Neville

Andrew Newbury

Sarah Newton-Scott

Laura Niall

Bruce Nicholson

Lynda Nicholson

Liz Nicolson

Kes Nielsen

Andy Nikolas

Anita Norburn

Gemma Norburn

Ruby Rae Norton

adele nozedar

Andrew Nunn

Jackie O'Brien

Mark O'Neill

David Oakes

Andrew Oates

Sarah Oates

Sandra Oberbroeckling

Kevin Offer

Will Ormsby

May Orr-Wilcox

Phil Orrell

Angela Osborne

Claire Owen-Birch

Paula Page

Dr Paisley

Ellie Palmer

Sarah Palmer

Gwen Papp

Megan Parnell-Bray

George Parr

Sarah Parry

Claire Parsons

Karen Paton

Trish Paton

Adam Ross Patterson

Clare Patterson

Gill Patterson

Giles Pattison

Gill Peake 1948-2022

Sharon Pearson

Janice Pedersen

Karie Penhaligon

Sarah Peters

Leslie Phelps

Alice Picado

Lisa Piddington

Karen F. Pierce

Elizabeth Pimley

Peter Pinkney

Denise Plank

Tim Plester

Jo Plumridge

Marcel Poitras

Annette Poole

Becky Potter

Kristine Heidi Pratt

Gemma Prothero

Christina Pullman

Kate Pyle

Ian Quelch

Peter Randall

Anooshka Rawden

Clare Rayner

Angela Rayson

Peg Reilly

Steph Renaud

Jane Renton

Mark Repsher

Marie Reyes

Debra Rhodes

Parker Rhodes

Julie Richards

Lizi Richards

Mark Richards

Karen Richardson

Laura Richmond

Meryl Rimmer

Nicola Rimmer

Kerry Rini

Lucy Rix

Robert Zara, Robert Zara

Catherine Roberts

Gemma Roberts

Amanda Robertson

Spencer Robinson

Rachel Robison

Karen Robson

Susan Rogers

Susan Rollinson

Eva Rose

Gary Ross

Billy Rough

Matthew Rowell

Rhona Rowland

Martin Ruddock

Sue Rupp

Karl Sabino

Matt Salts

Marie Sandland

Ingrid Sandstrom

Sherri Savage

Yvonne Sawka-Blick

Lisa Schaller DeCarbo

Julia Schlotel

Katee Schultz

Lisa Marie Sciberras

Devin Scobie

Christine M. Scott

Jenni Scott

Russell Scott

Sarah Scott

Andrew Seaman
Jonathan Seaman
Emma Selwood
Elena Senra
Neil Sentance
Andrew Sewell
Belynda J. Shadoan
James Sharp
Doug Shaw
Fiona Shearer
Elly Shepherd
Nicola Shepherd
Susannah Shepherd
Lucy Sheppard
Josephine Sherwood
Jane Shillaker
Alison Shore
Elizabeth Shostak
Laura Sibra
colin sinclair
Katie Singer
James Slade
Kate Sluka
SmallTeethingBeastie
(AVoelkel)
Bec Smith
Carolyn Smith
Charlotte Smith
Fiona Katherine Smith
Hannah Smith
Jay Smith
Lan-Lan Smith
Libby Smith
Mairéad Smith

Michael Smith
Nicola Smith
Nikki Smith
Peter Smith
Rosemary Smith
Simon Smith
LA Smith-Buxton
Julia Snell
Lauren Snyder
Michael Soares
Yve Solbrekken
Murielle Solheim
Roberta Solmundson
Sally Songer
Kit Spahr
Hetty Sparkles
Lyn Speakman
Rosslyn Spokes
Henry St.Leger
Judith Stafford
Susan Stainer
Andy Stainsby
Lisa Staken
Liz Stanley
Hannah Stark
Linsey Statham
Caroline Stead
Sarah Steer
Suzi Steffen
Julianne Stein
David Stemp
Rosalind Stern
Ruth Stevens
Sarah Stevens

Alistair Stevenson
Nic Stevenson
Shelagh Stoicoiu, Mary
  Stoicoiu
Melissa Stolberg
Carmen Stone
Gwilym Stone
Jon Stothard
Danu Stratton-Kent
Jane Street
Duncan Strickland
Rachel Stubbs
Nina Stutler
Julia Sullivan
Helen E Sunderland
Adam Sussman
Laurel Sutton
H. Svetcelnieks-Kalnina
HOPE SWANN
Laura Sweeney
Kirsty Syder
Angela Sykes
Mr & Mrs Tags
Tamaranth
Lizzie Tarling
Alison Taylor
Brigid Taylor
Dave Taylor
Garry Taylor
Kay Taylor
Shereen Taylor
Taz and Rikki
Dave & Jan Thomas
Donna Thomas

Victoria Thomas
Wendy Thomas
Ian Thomas-Bignami
Claire Thompson
Helen Thompson
John & Marianne Thompson
Frank Thomson
Ruth Thorne
Thomas Tiddlemouse
Lynne Tidmarsh
Geert-Jan Tielen
Karen Timm
Adam Tinworth
Helen Tipping
Joanne Todd
Pippa Tolfts
Amie Tolson
Deborah Toner
Angela Townsend
Christopher Trent
Simon Trevaskis
Stefanie Tryson
Joanna Tucker
Kate Tudor, Shirley Engel
Claire Tweed
Alison Twelvetrees
Sir Twonkalot
Anita Uotinen
Valerie
Sonja van Amelsfort
Fabio van den Ende
Chantal van der Ende-Appel
Shane Van Veghel
Anne Vasey

Sandy Vaughan
Elizabeth Vegvary
Kalle Videnoja
Sarah Vidler
Paul Vincent
Roz Vincent
Angela Vinci
Alice Violett
Aaron Voyles
Allyson Wake
Neil Waldrop
Jen Walker
Sue Walker
Niki Walkey
Heather Wallace
Rachel Walne
Michael Walters
Joolz Ward
Kezia Ward
Lee Ward
Kellie Waterworth
Christine Watson
Keith Way
M. F. Webb
Lisa Webster
Debra Weddall
Andy Weekes
Ange Weeks
Julie Weller
Clair Wellsbury-Nye
Benita White
Mark Whitehead
Annalise Whittaker

Helen Wild
Angela Williams
Caroline Williams
Finn Williams
Jim Williams
Robert Williams
Ross Williams
Julie Williamsom
Laura Willis
Tracey Wilson
Oliver Wilton
Tom Winch
Alice Winstanley
Mia Wolff
Anita Wood
John Wood
Matthew Wood
Peter Wood
Steve Wood
Steve Woodward
Jon Woolcott
Brenda Wordsworth
sOOz world
David Wrennall
Zoe Wrigglesworth
Jo Wynell-Mayow
Theresa Yanchar
David Yarrow
Jo Yeates
Doug Young
Michael Young
Donna Zillmann
Birgit Zimmermann-Nowak

A Note on the Author

Tom Cox was born in Nottinghamshire and now lives in Devon. His debut novel, *Villager*, was published by Unbound in 2022. He is the author of the *Sunday Times* bestseller *The Good, The Bad and The Furry* and the William Hill Sports Book-longlisted *Bring Me the Head of Sergio Garcia*. *21st-Century Yokel* was long-listed for the Wainwright Prize, and the titular story of *Help the Witch* won a Shirley Jackson Award.